IRISH VICE

IRISH VICE

A DIAMOND RING DARK ROMANCE

THE IRISH MOB TRILOGY
BOOK 2

ALIX KEY

DIAMOND
FREEPORT PRESS

Published by Diamond Freeport Press
P.O. Box 42133, Arlington, VA 22204

ISBN 978-1-95018-480-4

Discover other titles by Alix Key at www.alixkey.com

091825ak

ALSO BY ALIX KEY

Find a complete, up-to-date list of Alix's books at www.alixkey.com.

The Kidnapped Series

Diamond Solitaire

Rough Diamond

Conflict Diamond

Priceless Diamond

The Irish Mob Trilogy

Irish Brute

Irish Vice

Irish Reign

The Boston Mob Trilogy

Her Irish Savage

Her Irish Protector

Her Irish King

The Taming the Mob Princess Trilogy

Taken Enemy

Twisted Enemy

Tamed Enemy

The Sinful Mafia Series

Sinful Mafia Santa

Sinful Mafia Deception

Sinful Mafia Seduction

Sinful Mafia Salvation

WORD OF WARNING

Irish Vice is a dark romance.

It contains hard-to-read scenes, graphic language, and explicit sexual content.

A complete list of potential triggers can be found at:

https://alixkey.com/books/irish-mob-trilogy

Please don't read this book if you are sensitive to any of those triggers. But if you believe in the power of true love to bring joy and fulfillment to consenting adults, then this is the book for you.

Welcome to the Diamond Ring.

IRISH BRUTE, A RECAP

Have you read *Irish Brute*, the first book in the Irish Mob Series?

You can get your copy by typing

https://alixkey.com/PB4US

into your phone or computer browser.

If you don't want to read it—or if it's been a while—here's a quick summary of what happens in *Irish Brute* (minus, of course, the spicy scenes!)

∿

Having successfully represented Irish mob boss Braiden Kelly at a tax hearing, lawyer Samantha Mott receives a phone call from her cousin Eliza, who is being attacked by her Mafia kingpin husband, Antonio Russo. Samantha hears Russo murder Eliza in a horrific way.

Braiden drives a devastated Samantha home, through a

massive winter storm. The following morning, Russo insists that Samantha take Eliza's place, but Braiden intervenes, claiming he and Samantha are engaged.

Braiden and Samantha marry, although he secretly arranges for a defrocked priest to conduct the ceremony. They live at Thornfield Hall, accompanied by super-competent Fairfax (Braiden's chief of staff), mute Aiofe (Braiden's ward), and creepy Grace (Aiofe's nurse).

Samantha, still working for the tax-haven freeport, lives with strict self-imposed limits—only wearing black and white, never indulging in anything soft or feminine—to atone for something terrible she did "That Night", eleven years ago. Braiden adds his own house rules: Samantha must never touch the door that leads to the mansion's third floor. Also, she must eat breakfast every morning, end the work day by six o'clock, and wear pretty, floral skirts after hours (without panties!) Even as Samantha thrives under Braiden's imposed structure, she discovers the confusing pleasure of being punished for breaking his rules.

As Braiden and Samantha's relationship heats up, so does the gang war between Braiden and Russo. Russo attempts to blackmail Samantha with proof of what she did That Night, demanding that she give him Braiden's business contacts. Samantha resolves to face the consequences for her long-ago mistake instead of betraying her husband.

Braiden's boss in the Grand Irish Union forces him into humiliating peace talks with Russo. Moreover, Russo discloses Samantha's secret: While driving drunk and high, she killed three people in a hit-and-run crash.

Shaken by Russo's growing power, Braiden and Samantha turn on each other. Samantha flees Thornfield, seeking shelter in a cottage on the tax haven grounds. Miserable without each other, they become resigned to separation.

But when Braiden attends a client event at the freeport, he disrupts an attempt on Samantha's life. Disarming a hitman disguised as a waiter, Braiden kills the man (before, alas, they learn who sent the murderer).

Samantha returns to Thornfield. The morning after a joyous reunion, she sits down to breakfast with Braiden, only to discover an uninvited guest. Braiden reluctantly tells Samantha: "This is Birte Antóinín Mason. My wife."

1

SAMANTHA

~

"Samantha Kelly." My husband sounds stiff as he introduces me to the stranger in our dining room. "This is Birte Antóinín Mason. My wife."

My wife.

I start to laugh, because Braiden must be playing a joke. He's hired this bizarre woman to stand in our dining room, wearing her high-necked white gown, clutching her tiny gold cross, and chanting in her sing-song little voice.

But Braiden isn't laughing.

Last night, he killed a man for me. He was shot, his arm grazed by a bullet aimed at me. He acted without even knowing who sent the man with a gun. Braiden killed to save his wife. To save *me*.

Now, his voice cuts through the rabid-squirrel chittering of my brain. "Say something."

I can't piece together words, can't ask the questions I'm terrified of having answered. But Birte Antóinín Mason drops an obedient curtsey, as if she's just stepped out of finishing school or an etiquette class taught by the world's strictest nuns. "*Dia duit, Samantha,*" she says.

"English," Braiden says to his wife. And then, to me, "That means 'God be with you.' It's a common greeting in Ireland. Like 'hello.'"

It feels absurd to respond, as if this woman hasn't just turned my world upside down. But it's rude to stay silent. So I say, "Hello, Birte."

Braiden looks more relieved than he should at those two words. He glances at the pair of plates in his hands, at the neatly halved omelet he made for us in the kitchen. "Please," he says, gesturing toward the dining room table. "Let's eat."

I can't imagine shoving eggs into my mouth, chewing and swallowing like my stomach isn't folding into an origami crane. But I can't figure out what else to do, so I take my usual place at Braiden's left hand. I watch as Birte settles at Braiden's right.

Once he's put a plate in front of each of us, he retreats to the sideboard. It takes him an absurd amount of time to match two cups to their saucers. He adds four spoons of sugar to one cup and a splash of milk to the other. He tops both with tea.

Braiden sets our drinks in front of us before he sits at the head of the table. Birte gets the one sweetened for a child. I get the one for an adult.

Birte crosses herself and bows her head. I have a feeling she changes whatever she was going to say, translating from the Irish, or maybe from Latin. "Bless us, o Lord," she says. "And these, thy gifts, which we are about to receive from thy bounty. Through Christ, our Lord. Amen."

She crosses herself again and then looks at Braiden and me expectantly. I sat through enough blessings before meals at Zia Sara's house to remember to say, "Amen."

Braiden chimes in half a beat late. Birte frowns at him, but then she spears a bite of omelet. After chewing and swallowing, she says to Braiden, "Get some tea. Just like me. That's the key."

He leaps up like a Kentucky Derby favorite breaking free of the gate. He doesn't bother with a saucer; instead, he fills a cup almost to the brim with tea as dark as motor oil. He drinks it straight down, like medicine, ignoring the wisps of steam that curl around his face.

As he goes back for more, I finally find my own words. "Birte," I say. "Do you live on the third floor?"

"Third floor," she says, turning the words into a little song. "Locked door. No more."

Her weird little rhymes must exhaust her, because she settles down to a steady refueling, shoveling bites of omelet into her mouth so fast she barely takes time to chew.

"Braiden?" I ask.

He's the one who told me the door at the end of the hallway was forbidden. He spanked me for defying him, for testing the knob when I thought he wasn't watching.

He doesn't want to answer. I know him well enough by now to read that on his face and in his posture. But there's no way in hell I'm letting this go. "Braiden!" I say more sharply. "Does Birte live on the third floor of this house?"

"Yes," he says.

His flat answer ignites all my lawyer instincts. He sounds like every reluctant witness I've ever deposed, coached by his own attorney to limit his responses to single words as long as humanly possible.

There's a story I'm owed here. A story he's been covering up. A lie he's been living, that he's forced me to live from the moment I entered Thornfield.

"It was Birte I heard singing my first night here, wasn't it?"

He nods, but he doesn't answer out loud.

"Say it," I order. "I need to hear you say it."

"It was Birte."

"And it was Birte playing the piano?" It's strange to talk about her in the third person, as if she weren't sitting right across from me. But she doesn't react to her name. She merely hums to herself and sips her overly sweet tea, and I wonder what in the world could have happened to make her act so strangely.

"Birte plays the piano," Braiden says.

"And it was Birte I heard crying, the night…" The night Braiden and I first had sex. The first night I slept in his bed. When I sat up in the middle of what I thought was a dream, and Braiden calmed me. Soothed me. Lied to me.

"Samantha…" Braiden says, and I hear him searching for a path out of the crater he's blasted for himself.

"Stop!" I snap. He's the only one who calls me that, who uses my full name. I used to love it, because I'm Sam to the rest of the world. But now… "You don't get to say my name. You don't get to tell me more lies."

"I never meant—"

"How the fuck will you finish that sentence? You never meant to lie to me? You never meant to hurt me? You never meant for me to find out you have another wife living in your goddamn attic?"

I consider throwing my cup at him. It's filled with tea, after all, and he knows I hate tea. He only poured it out of habit, because he was serving her.

Forget about tea. I want to throw my plate. I want to hear the china shatter. I want to see egg and coagulated cheese slime the wall.

Even that isn't enough. I want to grab my knife, close my fingers around the grip, and press the edge against Braiden's throat. The blade is too dull to cut flesh, but I could lever it into his windpipe, cutting off his air so he'd never tell me another lie again.

But all of it—tea and egg and stupid useless butter knife— will just make a mess. Braiden will get up and walk out of the room. He'll go to his office and run his criminal empire, and I'll be left sitting at the table with Birte. Eventually Fairfax will arrive, the elfin man who keeps this entire household running like one of those printing presses that spits out sheet after sheet of perfect hundred-dollar bills.

As soon as I think of Braiden's chief of staff, I realize he's as guilty as my husband. Fairfax must know that Birte lives on the third floor.

Who else is in on the secret? Aiofe, Braiden's ten-year-old ward? Grace Poole, the Irish woman who looks after Aiofe? What about Braiden's brother, Madden? All his men, who are constantly in and out of the house for meetings?

"It's complicated," Braiden finally says.

"I'm sure it is." Each word is as bitter as cyanide.

I married Braiden because I thought I had no choice. Mafia kingpin Antonio Russo had just murdered my cousin and announced he was coming for me.

Braiden was the only man I knew who could keep me safe—and he got to goad his arch-rival at the same time. We had the ideal marriage of convenience, one made more perfect by the discovery that Braiden and I were more compatible in the bedroom than I ever could have dreamed.

Braiden likes to issue orders. And I—much to my surprise—like to follow them.

Liked to follow them.

I can't imagine getting down on my knees in front of Braiden Fucking Kelly ever again. I'll never put on the emerald collar he gave me. I won't submit to the twisted things he likes to do. The twisted things he taught me to crave.

I *trusted* him. I knew he'd never hurt me—not in any way I didn't long for. He was my husband. He called me *mo chailín maith*—his good girl.

His. Good. Girl.

I'm not any of those things.

I'm not a *girl*. I'm a grown woman who figured out how to escape my birthname of Giovanna Canna, how to flee my own Mafia-infested family. I left Philadelphia and took on a new identity—Samantha Fucking Mott. I put myself through law school and became general counsel of the largest, most prestigious freeport tax haven in the state of Delaware.

I'm not *good*. Eleven years ago, I made the worst mistake of my life—That Night. My college graduation, when I drove drunk and crashed my car and killed two of my cousins, along with a stranger. My secret was safe until five weeks ago, when Antonio Russo revealed it to the world. I'm still grappling with the fallout, paparazzi stalking me, my law license in jeopardy.

But more than anything else, I'm not *his*. Braiden doesn't own me. He never did.

I was an idiot, letting Russo reveal the truth about That Night. I thought I was saving Braiden. I thought I was protecting his criminal enterprise. I thought I was being true to the man I loved.

The only saving grace in any of this is that I never said those words out loud. I never told Braiden Kelly I loved him.

And now I never will.

2

BRAIDEN

W hen I catch the feckin' eejit who left the door open to the third floor, I'm sending her back to Ireland by the first flight from Philadelphia International Airport.

Her. Because I know this is all Grace Poole's fault. Once again, that drunken wagon forgot herself. Once again, she failed to turn the key. Once again, she let Birte wander free through Thornfield.

Plenty of men say I don't have a conscience, but they lie. I've got one. I just don't consult it much.

The one exception to that rule: The woman finishing her cuppa now, at my right hand.

I hold up a finger, begging a minute, because I can't have Birte hearing the things I need to say. Samantha's lips thin; she's clearly ready to argue. But she's not a wicked woman. She's not cruel, and it's clear something with Birte is off. Samantha gives me one tight nod, turning her back while I do what I must.

Birte Antóinín Mason is the biggest mistake of my life, the

great wrong I'll never atone for. She's the reason I've tolerated Grace Poole's incompetence in this house for seven long years. She's why I've paid a king's ransom to tutors, trying to care for Aiofe.

And she's the reason I test my voice in my head now, before speaking out loud. I know from past experience that a harsh tone will leave Birte sobbing for days. So I take extra care as I ask, "Ready for another cuppa, lass?"

She nods, her eyes as big as collection plates. I fetch her cup and fill it with tea, stirring in the four sugars I know she loves.

I can't send her into the kitchen, not with Fairfax taking his day off. The last thing I need is to put an unsupervised Birte anywhere near a rack of knives.

Swearing under my breath, I stomp back to the mudroom. Of course Birte doesn't have a coat there, but Fairfax has left one of his wool jackets. I check the pockets and find my first bit of good luck today—a pair of knit gloves.

Back in the dining room, I help Birte into the coat. I button it for her, and I help her slide her hands into the gloves. "Let's take your cuppa outdoors, then," I say. "Get a bit of sun."

It's not a perfect solution. If she spies a rabbit, she'll go chasing after it, hoping to find more in a den. But I put her in one of the chairs on the flagstone patio and give her my wristwatch. I tell her I'll be back in fifteen minutes, that she should drink her tea and watch the sky and see if she spies any hawks.

When I get back to the dining room, Samantha's pacing. I catch her dashing a hand against her face, and I know she's wiping away tears she doesn't want me to see. Whether they're from anger or sorrow, I can't say for sure, but I know I'm the source of them, and I hate myself a little more.

"All right," I say to Samantha, taking up a place by the window so I can keep an eye on Birte. "Ask me your questions."

"Are you really married to her?"

"Yes," I say, because the time for lying is long past.

"And you married me too?"

"Not exactly."

I intend my answer to buy me a few seconds to phrase a better one. I don't count on Samantha's frayed temper. "Don't fuck with me, Braiden."

"Father Brennan," I say. "Who performed our wedding. He's a defrocked priest, without proper authority to confer the sacrament of marriage."

"Just so we're absolutely clear, you knew that fact the day you dragged me into St. Columba's? You were one hundred percent aware our wedding was a fraud?"

She sounds like she's interrogating a witness on the stand. I sigh, but I don't try to duck the truth. "Yes."

"Why?"

It's a simple question. One word. Three letters. But the answer might take a lifetime to explain.

"I married you to keep you safe from Russo." But we're being honest now, so I have to confess more. "And to fuck with Russo's mind. To take something he wanted."

She takes the blow like a trained boxer. One breath, and then she's back to her inquisition. "When did you marry Birte?"

"Seven years ago."

"Why do you keep her locked in the attic?"

I swallow something that tastes like turned wine. "Look at her," I say, jutting my chin toward the window. "She's a danger to herself and to anyone around her."

"*Her?*" Samantha has a right to sound skeptical. She doesn't know Birte's physical strength, the hard muscles of a woman who worked on a farm. She doesn't understand Birte's rage.

"You've seen what she can do. The fire, in front of my office."

I see Samantha remember the blaze, the trio of altar candles and the stench of burned wood, the heavy scorched door hacked to pieces, after. That was the last time Grace forgot her duties.

No, not *forgot*. The last time Grace was so drunk that Birte escaped.

Samantha says, "Birte set the fire. Not Grace, like you said at the time."

"Yes. Birte did it."

"Why does she want to kill you?"

"I don't think she does. I think she was trying to save me. Trying to save my soul, at least. I asked her, but she couldn't explain. Or she wouldn't."

"What the fuck did you do to her?"

And now we're at the heart of it. I take a deep breath and start. "Birte and I met in Dublin. She was just up from County Cork, first time in the city. And I was working for my da."

I pause, praying Samantha will read between those lines. She knows what I do. What Da did. All the reasons a man might be in Dublin that he doesn't want to say out loud. She gives a single, stiff nod, which I take as permission to go on.

"For Birte and me, it was a crazy kind of love. She was young and sweet and innocent, not like girls here in the States."

Samantha rolls her eyes, but she doesn't cut me off.

"I fell for her, hard. And when she said I wouldn't get past her knickers without putting a ring on her finger, I was willing to take the leap."

"That must have gone over well with your father," Samantha says, like she's watching a trite old movie, giving it two stars in a devastating review.

"I didn't tell Da. Didn't tell Madden, either. I figured I'd bring my bride back after all was well and done, and there was nothing either one of them could do."

Christ. My voice breaks on that last word. All these years, and when I'm finally allowed to tell the story, I sound like a little boy who broke his Christmas toy before he ever got to play.

Of course Samantha hears. She's softer now when she speaks. "What happened?"

"Birte wore her mother's wedding gown. She had wildflowers in her hair. It rained that day, all morning long, but that was supposed to bring us luck. I didn't care that I had no family there, but Birte wanted to bring in American traditions. Her nephew, Finn, was our ring bearer. Her niece, Aiofe, was the flower girl."

"Aiofe," Samantha says. She looks toward the seat at the table, the one where Aiofe has sat for every meal we've shared as a family.

I nod, because that's easier than saying the rest out loud.

"Grace told me," Samantha says. "Finn was a year older than Aiofe. That he…what did she say? That he treated her like she was a daughter of King O'Hara. And Aiofe loved him like he put the green in shamrocks."

"Then you know what happened." I'm furious with Grace for sharing the story with anyone. But I'm grateful, too, that I won't have say the words out loud.

Samantha shakes her head. "She was telling me. In the greenhouse. But you found us and sent her away."

And tied me to an iron bench and ate me out till I came six times and begged for mercy.

She doesn't say it. She doesn't have to. We both know what happened that day. I sent Grace from the greenhouse. So I'm doomed to finish the story now.

"Birte's parents were gone, but her brother told her not to marry me. Niall said I was a criminal. Said I couldn't love her. Wouldn't keep her safe." Even after all this time, the words are ash in my mouth.

Samantha's waiting. I have to go on. She has to know what happened. "Niall couldn't poison Birte against me. So he did the only thing he could think of to stop our wedding. He showed up with a knife."

Samantha gasps. Whatever she's imagining, it isn't right. Isn't bad enough. Isn't the truth.

"Birte was prepared for trouble. She asked four strong lads from the village to wait by the church doors, to keep Niall from interrupting the service. They did as they promised. They kept him out of the church while we were wed."

I want to close my eyes. I want to shut away the memory of what happened next. But I can't do it. I can't look away from Birte on the patio. I have to keep her safe now, because I didn't keep her safe then.

"We left the church together, Birte and me. The sun came out while we were inside the church, and we were blind at the top of the steps. Niall hollered as he came at me, Irish words that Birte understood before I did. She stepped in front of me. Tried to save me."

It's all happening again, as bright as a big-screen movie. And I'm as powerless to make it stop as any ticket-buying jackeen.

"Niall saw her move. He wouldn't hurt his sister. He spun away. But he slipped on the wet stone, and he fell hard. It was just shite luck that Finn was in the way. That the knife was as sharp as it was. That Finn was looking up at his Da, craning his neck like that…"

Blood. So much blood.

I've killed more men that I'm willing to admit. Some of them I've wanted to hurt, wanted to make bleed. But I've never seen so much blood pour from so small a body.

I shake my head, trying to chase away the image. "Birte held him while he died. Niall saw what he'd done, and he turned the knife on himself. So then Birte held Aiofe while she screamed, while her father died."

"Oh my God," Samantha whispers.

I'm almost through now. She knows everything she has to, but I might as well wrap up the rest, bloody bow and all. "Grace practically raised Birte and Niall, watched over them when they were children. After…the wedding, she was the only one who could get Birte to sleep at night. The only one who could calm Aiofe."

"So you brought them all back here," Samantha says.

"It wasn't supposed to be this way. Wasn't meant to last this long. But Grace drinks, and Aiofe's mute, and Birte..." I shrug, gesturing toward the window.

"Seven years," Samantha says, as if I haven't already counted out every one of those days.

I have to risk it. I have to look away from Birte. I have to turn to Samantha to say the last bit. "So yes, Birte's my wife. She's never shared my bed. Never spent a single night alone with me. But legally, and before the eyes of God, we're married." That's it. That's the truth. I'm left with only a question: "Can you find it in your heart to forgive me?"

3

SAMANTHA

~

My fingertips tingle as if I'm arguing a case in court. The roof of my mouth is numb. I consciously force myself to inhale as deeply as I can, to hold my breath for a full count of ten before I exhale every molecule of air from my lungs.

This is Braiden. The man I trusted enough to marry. The Dom I've allowed to do things to my body I never dreamed I could accept.

I force myself to meet his deep blue gaze. I see pain in the lines around his eyes, a pinched expression so different from how he looked when I found him this morning in the kitchen, happily whipping up breakfast after our night of crazed lovemaking.

"I know you want me to say I understand," I tell him, as gently as I can. "You want me to excuse you. To say this couldn't be helped—your hiding Birte from me. You want me to say all is forgiven."

He's frozen. Every muscle in his body is stretched, pinned, waiting.

"I can't," I say.

"Samantha—"

"I listened to you," I snap. "Now you listen to me."

I cross the room to stand beside him. It's dangerous here. The heat of his body calls to me, the cedar and spice that ransacked my brain three months ago, rewiring everything I thought I knew about myself. I dig my fingernails into my palms as I look out the window at Birte.

She's sitting where Braiden left her, bundled in her coat and holding her cup of tea with both gloved hands, like a child afraid of spilling. The tumble of her hair matches Aoife's. She's not much taller than the ten-year-old girl I've come to know since moving into Thornfield Hall.

"She needs help," I say. "Both of them do."

"Doc Kelleher says—"

"They need a real doctor." I know Kelleher has his medical degree. But he's on the payroll of the Irish Mob, better at treating bullet wounds than managing any patient's day-to-day care. He administered contraception and handled my sprained shoulder, but I wouldn't come close to trusting him with a shattered mind. "They each need a complete physical. And serious, long-term mental health care."

"That can't happen," he says.

"You've kept a woman imprisoned for seven years! She deserves—"

"It's not a prison up there."

"What do *you* call it, then? She's locked behind a door that no one is allowed to touch."

"I'm protecting her! Keeping her safe."

"From what?"

"From herself. From the world. You don't understand how fragile she is."

"I understand that the first thing she did when she got out of her cage was to set your office door on fire, with you on the other side. You can't possibly say that's normal behavior."

"It's not a feckin' cage," he insists. "She's got windows and a piano to play and movies to watch. She eats the same food you and I do. Fairfax knows all her favorites. She has a chapel up there, with stained glass and a velvet-covered kneeler and candles to light every Sunday."

"Does a priest hear her confession?"

"She's in no state—" He bites down on his losing argument before he finishes making it.

"What about Aiofe?" I press. "She's ten years old. How traumatized was she by what she saw at that church?" I think of how withdrawn Aiofe is, how often she behaves like a child half her age. I remember the drawings I've seen, her beautiful sketches of a country chapel, of a bride, of a stuffed animal, and a horse cart. I'm willing to bet she carried that toy rabbit at the wedding, that she watched her aunt arrive for the ceremony on that cart.

"She has everything a child could ask for. New dresses. Countless toys. I pay good money for John Bell to tutor her five days a week."

"If her life is so perfect, why won't she say a word? Has she *ever* spoken to you?"

His own silence is my answer.

"They both need trained professionals who understand trauma."

"Impossible," Braiden says.

"How much can it cost? Ten thousand dollars? A hundred? You burn through that in a day."

"It's not the fucking money! I can't bring a therapist to Thornfield. How would I explain the security? Answer basic questions about my income?"

"You answer those questions all the time. You make donations to the Philadelphia Flower Show and say they're on behalf of Kelly Construction."

"How will I explain a shrink to my men? What will the security team think at the gate?"

"Whatever the fuck you tell them to think! You're the man in charge. You make the rules."

Rules.

That's what we have between us—all of Braiden's house rules. Eating breakfast every morning. Not working past six. Wearing flowery skirts instead of my severe black, white, and gray. Not wearing panties.

Braiden shakes his head. "I can't do it."

"You *won't* do it."

He shrugs.

He's stubborn. He's used to being in charge. He's built a life where no one ever tells him he's wrong. He's the best and the brightest and he always has the biggest dick.

Fuck. I will *not* think about his dick. I won't think about any of the things we've done in bed, any of the ways I've debased myself to please him, to satisfy the soft needy bits between my legs.

I turn to leave the room. I have to get my things. Call a cab. Get somewhere safe and figure out how to get Birte and Aiofe the help they need.

"Where are you going?" he asks before I reach the door.

"To pack."

"You're leaving?" He sounds astonished.

"I can't stay with a lying bigamist."

"I'm not a bigamist," he says.

Technically, he's right. Father Brennan wasn't a real priest. My marriage is a fraud.

"Fine," I say. "I stand corrected. You're just a liar."

I make it to the hall before he calls out, "I'm a liar who killed for you last night."

I turn back to look at him. He's standing between the table and the window, his weight evenly distributed on his feet. He's calm. Confident. Certain I won't go anywhere.

He *did* kill a man last night, a man who pointed a gun at my head. And he tortured his victim first, trying to find out who targeted me.

Braiden didn't care that he was covered in blood. Didn't care that he was grazed by a bullet, that his arm is wounded even now, bandaged beneath his dark tartan shirt.

He saved me.

But he didn't find out who sent the killer. If I leave this house, I'll be as vulnerable as the woman-child sitting on the patio. The second I step outside Thornfield's gate, anyone can come at me—including the paparazzi who've been swarming like starved goldfish since the story of my graduation night became public.

I'm a liar who killed for you last night.

The words hang between us. Absurd. Unanswered.

I can't go. I can't stay.

Before I can figure out how to respond, Braiden's phone trills. The ring-tone is U2's "Sunday Bloody Sunday".

I've heard it before. I've seen the cold shock on Braiden's face. I know he won't let it go unanswered.

Sure enough, he taps the screen and says, "Kelly." But he cuts off whoever's on the other end. His voice goes thick with his Irish accent and he says, "I'll be with ya in a second."

Pressing the phone against his chest, he makes a half-hearted attempt to keep from being overheard. "Don't go," he says.

It's an order. Another one of his rules. But I don't think I can play his game ever again.

"Please," he says.

And *that* breaks something inside me. That's the opposite of the voice he's used before, the crack of authority that sends me —literally—to my knees.

I don't have any good options. Stay with a liar who is steadily breaking my heart. Escape to a world where someone wants me dead, where I'm front-page news for every tabloid in the country, where I'm in danger of losing my law license and my job and my independence because of all the mistakes I made eleven years ago.

I look past Braiden, through the window to where Birte sits in the cold March sun. She's huddled in her coat, in her strange white dress, in her flimsy slippers. Beyond her is a low stone building—the pool house. It's safely behind the front gate. It's not under this roof. It's a port in a storm, the best I can come up with on short notice.

"I'll be in the pool house," I say.

He opens his mouth to argue.

"That was a statement, Braiden. Not the start of a discussion. Take your call. And here's a new house rule: Don't come in there without my express permission."

I leave before I can see his reaction.

4

BRAIDEN

~

I've kept Kieran Ingram waiting for longer than any sane man would dare. But in for a penny, in for a pound. "This isn't a good time," I growl into my phone. But I'm not suicidal. I add his title at the end of my complaint: "Boss."

"If I waited fer ya t' tell me when th' time is good, I'd be a carcass rottin' underground." The General of the Grand Irish Union sounds like he's gearing up to take a hit out on me. Ingram is in charge of Boston's Mob, but he's also the head of us all—New York, Philadelphia, Chicago and all the rest.

My wife is freezing her arse off in the garden, singing songs to herself and staring at the sky. The woman I love just traded my bedroom for the feckin' pool house so she won't have to put up with the likes of me. The child I'm responsible for is nowhere to be seen, and I can only hope she's being cared for by the drunk I've hired to do the job.

My life's in the jacks, so it doesn't seem like much of a risk to say, "I'll call you from the office tomorrow, Boss. When I can talk freely."

I don't bother filling him in on the details—the office I worked out of for years is wrapped up in yellow crime-scene tape, while Philadelphia's finest drag their feet investigating who burned it to the ground.

I know who torched the Hare and Harp. The same man who stole a quarter of a billion dollars worth of cocaine from me five weeks ago. Antonio Russo. It's always fucking Russo.

Not that Ingram gives a shite. "Ya'll talk t' me now, boyo, or I'll put someone in Thornfield Hall who understands th' way things work."

His threat ends with an explosion of coughing. The gombeen smokes three packs a day, and his lungs have turned to porridge.

Waiting for him to catch his breath, I remind myself that Ingram's never made an idle threat in his life. When he can breathe and I can talk without a sarcastic sneer, I say, "What can I do for you today, Boss?"

"Fiona's arrivin' at noon."

Fiona. His daughter. Ingram's used her as a weapon against me before. "Arriving where?" I ask, even though the stone in my belly says I already have my answer.

He ignores my question, as well he should. "Ya'll show her how ya run things there in Philly."

Issuing his order triggers another coughing jag. While Ingram hacks up half a lung, I review my sorry options.

I'm a Captain in the Irish Mob. I rule Philadelphia, same as my da did before me, and his da before that. I choose my men, from my Clan Chief to my driver. If I don't trust someone, he doesn't sit at my table.

And I don't trust Fiona Ingram. She's a schemer, a spy intent on proving herself to her dry shite of a da. Ingram sent her down here a month ago to broker a peace with Russo, and the chaos coming out of that meeting nearly cost me Samantha.

Samantha. The woman I took a bullet for less than twenty-four hours ago. The woman who just moved into my pool house because my life's a fucking mess.

Kieran's finally breathing again, so I take the opportunity to bargain for more time. "Noon is too soon," I say. "I've…complications to attend to."

"Yer whole life is complications, boyo. Let Fiona help with that. She's got a good head on her shoulders."

Not for the wreck of my home life. And I'm not about to open up every corner of my business to Ingram and the Grand Irish Union. I'll hand things over to Russo first.

So I shoot in the dark. "What does Fiona say about coming down here?"

"She'll do as she's told. Always has. Always will."

Rumor has it that in the past, Fiona's been told to kill four men. She's added to the list herself; her total's closer to seven.

And after Fiona's explored my Fishtown business inside and out, she won't hesitate to make it eight. Take over Clan Kelly once and for all. Name herself first woman Captain in Philadelphia's history, and any of my lieutenants who don't like it can answer to her and Ingram both.

"Do we have an understandin' boyo?"

"Yeah," I lie. I understand. I just have no intention of obeying. I can't keep Fiona out of Thornfield, but I don't have to give her a glimpse of my business operations.

"What's that?" he presses.

"Yes, Boss."

"Treat Herself proper," he says. "Like ya'd treat me, if I came down there."

He makes me scrape and bow a few more times before he ends the call.

Miracle of miracles, Birte is still sitting in her chair. Keeping an eye on her, I jam my finger, placing a call on my phone.

"Mr. Braiden," Grace answers on the fourth ring. She slurs my name. It's not yet noon, and she's drunk.

"Who do you think was standing in my fucking dining room this morning?"

She figures it out faster than I thought she would. "Not Miss Birte!"

"One and the same."

Her excuses pile up, half in English, half in Irish, all soaked in the stolen whiskey she keeps hidden in a hip flask.

"The last time Birte got out, she set my office door on fire. You're lucky she didn't burn the house down today."

"Mr. Braiden," Grace starts again. "I'm so sorry. It won't happen again. You know I love that girl like she's my own. I prom—"

I cut her off mid-word. "Come up to the house. Bring Aiofe with you. One more slip, and I send you back to Dublin."

"But Miss Birte—"

"She'll learn to live without you if you so much as drop a saucer."

Fairfax is next. It's his day off, but I've called him back to the house on plenty of Sundays before. As I expect, he answers on the first ring. "Sir?"

"Going forward, the door to the third floor will remain unlocked."

"Sir," he says, and I can't tell if he approves or not.

"And Birte will join us for meals."

"Sir," he says again, and if he thinks Birte can't handle the stress, he's smart enough not to voice his concerns out loud.

"Also," I say. "As of this morning, Samantha has decided to move into the pool house."

"Th— the pool house, sir?" In any other man, that stammer would be a fierce outcry, accompanied by enough curse words to singe the sky. I'm certain I've never before knocked Fairfax so far off-balance.

"I want her belongings moved from my bedroom by three," I say. "She'll need a bed out there. By tonight."

"Very good, sir," he says, as if I haven't demanded the

impossible. "Do you want appliances installed as well? At present, there's a mini-fridge and a microwave."

"No."

I'll give her the distance she demands. She can take some time to come around. But my house rules aren't as easy to get around as she thinks. She'll eat breakfast beside me here in the dining room and dinner too—every feckin' day.

Still, I'm not a total monster—multiple marriages to the contrary. "Have a coffee maker installed. And lay in a supply of the Jamaica Blue she likes."

"Yes, sir."

"And one more thing. We have a new houseguest arriving today—Fiona Ingram. I suspect she'll stay for several weeks."

The long pause is the most eloquent protest I've ever heard Fairfax make. He's worked for me, and for my father before me, long enough to know the Ingram name. He's heard all the rumors, and I'm sure he has his own share of facts.

But he finally says, "And where will Miss Fiona be staying?" Another pause, but he maintains his professionalism by adding, "Sir."

"In one of the guest rooms." And then, as if it's an afterthought, I add, "Not the one Samantha used." Before she moved into my room. Before she became mine.

"Very good, sir."

I thank him and end the call.

My fingers go to the fresh bandage I wrapped around my forearm when I woke this morning. That was when I thought the worst part of my day would be managing a seeping wound, reminder of a wayward bullet meant to take Samantha.

I trace the outline of an older wound beneath the gauze, a scar I've carried since I was six. A madman trapped me in a closet then, murdering seventeen of my classmates and five innocent nuns. I've long grown used to the acid burn deep in my ruined skin, to the bitter taste of failure. I should have stopped the killer. Twenty-two tombstones measure how I failed.

I stop myself from scratching as Aiofe and Grace appear in the garden, rounding the corner of the pool house. When Aiofe catches sight of Birte, she flies across the lawn, her small features lighting with joy. Grace plods along after, her plain face tugged into sullen lines.

Before I can see how Birte responds to the attention, my phone rings again. It's a blocked number, one I'd ignore if this were a day my life wasn't falling apart. Instead, I answer: "Kelly."

"Tell your guard to let me past the gate."

"Fiona." She's hours early, which can't be a mistake.

"*Boss*," she prompts me.

"I'll not call you Boss in my own home."

"You'll give me the honor I'm due."

"Your da's my General, and I call him Boss. You only get the title when you act in his stead."

"I always—"

I make a point of cutting her off. "You're here to learn, your da said. Lesson one. I make the rules at Thornfield." I tap my phone, opening the front gate. "Come on up to the schoolhouse, Fiona. Make yourself at home."

5

SAMANTHA

Alec Fairfax is a marvel.

When I arrived in the pool house this morning, I found a building that hadn't been touched in months. While the floor-to-ceiling windows looking over the pool provided stunning light, their water-spotted panes hadn't been cleaned in ages. There were visible gaps between the door and its frame. The dorm-size refrigerator and microwave seemed functional, but I had a choice of sleeping on a too-short couch, a pool table, or the floor, with a stack of brightly colored beach towels as my only linens.

By the time the sun set over the main Thornfield house, a complete transformation was made. Fairfax commanded a small army of specialists—a carpenter to install weather-stripping and window shades; housekeepers to dust, mop, and polish the windows till they gleamed; multiple teams of delivery men bearing a king-size bed complete with wrought-iron headboard and footboard, a pair of nightstands, a mahogany armoire and matching chest of drawers, an overstuffed armchair perfect for reading, and a full array of lamps. The last crew to arrive brought towels and sheets and blankets, along with a duvet covered in a honeysuckle-and-tulip print.

The floral design is gorgeous, a classic pattern in greens and blues and cream. It's prettier than anything I've owned in years.

I shouldn't like the duvet. I shouldn't allow it. I should have the discipline to stick with the plain solid colors I deserve. But I can't stop staring at the beautiful flowers—one good thing to come out of today's chaos.

Fairfax himself brings my clothes from the house—four suitcases that he must have ferried in stages before knocking at the pool house door. "Would you like me to unpack for you?" he asks.

"No," I say, reaching out to take one of the bags. "I'll do it."

He shifts his weight from one foot to the other. "Miss Samantha—" he starts.

"Please. Just Sam. Like before." Before I moved out of the house. Before I found out my husband had another wife.

"Sam," he starts again. "I owe you an apology."

"No, you don't."

"An explanation then."

"Your explanation is that you work for my husband." That's not exactly true. Braiden and I are not married.

Fairfax threads that needle delicately. "Nevertheless, I regret I did not tell you about the first Mrs. Kelly."

The first Mrs. Kelly.

I shake my head, because we're all trapped in these lies together. "Thank you," I say. And then I purposefully try to brighten the mood. "I can't believe you've done all this in just one afternoon."

He dusts his hands after rolling the last suitcase to the foot of my bed. "Where there's an unlimited bank account, there's a way."

I frown. I don't want any more debt on my account with Braiden. But I say to Fairfax, "I know this was supposed to be your day off. I truly appreciate everything you've done."

"My pleasure," he says, with such a sincere tone I almost believe him.

After he leaves, I unpack. I'm astonished by Fairfax's thoroughness. He tracked down every item of clothing I had in the closet I shared with Braiden. He sorted the master bathroom, bringing my cosmetics and my bottles of shampoo and conditioner. I blush when I realize he emptied my nightstand as well, rounding up my nail file and cuticle scissors, a notepad and pen, and a half-full bottle of lube.

He wasn't just busy packing. He's laid in a supply of my favorite snacks—wheat crackers and dark chocolate Kisses and a bowl of tart little apples. He stocked the shelves with liquor too —all high-end bottles, with glasses to match. There's a small bowl filled with lemons, limes, and oranges.

It's nearly seven o'clock when I shove the suitcases into the storage closet, next to pool noodles and kickboards and a mind-numbing array of inflatables. I lower my new window shades against the twilight.

When I was a single woman living in my Delaware condo, I was rarely home at this time of day. I worked long hours at the freeport, poring over legal documents until nearly midnight. When I finally made it home, I changed out of my black suit and got ready for bed.

But Braiden made me sell my condo. And by Braiden's house rules here at Thornfield, I'm not allowed to work past six. After hours, I'm required to set aside my plain clothes. I must wear one of my floral skirts.

Braiden is a liar. He tricked me into marrying him. He made a fool out of me.

But three months of living as a Kelly has changed me forever. It feels wrong to wear my skinny black jeans at the end of the day.

Refusing to think about how thoroughly Braiden's gotten under my skin, I turn to my wardrobe. I swap my black cashmere sweater for a soft pink shell. I shimmy out of my jeans and select the brightest skirt I own, a riot of roses in amethyst and magenta and a heart-stopping fuchsia.

I hesitate once the waistband settles over my hips. Braiden demands I wear my skirts without panties. The house rules have been drilled into me so thoroughly that it feels wrong to be fully clothed.

Closing my eyes, I touch my forehead to the armoire. I don't want to be this woman, bound by a man's rules. I don't want to be so weak. So controlled.

But the thing about my underwear, the reason for the rule: No one else in the house knew about it. It was our secret, Braiden's and mine. I did it for him, and he knew it, and that gave *me* a certain power.

I reach beneath my skirt and hook my fingers into the elastic waistband of my panties. Before I can pull them off, though, there's a knock at the pool house door.

I startle as if I've been caught doing something nasty, like masturbating in the middle of a train station. The elastic snaps back to my belly in punishment, and my heart pogo-sticks my sternum.

It must be Braiden out there. He's come to survey his handiwork—this retreat that he ordered up in less than a day. He'll tempt me as he always does, with a knowing look and a wicked grin.

But I'm ready for him. I'm not giving in without another conversation, and another, and another, until he does what's right for Birte and Aiofe. I set my jaw against the commands he's bound to issue. I close my ears to the special voice he uses, the tone that runs a direct line to every screaming cell in my body.

Before I open the door, I remind myself that I'm a strong and independent woman. I'm a member of the Delaware bar—

at least for now, until the ethics office decides if That Night will cost me my law license. And if worse comes to worst, I'll build myself another profession. I can do anything, once I've set my mind to it.

I turn the knob and raise my chin to meet my fate.

Madden Kelly looms in the doorway.

Madden is tall like his brother, and he's got Braiden's wide shoulders. But where Braiden's eyes sparkle like matching star sapphires, Madden's have the sheen of day-old coffee. Braiden's hair is so black it's almost blue, but Madden's is the matte brown of a scarred oak trunk.

"What do you want?" Madden's the one who told Braiden I was working for Russo. Sure, he was duped by the Mafia don, and he was only trying to protect his brother. But Madden's mistakes sent me fleeing Thornfield for five long weeks, and I haven't forgiven him yet.

"Is that any way to greet your kin?" He pushes his way past me like we're old friends.

"I'm sure you've heard the news by now." I watch him survey my new home. His eyes sweep like a stopwatch, tallying up the changes. I remind him: "You're no kin to me. You never were."

Madden slinks across the room like a cruising coyote. Pausing by the rack of pool cues, he picks up a cube of green chalk and rubs his thumb over the surface. "Ach," he says, sounding more Irish than Braiden ever has. "You've learned the truth about poor Father Brennan."

"You *knew*." I'm unable to keep bitterness from my voice. Madden was Braiden's best man. And when Russo launched an attack on our wedding day, Madden was the man Braiden trusted to rush me into Thornfield's safe room.

He's gloating now. "Of course I knew."

"And the rest of Braiden's men? Have you all been having a good laugh behind my back?"

Madden smirks. "Not because the priest who married you

was false. But more than one lad has commented on the boss stinking like fish these past few months."

"You're disgusting," I snap.

He moves faster than my eyes can follow. I don't realize he's grabbed a cue until the maple rod is pressed against my throat. Madden's trapped my body with his; my shoulders are crushed against the solid wood door of my wardrobe.

I react automatically, falling back on self-defense training I mastered when I was in law school and returning home alone from the library, well after midnight most nights. Stiffening three fingers, I drive at Madden's throat, putting all my strength into the short, sharp jab. At the same time, I grip his left wrist, turning into his arm and forcing my body weight against the joint of his elbow.

He drops the cue in surprise. It's still rattling on the floor when I bring my knee up hard, smashing into his nose. Blood starts to flow as I stretch for the cue. He gets there first, but I kick at his wrist before he can bring the wood up between us.

He staggers back three full steps as I scream, "Get the fuck out of here!"

This time, I see every move he makes. His knees dip. His hand grips a holster at his ankle. Light flashes cold on steel as he comes up with a pistol.

"Not so brave now, are you, cunt?"

By reflex, I hold up both hands. His laugh is liquid as blood drips down his chin. He saunters forward one step, two. I back away until I'm once again stopped by the armoire.

The gun is ice against my carotid, so cold the muscles of my heart start to freeze. My eyes are open as wide as possible as I try to glimpse his finger on the trigger without turning my head. He raises his wrist, pressing harder into my throat. I barely feel his knee digging between mine.

"I know what you're up to, bitch." His spittle lands on my cheek. "You're fucking my brother and running back to Russo.

Take the Irish through the front door and the guinea up your arse. But when I catch you with that Italian gobshite, I'm blowing your fucking brains out. Got it?" The nose of his gun carves a divot in my throat. "Got it, bitch?"

I swallow, which only makes me feel the gun more. He's delusional, but that won't save me if he decides to pull the trigger. I nod my head once. My lips form the words, but I can't make myself say them out loud. "Got it."

Madden shoves one more time before backing off. "Christ," he says, pressing the back of his hand to his nose. "Look what you did."

As he stalks into the bathroom, I slide down the door of the wardrobe. I end up with my head between my knees, my neck bowed as I try to remember how to breathe.

A few minutes or an hour or a century later, Madden comes back to the main room. He throws a bloody washcloth at me. It's one of the new ones, lavender now splotched with crimson. I cringe as it hits the floor beside me.

"Let's go," he says.

"Go where?" I'll never get in a car with him. I wonder what other weapons he's carrying.

His laugh is cruel. "To the main house. Braiden sent me to fetch you to dinner."

"I'm not hungry," I say automatically.

"He said you'd say that. I have Himself's permission to throw you over my shoulder and carry you to the dining room."

As if you need permission.

I think it. But I don't say it out loud. I won't do anything more to taunt the time bomb in front of me.

Instead, I push myself to my feet. I run a hand through my hair. I tug on my skirt, settling it firmly over my hips.

Madden nods approvingly. "You'll want to look your finest," he says. "We'll have the whole family sitting around the table. Along with a very special guest."

I refuse to ask. Instead, I concentrate on making it to the main house under my own power, trembling legs and all. Every step, Madden follows behind, breathing noisily through his swollen nose, and I know he's my enemy for life.

6

BRAIDEN

~

Dinner is the single longest meal of my life.

Despite coming in on his day off, Fairfax has worked his usual magic. He serves up a full Sunday roast—leg of lamb, potatoes, the spring's first asparagus, and Yorkshire pudding. I keep Aiofe in her place to my right and Samantha to my left. Birte sits by Aiofe, Madden next to Samantha. I put Fiona at the foot of the table.

She can report back to her da that she has a place of honor. And she can't get close enough to put a knife between my ribs.

She *claims* she's only here to learn how I run the Fishtown Boys. She *says* her da means to make her captain of the Boston crew after he's gone, may that be many years in the future. She *insists* she'd be a fool to stir up trouble for me down here.

I don't trust a word she says.

So for five full minutes, the only sound in the dining room is the scrape of silverware on plates. All six of us eat like we're training for the Olympic gold medal in Family Meal.

No one looks up from Fairfax's feast. I try to ignore the itch of my bandaged wound, pulled tight by the flex of my fingers. The more I try to forget the ache of the scar that frames it, the more my flesh burns.

Fiona fortifies herself with a massive gulp of Bordeaux before she finally says, "My, what lovely weather we're having lately."

Madden snorts as he forks a huge bite of lamb past his lips. The sound comes out liquid and clogged, and I realize his nose is swollen. It wasn't that way when he arrived this afternoon, answering my summons when I realized there's no way I can ship Fiona back to Ingram. Not yet, anyway.

"What happened to you, *dearthair*?" I ask.

He scowls, as if my calling him brother is an insult. "Walked into a wall," he mutters, savaging a roasted potato with his fork.

Aiofe giggles until Madden glares at her. I tap my knife to put him back where he belongs. He pours half a bottle of wine into his glass, but he keeps his mouth shut.

I can't remember ever hearing Aiofe laugh before. Her color is high. She's eating her vegetables without my reminding her. I don't know what's set her right—having Samantha back after five weeks of separation, eating with her auntie at her side, or basking in the novelty of Fiona's cool stare from the foot of the table.

We pass another few minutes in silence before Fiona tries again. "Are the rumors true about that heroin bust? Did the police really pick up three of your corner men?"

I attempt to incinerate her face with my stare. "We do not discuss business at the dinner table," I say.

"At the table," Birte repeats. "On the cable. In the stable."

Aiofe beams at her, as if Birte just recited one of Yeats' finest poems.

"Fairfax!" I holler. When he glides in from the kitchen, I plead, "Have you made us a sweet?"

He carries in an enormous trifle, soaked in enough sherry

that I can smell it from the doorway. The dessert proves enter-
tainment enough to carry us to the end of our tortured meal. I
can't help but notice Samantha's barely touched her food—
dinner or dessert. My own appetite died with the first endless
silence.

As Fairfax starts to clear the plates, Fiona looks out the
window. "Anyone care for a stroll?" she asks. "I haven't seen the
grounds yet."

"Of course you haven't," I growl. She spent the entire afternoon shadowing me.

Madden stands to accompany her, saying, "He only *sounds*
like a bear with a sore paw."

"I don't know," Fiona says, looking over her shoulder.
"Those teeth he's grinding look rather bearish to me."

They laugh and head toward the mudroom. I trust Madden
will get her a coat so she doesn't freeze her arse off, first night on
my watch. Then again, maybe she'll go back to Boston under
her own power if she suffers a little frostbite.

Birte is humming to herself, pleating and unpleating the
napkin in her lap. I turn to Aiofe. "You've got half an hour
before bed. Why don't you show Auntie Birte the nursery?"

Aiofe beams, taking a willing Birte's hand and leading her
toward the stairs.

That leaves Samantha and me. Exactly as I planned.

"That wall Madden walked into," I say. "Is it a problem?"

I see her start to lie, to tell me all is grand. I know how to
read every line of her body. But this time she chooses the truth.
Or something close to it. "I've got it under control. For now."

I want to tell her she's safe here.

I want to tell her I've killed for her once, and I'll do it again,
once my runners track down whoever sent the man to the
freeport.

I want to tell her I hate having kept Birte a secret, that I
should have told her the truth when I gave her my ring, the day
I asked her to marry me.

I want to tell her I'm sorry.

Instead, I say, "You left something in the bedroom upstairs. Come fetch it before you go back to the pool house."

She's wary, precisely the way I knew she would be. "Fairfax brought me everything I need."

"So now you're scared of me?"

That gets her back up, just as I planned. She pushes her chair away from the table and throws her shoulders back, leading the way upstairs like she's Washington crossing the Delaware.

Was it only last night that she was attacked at the freeport? That she ended five weeks of exile and agreed to come home? That I tied her to the bed and put her in a blindfold and made her beg for the slap of my riding crop?

Was it only this morning that she found Birte in the dining room?

This day feels like it's lasted twenty-five years.

I've spread her gray nightshirt on the hunter-green duvet. She stiffens when she sees it. "Fairfax must not have realized it was here," she says, crossing the room and snatching up the soft jersey garment.

Or I ordered him to leave it behind when he collected the rest of her belongings. Faced down his most fierce frown about it, too.

"I'm sorry to have bothered you," she says, turning toward the door.

"You're never a bother, *piscín*."

She flinches at the pet name. *Kitten*. Mine to hold. Mine to tame. But I always have to mind her claws.

"Let me go, Braiden." Her voice trembles.

"I'm not stopping you."

She can walk past me. Through the doorway. Down the hall. Back to the pool house.

She doesn't move.

When I close the distance between us, I can smell her

shampoo—honey and berries from a bottle Fairfax carried out to the pool house. I see a mark on her throat, a red welt as if she's pressed the handle of last night's crop into the soft hollow beneath her ear.

I touch it with my fingertip, and her pulse takes off like a flag fighting a hurricane. I cup her jaw, and she leans into my hand.

"Stay," I whisper.

She nods, once.

I hate to pull away, hate to lose the heat of her cheek against my palm. But I close the door before she changes her mind. When I shoot the lock, my fingers are strangely clumsy.

There's one more thing I kept from Fairfax when he packed up all her belongings.

The velvet box is in my top dresser drawer. When I open it for Samantha, I feel like I'm displaying the contents the very first time. The emerald at the heart of her collar catches all the light in the room, gathering it and concentrating it and distilling it into something more.

It's too much. Too fast.

She crosses her arms, her fingers still knotted in her night-shirt. The gray fabric bunches across her chest like the most fragile shield in the world.

"I can't," she says. Then she shakes her head like I've challenged her. "I won't."

I close the box.

"I *trusted* you," she says.

"I know."

"It was all too easy. You said you'd marry me, and I said yes. I thought it was the perfect way to avoid Russo. To be safe."

"It was. It is."

"It *isn't!*" She's loud enough that I'm glad I paid handsomely to soundproof this room. "You lied to me!"

"I never meant to hurt you."

"Bullshit!"

"Samantha," I say, pitching my voice to the level I wish she'd use.

She may not realize it, but she lowers her voice. "You found a fake priest to marry us. You let me stand in that church and say my vows and believe it all was real. You actually thought that wouldn't hurt when I found out?"

I prayed she'd never learn the truth. But now I say, "I was trying to protect you."

She snorts in derision. "You wanted to make sure I have no claim on you. So you can walk away whenever you want."

I shake my head. "I never want to leave you." In my head, in my heart, I was trying to do the right thing. I was trying to keep her from wedding a married man. "What do you want?" I finally ask. "How can I make this right?"

"You can't!" She spits the words. That venom's intended for me, but there's a healthy dose of loathing for herself.

"None of this is your fault," I tell her.

"I want to believe that."

"It's the truth. You didn't know. You couldn't have done anything different."

"But I can now." She says the words like they're a curse. "I should leave. Walk out that door and never set foot in this house again. I should sleep in my car or go back to the freeport or stay in a fucking hotel. I should..." She swallows the rest of her sentence, as if there are too many words, as if they're too hard to say out loud.

She has too many options. Too many choices. Too many decisions to make.

She became my sub because I told her exactly what to do. I gave her one clear path. I carried all her burdens for a while, giving her a chance to rest.

And I can do that again.

So I say, "Drop that goddamn shirt." I use my Captain's voice, carving away every path but one.

She hesitates for long enough that I think I've made the biggest mistake of my life.

No. It would only be the second biggest. Hiring Father Brennan was worse.

Still no. Third biggest mistake. The worst was failing to tell her about Birte from the very beginning. And I'll live with that for the rest of my life.

But then Samantha drops the shirt, and I glimpse a narrow path toward redemption.

"On your knees," I order, pointing to the floor.

She's about to do it. Her face clears. Her knees sway.

But she pulls herself straight before she gives in. She closes her hand over my wrist. "If I do this," she says. "You have to do something for me."

"I'll do something for you," I growl.

She shakes her head. "Promise," she says.

This isn't right. She's my sub. I'm her Dom.

But she isn't wearing her collar yet. And she'll never put it on if I don't ask, "Promise what?"

"If you won't get a doctor in here for Aiofe and Birte, bring in someone they can trust. A priest. A real one. Not Father Brennan."

I start to protest. I need to protect the Fishtown Boys, keep prying eyes from Thornfield.

But there are two reasons I'll do it. One: Samantha is the one who asked. And two: It's the right thing to do.

"Fine," I say. "I promise. I'll bring someone in tomorrow."

She stares at me, like she's trying to read my mind.

I've lied to her before. But my arm is still bandaged from that bullet. I'm not lying now.

"Fine," she says, carefully matching my tone. And she sinks to the floor, her flowered skirt floating prettily around her knees. She looks up at me, her face open. Honest. Free.

"I need my collar," she says. And then, after the slightest of pauses, she adds the word my heart covets most. "Sir."

7

SAMANTHA

He locks the emerald around my throat. My pulse beats hard against the stone, telegraphing an awareness to every cell in my body.

I shouldn't be here. I shouldn't give in to my body's physical needs. But when Braiden issued his command—*drop that goddamn shirt*—everything became clear in my head. All the noise, all the doubt, all the questions I've asked myself since I first saw Birte in the dining room—everything dropped away, like sugar crystallizing at the bottom of a cup of too-sweet tea.

Braiden walks around me now, studying me from every angle. I want to say something, beg him to tie me up, plead with him to go down on me. But I'm wearing the collar now. I don't get to speak.

No.

I don't *have* to speak.

I don't have to make any decisions. I just have to do what I'm told to do. That's the bargain we've made.

But does the collar still work, now that I know he's lied to me? He's covered up his past. Can I forget that for long enough to silence the voice nagging at the back of my head—the one that says I need to take charge, need to put the world in order, need to advocate for everything I believe in?

What will happen if the paparazzi learn about the things I've let Braiden do to me? How many stories will I face in the press then? What if the ethics board concludes I'm sexually depraved? Will that be the last straw before they yank my law license?

Braiden snaps his fingers, a bare inch from my nose. "Stop thinking," he commands.

He's told me that before. Then, I didn't think it was possible. I didn't believe I could unzip my brain, that I could step outside my circling thoughts.

But now I try to focus on my body instead of my mind. My nipples tighten against the satin cups of my bra. A slow ripple of desire churns through my belly and tension tightens my thighs, settling into my knees' soft ache.

A door slams somewhere in the house, a vibration I feel instead of a sound that I hear. I wonder if Birte's up to some mischief with her newfound freedom from the attic. If Aiofe's protesting her bedtime without saying a word. If Fiona's marking her territory, or Madden's making sure he isn't forgotten in his brother's house.

Or maybe it's just the wind.

"Eyes on me," Braiden says, and I realize I've been staring at the door, waiting for someone to turn the knob, to test the lock.

I swallow hard, but I do as I'm told. I meet his fierce gaze.

"My God," he says. "You're gorgeous." His fingers find the sore spot on my throat, the place where Madden pressed his pistol. "What happened here, *piscín*?"

I could tell him. I could let him know Madden threatened me. But if I say that, I'll have to admit Madden still thinks I'm spying for Russo.

I don't want Antonio Russo in this bedroom. I don't want to think about what he did to my cousin. I don't want to remember how he released my darkest secret to the entire world. I don't want to wonder if the man who tried to kill me last night was sent by Russo, if the truce between the Mafia don and Braiden is over and now we're back at war.

Swallowing hard to drown out the long-remembered scent of Russo's Acqua di Parma cologne, I shake my head. "It doesn't matter."

"It does to me." He presses a little harder into the bruise.

"No. It really doesn't," I say.

"You're the girl on her knees. You don't get to decide what matters and what doesn't."

If I say what Madden's done, Braiden will leave me here and chase after his brother.

And I don't want to be left alone.

So I press my lips together, and I shake my head—one tense, tight toss.

Braiden strikes like a mamba. His fingers dig into my armpits, hauling me to my feet and shoving me toward the bed. I stumble a bit, which only seems to stoke his rage.

He folds me over the edge of the mattress, pressing my face into the dark green duvet. My feet are still on the floor, spread for balance. He kicks at my ankles, forcing them wider. He pushes against my ass, and I feel the swell of his erection through his pants as he leans over to whisper in my ear. "Tell me what Madden did, *piscín*. Or I promise you'll be punished."

Punished. The word sparks through my blood like a fever. He could offer me a million dollars now, say he'll buy me a house, suggest a vacation to all the capitals of Europe, and I wouldn't say a word. There's something I want more than all that. Something I need.

He shoves off my spine, and for a devastated heartbeat, I think I've lost this round. But then I hear his belt slither free from his pants.

"You know the rules," he says. "Say *red*, and we're done." My knees melt, even as I shake my head. I'm never saying *red*.

He backs off enough to grab the hem of my skirt, yanking the fabric over my ass. The backs of my thighs tingle at the touch of cool air.

"Oh, *piscín*," he says. "And here I thought you were a clever girl." He plucks at the top of my panties, letting the elastic snap back. I catch my breath, surprised by the sharp sting, which must be why he does it again.

"I'm a simple man," he lies. "With simple rules. And you should know by now that knickers aren't allowed. Not with a skirt. You sat at my table for an entire meal, disrespecting me. And now you have to pay."

He stalks over to the nightstand and yanks open the drawer. It only takes him a moment to find the shears he keeps there, the ones meant to slice through rope in an emergency.

The steel is so cold against my hip that my leg starts to spasm. He plants a hand on the base of my spine, calming me, stilling me, and then he makes a single, devastating slice. I hear each fiber of my panties shred, first on the right side, then on the left.

My thighs tremble as his fingers close over the ruined satin. He pulls the cloth at an angle, sawing against my throbbing clit, through the needy folds of my pussy, against the crack of my tightening ass. The pressure is nearly enough to break me, and then it's gone too soon.

"Such a naughty girl," he says.

Everything about this is wrong. I should leave this room and go to the pool house, just like I did this morning. I should have more self-respect.

But my body's demands are louder than my brain's. I need to trigger him. I need to earn my release. So I fight back with words I know will earn me discipline. "I'm not a girl."

He laughs. "You're *my* girl," he says. And before I can

protest further he shoves the soaked scrap of satin against my face. I twist my head, trying to get away, but he easily overpowers me. My nose is filled with the scent of me, the salty, briny, slick he raised in me. I open my mouth to protest, and he pushes the cloth past my lips, driving it in with his fingers until I have to suck on my own juices.

I'm still working my jaw, trying to spit out the gag, when he lands his first blow. He uses the tongue of his belt, a full handlength of leather. The end bites deep, and I feel the double slash from the sides, parallel stripes on my already overheated ass.

"Count," he says.

"One," I grunt. The word is muffled by satin, but it's clear enough for him to know I'm counting. I'm not saying *red*. I'm not telling him to stop.

The belt lands again, lower this time. Twin lines of fire sizzle toward my clit.

"Two." I know the word I'm saying. I know the sound he wants.

A third blow, across the tops of my thighs.

I hold off on the number because that's not what I want. If he's going to spank me, I want his attention on my ass.

"Count," he says again, his voice deadly still.

I stay silent.

"Say it, lass, or I leave the room right now."

He'll do it, too. I have no doubt. Braiden Kelly is a master of control. Even if it means going without his own satisfaction, he'll leave me sprawled here, desperate and alone, just to teach me a lesson.

"Three," I say, the word almost lost in drenched cloth.

I don't know why I want this. Why I need this. Why Braiden's violence is the only thing that makes me truly whole. All I know is this is what I truly desire. This is right. This is *me*.

The fourth blow lands higher than the first. The fifth stripes my right ass-cheek. The sixth hits my left.

My eyes are closed. My jaw is stretched. I'm wound tight, waiting, waiting, waiting, knowing the next touch will send me over the edge.

I barely hear the rasp of his zipper. The belt trails between my shoulder blades and down my spine, over the arch of my hot, bruised ass. He pulls it away as he shifts his weight, leaning back from my body.

And when the belt falls this time, it's the hardest blow yet, cutting deepest, slashing across all the other lines. My muscles clench. My nerves scream. My clit goes incandescent and there's a word I'm supposed to say, a number I'm supposed to know, but I've forgotten how to count, forgotten how to speak, and all I can do is spin tighter and tighter and tighter.

Just as I fall off the edge of darkness into blinding light, Braiden presses into me. His cock fills me, completes me, merges into my spiraling spine. I'm seizing, sobbing, desperate for more as his fingers clutch my hips. His thumbs dig into the searing lines he's carved into my flesh.

I drown in my orgasm, losing myself, losing him, and just when I think I must spin back to earth, he thrusts even harder, and I crest a brand new peak.

This time, I feel his cock in my belly, in my lungs, in my brain. He plows the deepest, darkest parts of me, pushing hard, moving fast, and when he comes—swearing Irish oaths I'll never understand—I fold around him a third time, each ripple, every roll carrying me farther than the one before.

I black out, or maybe I really am transformed into something more than human.

When I come back to my senses, we're both on the bed. Braiden leans against the headboard. He's cradling me, my back against his chest, his arms tight around me. My soaked satin panties are nowhere in sight.

"*Mo chailín maith*," he says.

His lips are lost in my hair, and he tells me I'm safe, and I don't know why I was in danger, and he tells me he's sorry, and I don't know what he's done. His thumb is soft on my cheek, and I realize he's wiping away tears I didn't know I shed.

I can't tell how much time passes before he pulls a blanket up to my shoulders. He reaches to the nightstand and helps me with a glass of water. As I sip, he reaches into his nightstand drawer, coming up with arnica gel that smells like rosemary and sage.

He smooths it into my throbbing skin, the heat of his hand a second type of salve. He whispers as he tends to me, telling me I'm gorgeous, telling me I'm his.

When he's finished with all the stripes he gave me, his hand moves to my throat. He slips past my collar, past the platinum that has heated to match my blood. He finds the bruise on my pulse point, the place where Madden pressed his gun, and he soothes that too.

I sleep for a while, but I don't remember any dreams. When I wake, he's sitting beside me, propped against the headboard, his hand splayed over my hip.

I reach for my throat, slipping a finger beneath the emerald nestled there.

"Go back to sleep," he says.

But I shake my head. I tug at the collar, feeling the lock at the nape of my neck.

He sighs and finds the key. When the hasp springs loose I snag a deep breath.

"Sleep, *piscín*," Braiden says, setting the collar on the nightstand.

But I don't sleep. I stand. I take a step in my bare feet. Another. I find the shoes I don't remember shedding. I smooth my hands down my rumpled skirt.

Braiden could stop me. He could drag me back to bed. Tie me up if I fight him. Break my body and my spirit with another shattering orgasm.

But he doesn't do any of that.

He lets me go.

So I unlock the door. I make my way through the darkened house to the mudroom. I cross the garden. And I enter the lonely pool house I now call home.

8

BRAIDEN

Six weeks ago, I kept an office in downtown Philadelphia, at the back of a pub. My grandad was the first man to pour Guinness at the Hare and Harp, long before the mahogany bar was scarred by decades of drunks. My da was the man who built out the basement, adding soundproofing and a drain so the Fishtown Boys had a place to do their wetwork.

And I'm the man who lost the place, saw it burned to the ground, victim of a skirmish with Russo. I took a baseball bat to his prize Lamborghini. He torched the Hare.

I came out the worse in that exchange. Especially because I'm still working out the cost for the fire commissioner to forget that basement room. In the end, I'll pass the debt on to Russo, I've vowed that. But for now, he's made my life a feckin' hell.

And I'm taking all my meetings at Thornfield.

My home office is any working man's dream—a leather chair behind the desk big enough to handle my large frame, two chairs for visitors in a dark green plaid, with a matching couch long enough to stretch out on when I need a kip. My favorite books line the walls, and a pair of windows look out over the drive so I get fair warning of anyone allowed past my guarded gate.

So that means I can watch Father Regis make his way down the drive after a morning of visiting with Birte and Aiofe. I'm not sure things went as Samantha hoped. Birte spoke in rhyme when she bothered to say anything at all, and Aiofe didn't say a word. But the good father prayed over both of them and said he'll be back soon.

At least I've kept my promise.

I'm still at the window when Madden arrives, climbing out of his acid-green McLaren, a car so flashy it makes my eyes bleed. My brother stretches like he's made a cross-country trip, then he plants his hands on his hips and looks around the courtyard like he owns the feckin' place.

I consider walking down the hall to see if Samantha's eyeing the eejit from her own office. I'm man enough to know I don't care if she's watching the show. I just want to see her.

I want to see her smile, same as she did when she came to breakfast this morning. I want to see her shift on her chair, trying to find a comfortable position, given the arse I striped last night. I want to see her blush as she remembers how I used her, how she let herself be used.

I want to see her.

Which is reason enough for me to stay in my own bloody office. I have an empire to run. I pace away from the windows, flexing my knees to ease some of the pressure my zipper has placed on my cock.

Coming upstairs, Madden takes the steps two at a time, sounding like a T-Rex crashing through a jungle. He whistles as he's walking down the hall, which gives me plenty of time to cross to the door. "What's the cr—?" he starts to say, striding into the room.

Craic. He's about to say *craic.* But the word dies in his throat as I catch him in a headlock, partway over the threshold.

He's slow going for my wrist, so he doesn't stand a chance. I use my weight to press his temple against the doorframe, adding pressure until he goes limp in surrender. I ignore the twinge as my barely scabbed wound breaks open beneath its bandage.

"What the fuck?" he complains.

I'm out of line. Samantha said she had everything under control. But I growl, "Touch my wife again, and I'll break your fucking neck."

I'm cutting off my brother's idiotic obsession right here, right now. He came at me with a bundle of lies the night we met Russo at the Rittenhouse. Foolishly, I listened to him then, and I lost five weeks with Samantha.

I know Madden's only carping because he feels cornered by the Mafia don. He hates that Russo's won the last few rounds. But I won't let him put the blame on the woman I love, not when I finally have her home. Well, in the pool house. At Thornfield, anyway.

Still pressed against the door, my idiot brother proves he has more bollocks than brains by asking, "Which wife?"

Before I can rip those shriveled stones off him and make him eat them bite by bite, there's a voice from the hallway. "Oh, joy. The circus came to town, and I'm in time to see the clowns."

I give Madden one last shove before I push off him. Fiona's standing in the hallway, dressed like she just stepped off one of those fashion runways in Paris. The crimson of her trousers looks like she dipped them in blood. Her jacket closes with a single button across her flat stomach, pretty much engraving an invitation to check out her tits. Her bra isn't up to the challenge even though—or maybe because—the lacy cups are dyed to match the trousers. She's finished the outfit with four-inch stilettos.

This is the first I've seen of Fiona Ingram this morning. She was under no obligation to come to breakfast—I have neither the jurisdiction nor desire to insist on house rules for her. But she clearly detoured by the dining room before coming to this meeting. From the smell of it, her expensive insulated mug is filled with coffee instead of the tea a good Irish girl should drink.

I growl at the pair of them and stalk over to my desk. Madden throws himself into one of the plaid chairs. Fiona takes over the couch. Fair play to her, choosing a seat that forces Madden to twist half-way round to keep an eye on her.

"Cards on the table," I say, leaning back so they know I'm not intimidated by either of them. "Last month, we met with Russo's bunch at the Rittenhouse." I point at Fiona, knowing the gesture's rude and not giving a shite. "You had marching orders from your da. You cut a deal with Russo's boss before we ever sat down to the bargaining table."

She doesn't try to argue—just salutes me with her coffee before taking a sip. I fight a swell of irritation. I want her to lie, just so I can give out to her, put her in her place once and for all.

But I go on, because that's the only option she's left me. "For almost six weeks, I've worked under the peace treaty—no business west of Tenth Street, nothing from the port, no new corner boys. I've lost a third of my protection money, two whorehouses, and a gambling club, not to mention after-hours pours at all the bars. We're running in the red."

Fiona merely studies her nails. "A good Captain has a backup plan," she says.

"My *backup plan* was boosting a shipment of cocaine from the Philadelphia port the night of the summit. The Germans were bringing it in, rebuilding after their own upsets last year."

I witnessed part of that *upset* personally, a dry shite butchered for his poor choices in life. His business partners met their own bad ends shortly before Christmas, leaving a vacuum on the docks. And as the good Jesuit brothers taught me at St. Ann's, nature abhors a vacuum.

I should have had a quarter billion dollars of coke free and clear last month.

"Russo hijacked the truck," I say, just in case Fiona's forgotten that little detail. "I'm still digging to find out how he knew about the shipment, how he traced the Fishtown Boys."

"I've already told him how," Madden says to Fiona. He has to look over his shoulder to talk to her, which makes him look scared. Scared as well as stupid, because he chirps the same song he's tried before. "Sam's feeding information to that goombah."

For one blinding moment, I consider shutting his eejit mouth forever. Or at least knocking his teeth down his throat. Breaking a few bones. Carving a reminder on his feckin' chest so he drops his line about Samantha forever.

After all, why should I keep a hospital-grade surgery in the house, if I'm not prepared to use it? Why should I keep Doc Kelleher on retainer if I don't create an emergency or two on the regular?

But I've got legitimate business to get through this morning. So I lower my voice to barely a whisper and deliver a different threat: "Say it again, and you're out of the Boys."

Madden opens his mouth. Shuts it. Sits back in his chair with the exasperated tongue-click of a teenage girl. I watch him consider half a dozen responses—lies about Samantha, all—but he chooses a wiser course of action.

He says: "I know how you can make up the shortfall."

He's my feckin' Clan Chief. I need to take my second-in-command seriously. "I'm listening," I say. Fiona glances between us, like she's watching a tennis match on the telly.

"Explosives," he says.

I'm not sure I heard him right. "Explosives?"

"Bombs," he says, like I might have stumbled over the three-syllable word.

"What the hell do the Fishtown Boys know about bombs?"

"The Boys don't," Madden admits. "But *I* do. I've learned a lot from the boys in Dublin."

Madden's always been fascinated by the old country. There're plenty of old-timers there, happy to talk about the Troubles over a lash or ten. Madden planted three pipe bombs for me back in February, one of the first skirmishes in our war with Russo.

Now I eye him with curiosity. "So, you're the Mad Irish Bomber now?"

He shrugs. "I've been reading some things. Experimenting."

"And how, exactly, will we make money with explosives?" I give all three syllables equal stress before I say, "Assuming you don't blow your fucking hands off."

"My hands are in perfect working order." That sounds like a boast, like he's keeping a harem of needy women satisfied.

Fiona scoffs.

"The money?" I remind him.

"We can hire out our services—anyone going after a bank, an armored car, any sort of safe. Or we can work as middlemen, start with raw materials and send out finished bombs. I've only been working with dynamite so far, but I have a line on military-grade goods. C4. That type of thing."

I'm surprised. Madden's never shown this much initiative before. But I imagine the thought of blowing up shite puts some iron in his prick. I'm just not sure it's a good idea to set my brother loose with that type of power.

Fiona seems to notice my hesitation. She offers a pointed smile over another sip of her coffee. "Or not," she says, as if I've already given Madden an official shut-down notice. "What's your plan, Captain?" she says to me. "You've got limited territory. Reduced earnings. A stolen shipping container. What are you going to do?"

I don't want to tell her. I don't want her learning the first thing about my operations.

But she's here, and she's staying, at least for now. And if I don't give her *something* to pass on to her da, I'll only face more grief down the road.

So I open the door on my latest operation, one that sounds so outlandish Boston'll never buy in, nor anyone else in the Grand Irish Union. "To start with," I say. "Counterfeit goods. Butter."

"Butter?" She's careful not to laugh out loud. Madden sulks as I refuse to engage on his grand scheme.

"Home cooks'll pay twice as much for something labeled Irish as they will for domestic."

"Is there any difference?"

"Irish butter is more yellow. And it has a higher fat content. But with a little food coloring added in, who's to know? The Mafia do the same with olive oil—buy cheap stuff and label it extra virgin."

"There's money in it?" she asks.

"Twenty billion a year, for the oil. No one knows how much for butter. Yet."

She nods like an accountant flashing fingers over an adding machine. She's taking me seriously. "You'll need a strong supply chain. And dedicated distribution."

"Working on it," I say. She isn't telling me anything I don't know. I'd have the system in place already if I wasn't so busy recovering from the blow she dealt me at the Rittenhouse.

"What else've you got?" she asks.

I've been saving this one. Even Madden doesn't know. And it's safe to share in front of Fiona, because no one else in the Union can ever make a similar deal.

"Imports," I say.

My brother's still out of sorts, so it's Fiona who feeds me a skeptical opening. "Imports?"

"I've got a contact back home." Eighteen years I've lived in Philadelphia, and *home* is still an ocean away. "In County Sligo. Near Skreen."

Madden starts humming *Danny Boy*. I ignore him.

Fiona continues with the heavy lifting. "What sort of contact?"

"The sort that sweeps floors in a cold country church. The sort that opened a storage closet a few weeks back, when ancient Father Donall died, may he rest in peace." I cross myself, just so I can see them ape me. Fiona complies, annoyance plain on her face. Madden doesn't bother.

"The good father was holding out on his parishioners," I say. "Never gave a hint about what he was hiding."

Fiona's tired of playing my game. "Enough," she says. "What are you bringing in?"

I turn around my monitor, so both of them can see. The pictures are poor quality. My man on the inside has a phone that's ten years old.

It's a book. Judging by the five-pound note in the frame, it's as long as my forearm and two hands wide. The cover looks like wood, embossed with tarnished silver and latched with gold. It has iron hinges, two of them, and the pages lie almost flat when it's open.

I'm no expert on bibles, and I can't read Latin with a gun to my head. But every good Irishman has heard of the Book of Kells, and a little Internet research pointed me toward the Lindisfarne Gospels too.

The Book of Skreen was made thirteen hundred years ago. The colors look as fresh as yesterday's paint. The designs are so complex my eyes cross tracing them.

"It must be fake," Fiona says.

I shrug. "Father Donall didn't think so. He kept it hidden away. There was a curse on the book, one that said the man who opens it will burn in Hell forever."

"Please," Fiona says, pursing her very modern, very cosmopolitan lips.

"We'll see what it's worth when it gets here."

"Which will be?" She's all business now. As if she has a better meeting to get to.

"I've sent Patrick Moran to fetch it."

That gets Madden's attention. I wouldn't send my Warlord, my chief enforcer, if I didn't think the book was real.

"He's bringing it here?" Madden asks. I can already see him plotting to get it away from me.

I shake my head. "It's going straight to the freeport."

"The freeport?" Fiona asks.

"Diamond Freeport. In Delaware. A domestic tax haven where I keep a gallery for things I want kept secret."

"I know *what* a freeport is. I didn't know which one you use."

"Sam works there," Madden says. He sounds like a kindergarten brat tattling on the girl who made him eat paste.

"Samantha's General Counsel there," I clarify. "She knows what's what. She'll get the book appraised. Help with an auction when we're ready to move it."

"She'll *help* all right," Madden says.

I shoot him a look designed to shrivel the worm that passes for his prick. Fiona actually cracks a smile as he shifts in discomfort.

"It sounds like Samantha and I have a lot to talk about," Fiona says.

I don't like the tone of her voice. I like her words even less. But I can't think of a single reason to forbid her to talk to the woman in the office down the hall.

"Do what you must," I say, like I don't care.

"You should know by now, Captain. I always do."

Fiona's lips curl as she takes another sip of coffee. It's the smile of a lioness. I'm just not sure if I'm a lion or a gazelle.

9

SAMANTHA

～

Everything's different. Everything's the same.

It shouldn't matter that the door to Birte's refuge on the third floor is open. Now that I know Braiden's first wife—his only *legal* wife—lives up there, I shouldn't still be drawn to the end of the hall. I shouldn't need to take careful steps over the runner, testing the floorboards for squeaks. I shouldn't be sneaking around Thornfield.

But I do slink down the hall. I dart past the door to the infirmary as if monsters lurk under the hospital bed, waiting to suck me inside. And I don't realize why I'm so on edge until I'm hovering outside Braiden's office.

Braiden is meeting with Madden and Fiona. They're talking Fishtown Boys business. The criminal empire is unfolding in that office, and I'm drawn like a lemming to a cliff.

Murder. Extortion. Racketeering in all its gritty filth—the sort of dangerous business that makes Thornfield's electrified fence necessary, that accounts for the gatehouse with its armed men, that justifies a presidential-grade safe room and an armory to match.

I've been with Braiden for nearly three months, and I still don't understand all he does to maintain his illegal domain.

I catch my breath to better hear what they're saying.

Braiden is talking about *butter*.

After a minute, it makes more sense. He's talking about counterfeit goods. About defrauding home cooks, maybe some restaurants. His plan might affect legitimate dairy farmers; he might cut into the profit of the dairy lobby.

But I'm ashamed when I imagine all the terrible things I *thought* they'd be discussing.

Before I can head back to my office, Fiona laughs. The sound is deep and throaty. I immediately picture her long limbs in a man's silk pajamas, the top hanging open seductively.

On paper, Fiona and I are so similar we could be twins. Both of us were raised in the heart of organized crime. We're accustomed to making our way as women in a world ruled by men. We speak up when we need to, and we fight for what we want.

In person, though, I can't imagine a woman more different from me. I've spent the past eleven years filing off the serial numbers of my childhood. I've narrowed my life to black and white and gray, all I deserve after That Night.

Fiona, to the contrary, has apparently never doubted her value for a second. She's jewel tones and leather, stiletto heels and hundred-dollar lipsticks. She takes what she wants, never doubting it's hers, never questioning if she's worth it.

And when Fiona laughs, I know I have no place in Braiden's office. That meeting isn't meant for me.

Down the hall, my own office feels cold and empty. I bring up a series of emails from Sonja Heller, the junkyard-dog lawyer I've hired to represent me in the proceeding that will determine whether I keep my law license. The ethics board has sent a list of demands. They want me to answer dozens of questions. There are hundreds of documents they want to review. They want medical records and pay stubs, and confirmation of dates of employment for every job I've ever held, including two weeks that I scooped ice cream during my sophomore year in high school.

And that's only the start.

The board will decide if my hiding the drunk-driving deaths of three innocent people is a crime of "moral turpitude". They'll decide if what I did is so repulsive I can no longer be trusted as a lawyer.

I've done some legal research.

I haven't found a single case where any other lawyer in any jurisdiction did what I did. It's not just the three people who died. It's the fact that I was drunk and high while I was driving. That I covered up the crime. That I kept it secret for eleven years, and would have hidden it for longer if a private citizen hadn't made the details public.

It doesn't help that I used Mafia money to cover up what happened in the first place. And my current employer is a corporation created specifically to protect billionaires from tax obligations. And my so-called "husband" is a Captain in the Irish Mob.

But most damning of all: Every last detail of my case continues to be front-page news on an almost-daily basis, because headline-crazed paparazzi follow me around like wolves chasing a wounded sheep.

It's just a matter of time before I'm taken down, left without a law license, without a job.

The tip of my nose is icy. I realize I need a sweater, so I make my way to the pool house, squinting in the brilliant morning sun. I'm concentrating on the tarp that covers the pool, studying the stones that anchor its swooping edges. That's my only excuse for not noticing the open door until my hand is on the knob.

The pool house is meant for guests to use. There's no lock

on the door. No privacy. I didn't think that would matter, not when Braiden runs all of Thornfield.

"Hello?" I call, pausing in the doorway.

It takes a moment for my eyes to adjust to the dim light. The inside of the pool house is as cool and dark as a cave. I left the window coverings down when I went to breakfast.

I catch a flash of movement by the counter. Blinking, I step to my right, letting more sunlight stream inside.

Grace Poole stands by the liquor bottles Fairfax left yesterday. She has one claw wrapped around the Belvedere. The other holds a battered, dented hip flask made of steel.

"What the fuck are you doing?" I shout, my voice even louder and harsher than I intend. I storm into my home, carried on a tide of raw rage.

She ducks her head like she thinks she'll be smacked. Shielding her face with one hand, she pulls the full fifth of vodka close to her body.

No. It's not full anymore.

Half the bottle's been drained away. Even if her flask is filled to the brim, Grace has downed enough booze to pickle a rat.

"Ma'am," she says, dropping the old-fashioned curtsey she uses like a weapon. "I thought ya were a' th' house."

I could get drunk from the fumes on her breath. "I'm sure you did," I say. "Who gave you permission to come in here?"

"No one, ma'am. I were checkin' th' linens. Makin' sure ya have yer flannels and towels and whatnot."

"You're lying!"

"Ma'am!" She cringes like she thinks I'll beat her.

"You're supposed to be with Birte. Where did you leave her? Why aren't you keeping an eye on her?"

"Miss Birte's with th' wean."

The wean. That's what Grace calls Aiofe. I remember from the day she cornered me in the greenhouse. "It's Monday," I say. "Aiofe should be with her tutor, now that Father Regis is gone."

"Mr. John called out sick. Brown bottle flu, I say."

Completely missing any hint of irony, she sniffs like she smells something rotten before she mimes taking a drink. She seems surprised to find her flask in her hand.

"Grace, this is absolutely unacceptable. Now that Birte is allowed access to all of Thornfield, she needs *more* supervision, not less. You absolutely cannot let her wander the grounds alone."

"Miss Aiofe is with—"

"Aiofe is a child! A sick child who can't watch over a grown woman. What if Aiofe needed to shout a warning? What if she needed to call for help?"

"Th' first Mrs. Kelly—"

"Stop," I say.

"But Miss Birte *is* th' first—"

"Not another word."

"Miss—"

"Enough!" I shout. "You're supposed to be watching a fragile woman who's roaming outside for the first time in years. You came in here without permission. You lied about why you were here. You stole liquor and now you're drunk and you're arguing to cover up the fact that you've endangered the life of a child."

With every statement I make, Grace shrinks a little more. Her shoulders slump. Her chin digs into her chest. Her fingers curl into talons, clutching the only thing she cares about: Her flask.

Her weakness make me furious. I want to scratch her sullen face. I want to rip out her dull, matted hair.

If Grace had done her job properly, Birte would never have appeared in the dining room. I never would have discovered Braiden's lies.

A tiny voice of reason whispers in the back of my mind: I should be grateful I found out now. Because of Grace, it's not too late.

Too late for what? I just want to stop hurting.

"I'm going to Braiden right now," I say. "I'm telling him to fire you."

"Ma'am!"

"I want you out of here tonight."

She starts to sob, a terrible sound, like pigeons boiling in a pot. "Ma'am," she chokes out.

"On the next flight to Dublin," I say.

She sinks to her knees. Grabbing the hem of my pants, she pleads in an unholy mixture of English and Irish. I stagger back, trying to escape the clutch of her fingers. I stumble, though, because someone's standing behind me.

It's Aiofe.

She's wearing her puffy purple coat with the bright pink zipper—security against the occasional gust of March wind. Her hair is woven into two braids, with soft curls escaping at her temples and the nape of her neck. Her eyes are bright, almost feverish.

She gapes at Grace in shock. Her lower lip starts to tremble and two fat tears trickle down her cheeks.

Grace clambers to her feet. She drags the back of one hand across her face, scraping away tears and snot. With the other, she shoves her flask deep in her apron pocket.

"Hey ho, wean," she says, shaky on the first two words, but smiling by the third.

Aiofe looks from Grace to me and back again. Her forehead puckers in confusion.

"Don't ya worry, lass," Grace says, patting her shoulder. "Herself and me, we was jus' talkin'. Not t' fear, wee one. Ya got nothin' t' fear."

Aiofe nods as if she's finished adding up a massive column of numbers. Her smile, when she manages one, is like the sun coming out from behind a bank of clouds.

As I watch, astonished by the transition, she unzips her jacket. Nestled inside, crushed against her dark blue cable-knit sweater, are a dozen flowers—tulips in pastel shades of pink and yellow and lavender.

I stare at the miniature turbans of the flowers' tight-wrapped petals. Aiofe gathers them together and shoves them toward my hand. When I still don't understand, she moves them from her heart to mine.

"They're for me?" I ask.

She nods, as seriously as if she's passing me a Nobel prize. She points toward my duvet cover, with its stylized tulips woven between banks of honeysuckle.

"Thank you," I say. "They're beautiful."

Aiofe's smile turns shy. She ducks her head and looks up at Grace through her lashes.

"I tol' ya," Grace says to her. "Posies make a house a home. The missus knows that, same as anyone. G'wan now. Put 'em in water, 'afore they wilt." She points toward the highball glasses next to the liquor bottles.

Obediently, Aiofe takes one and holds it under the faucet until it's half full. She sets the stems in the water carefully, like they're made out of spun sugar and might shatter. Biting her lip, she takes her time arranging them, moving the colors around to make a secret pattern.

When she's finally finished, she looks at Grace, her wide eyes clearly seeking approval.

Grace nods. "That's savage, lass."

Aiofe grins again, pride puffing her narrow chest. She hands me the glass with two hands, bowing a little in her excitement at presenting her gift.

"They're perfect," I say. I set the flowers on top of the microwave, where they can be seen from every point in the room.

When we're all through admiring them, Grace says to Aiofe, "Now where's yer Auntie Birte?"

Aiofe moves her hand in a waving pattern, shifting from side to side like a salmon swimming upstream. I don't need words to understand that Birte's in the greenhouse, watching koi in the Irish garden fish pond.

"Shall we get her, then? Bring her back t' th' house fer a cuppa 'n' one o' Fairfax's biscuits?"

Aiofe shakes her head fiercely, then holds up two fingers.

"Two biscuits?" Grace asks. "Have ya been good enow fer two?"

Aiofe points emphatically to my flowers.

"A gift fer th' missus. Yer right. Ya should get two biscuits fer that."

Aiofe heads for the doorway, but Grace calls her back. The woman reaches for the pink zipper and slides it up to the top of the purple jacket.

"Don't want ya catchin' yer death o' cold," she says, even though it's pleasantly warm in the sun.

"Aiofe," I say, just before she steps outside. "Thank you again. The flowers are lovely." She nods and slips her hand companionably into Grace's.

Before they can leave, I call out, "Grace?"

The woman stops in the doorway without turning to face me.

"Forget what I said earlier. You can stay. Keep an eye on Aiofe and Birte, both."

Something unhitches in her shoulders, and she takes a step forward.

But I call out again: "Grace? Leave the flask behind."

For a moment, I think she won't do it. But then she reaches into her apron with her free hand, the one Aiofe hasn't caught. She fishes out the flask and stoops to set it on the threshold before she lets Aiofe drag her into the sunshine.

I don't trust Grace Poole. She's a drinking alcoholic who's overmatched by her job.

But as I pour the vodka down the drain, I have to admit that Aiofe loves her. Aiofe *needs* her. And if there's anything I can do to ease that poor child's life, I'll do it. No more questions asked.

10

BRAIDEN

Tuesday morning, Fiona steps in front of the Jeep as I take the wide turn from the garage toward Thornfield's front gate. She has a greater confidence in mechanical braking than I have, or maybe she trusts her father will string me up by my thumbs if I don't stop in time.

Climbing in on the passenger side, she asks, "Where to?"

"*You're* going back to the house. I'm making the milk run."

"Your Fairfax doesn't keep your pantry stocked?"

I can't tell if she's yanking my chain, or if she really doesn't understand. "I make the round for collections once a month. Keep my eye on the business. Make sure no one forgets me."

She gives me a crafty side-eye. "No one's forgetting *you* anytime soon."

She might be flirting under orders from her da, or maybe she's really interested in having a go. But I've already got two women wearing my wedding bands, and I'm not looking to add another. "Go on then," I tell her. "Back in the house."

"I'm coming with you."

I tighten my hands on the wheel. She's wearing black leather pants and a matching corset laced up the front. Her stiletto heels look like they've dug into more than one man's dangling bits. I can't see where she'd hide a riding crop, but it's all she needs to complete her little dominatrix outfit.

"Not dressed like that, you aren't."

I know it's the wrong thing to say the instant the words are out of my mouth. So I'm not surprised when she curves her scarlet-painted lips and says, "Fuck that," she says. "You're not my da."

If she were Samantha, I'd turn her over my knee.

If she were Samantha, I'd punish her for weeks, just for showing off her wares like that.

If she were Samantha, I'd never be having this conversation.

But she's not Samantha. She's a business associate, with hopes of learning from me about how I manage my billion-dollar cartel. And she's making me late for a whole round of meetings.

"I'm not your da," I agree. "But I'm responsible for keeping you safe as long as you're in Philly. Change your clothes or stay at Thornfield."

She considers fighting back, but it seems that Fiona Ingram is ultimately a practical businesswoman. She opens the car door and slips off the seat.

"I'm leaving in five," I warn.

She replies with a single jutting finger.

I lean back while I wait, banging my head against the padded headrest.

Fiona Ingram is feckin' trouble, with a capital, hand-lettered F. My goal is to show her how boring life is in Philadelphia. There's nothing for her to learn about my operation. She might as well go home and pester her da for a role in Boston.

The sooner I can convince her of that, the better. The trick will be getting Ingram to accept her return without starting a war.

Another war.

Russo's already chewing away at my right side. I can't afford to have the Grand Irish Union go after my left. Because Ingram's exactly the type of spiteful shitehawk to have a go at me, if he thinks I've insulted his daughter.

Fiona's got one thing going for her—she's a quick dresser. She's back in the Jeep in little more than a minute. She didn't bother swapping out those leather fuck-me pants. But she's put on a sapphire-colored jacket that covers her from chin to thigh. It's got five buttons and every one of them is done up. And it isn't even leather.

It's cut tight enough that I can guess her feckin' bra size, but I'll count this one as a win.

"Tame enough for you, old man?"

I don't take the bait. Instead, I put the Jeep in gear and head toward Fishtown.

But her taunt sticks with me, as I merge into the fast lane on 30. I'm only thirty-five. Hardly ready for a walker and adult diapers.

"How old are you, then?" I ask, like I haven't been brooding for the past five minutes.

"Twenty-four." She sounds defensive.

Younger than I thought. But I ask, "Why hasn't your da married you off by now?"

"He's tried."

We cover a few miles, but she doesn't share any details. I'm not opposed to digging. "Kieran Ingram's Captain of the Boston Mob," I say, like it's news to her. "General of the GIU. I'd expect him to have some strong feelings about your future."

"What's that street sign say?" She points to a black and white shield ten yards down the road.

"Highway 30?"

"*U.S.* Highway 30," she corrects. "We're not in the old country. Da can't tie me up and drop me on the steps of some church and expect the priest to look the other way."

She's wrong. Ingram could do exactly that. Money talks. And Mob money has a louder voice than just about anyone else's.

I should know. That's how I got my ring on Samantha's finger.

But there's no reason not to humor Fiona for now. "What are you holding out for then?"

She spares a sly smile. "True love and ten dozen long-stem red roses."

"I didn't count you as a woman to sell yourself cheap."

"Have you checked the price of flowers lately?"

"There's that," I say, as if I'm agreeing. I have no idea what roses cost, any more than I can quote the price for a gallon of milk. I sent three dozen roses to Samantha her first day back at work after our honeymoon. Sounds like I should have quadrupled the order.

We get to my first stop—a basement gambling den on Wildey—and I park in front of a fire hydrant. Most of the ticket writers know my Jeep by sight. If someone makes a mistake, well, that's why I fund City Council campaigns. I know plenty of people who can make a fine disappear.

"Watch," I say as we head down the steps. "Don't talk."

I'll give Fiona credit. She's quiet as my shadow, standing back and letting me take care of business. Mikey's worked with me for donkey's years now. "If it isn't Himself," he says, handing over the envelope that's waiting on the corner of his desk.

"Feels a bit light," I say.

Mikey looks like a Bassett hound caught in a rain storm. His jowls slosh as he shakes his head. "Business has been off all month. Some of it's Lent, good Irish lads passing up the cards."

"And the rest of it?"

He sighs. "This war you're in with the goombahs. No one wants to get caught in the crossfire."

"We're in a truce now, Mikey. Have been for a month and a half."

"The boys who come here want to gamble on a royal flush. Not on how long those guinea shitehawks will honor a feckin' truce."

Money's getting tight. Russo drove off with two hundred and fifty million dollars of my cocaine. I'm looking for a new place to rebuild the Hare. I've got a constant stream of payments, getting city officials to look the other way, and business has been lighter than usual at Kelly Construction.

But Mikey isn't responsible for any of that. I slip his envelope into my breast pocket. "Pleasure doing business with you," I say.

Fiona waits till we're back in the car to speak. "You don't worry he's skimming?"

"Mikey's brother was a runner for me, years back. Till he decided it was easier to snitch to the feds than face a heroin rap. He ended up in the Schuylkill with a rat in his mouth." I tap the envelope through my jacket. "Mikey knows the cost if he skims."

I skip my other gambling spot, and the after-hours bars too. No reason to serve up my entire list to Fiona on a silver platter.

We hit a couple of restaurants, spread out over a dozen blocks. By the time we get to McKinley's, word's got out. Everyone knows the boss is making today's run. I'd rather catch them unawares, but I'll settle for seeing them on their best behavior.

I save the girls for last. Part of me is hoping Fiona'll get bored, that she'll decide to take an Uber back to Thornfield. Not feckin' likely.

At this hour, the working girls are still asleep. Mimi's nursing a coffee that looks like it's half Bailey's. It smells like pure booze.

"Your cast is off," I say, as she raises her mug in greeting. One of Russo's thugs broke her arm before our peace talks at the Rittenhouse.

"Good as new," she says, opening and closing her fist. I paid for her to see one of the best orthopedists in the city. And I picked up her tab for a week in Atlantic City when she was too sore to work. "Here you go," she says, handing over her envelope.

"Good week," I say, because Lent doesn't seem to have made a dent in the whorehouse business.

"Spring break. God bless the frat boys of St. Peter's University." She makes a half-hearted sign of the cross before she nods toward Fiona. "Who's your lady friend?"

"Just a visitor from out of town."

"Showing her all the top tourist sites, eh?"

"The Chamber of Commerce says I'm a model citizen."

When we get back to the car, I decide to skip the strip club. Madden can pick up Jacko's envelope later, along with all the other stops I've driven past.

We're back on 30 when Fiona says, "So I'm your dirty little secret?"

I wondered how she'd take my keeping her name out of it. "No reason to paint it on the city walls—Kieran Ingram's got my bollocks in a vise."

"You think that's what's going on here?"

"It isn't?"

"If Da wanted to dig in his claws, you'd be talking to his Warlord, not to me."

"Sending his chief enforcer might make too loud a statement."

She cocks her head to one side. I don't know how she gauges it, but a shaft of sunlight falls straight on her slick red lips. "I can be plenty loud."

With that tone, she intends her words to go straight to my cock. She wants me to shift in discomfort or—better yet—come back with a promise of all the ways I'll make her scream.

I've been talking dirty since she was eight years old, and I always deliver on my promises. But I won't be playing her game today.

"Your da's using you," I say.

"My da trusts me to build his empire."

"By spreading your legs for the likes of me?"

She flushes so hard her cheeks match her lips. I don't think she knows the meaning of the word shame, so I'm guessing that's anger I see. "By serving as his Clan Chief. I'll be in charge of Boston one day."

"Not unless you grow a prick down there. How long did he give you to land in my bed?"

"Jesus, you're an asshole. I just thought the two of us might have some fun."

"Your type of fun leaves a man looking for a new line of work."

"I'll need a Clan Chief once I'm in charge."

I suspect she doesn't mean me to laugh. And I'm not sure the harsh bark that squeezes out of my chest even counts as amusement. So I make my voice deadly serious to avoid any misunderstanding. "I won't be anyone's second in command."

"You go on telling yourself that," she says.

She reaches out and slaps down the sun visor. Neither of us says another word until we're back at Thornfield. I work the security at the gate, masking a wince as my bandaged arm stretches for the biometric reader. I start the long drive up to the house.

"Let me know when you're ready to head back to Boston," I say.

"I don't need your permission to travel."

"No. But you need my permission to stay."

I wait for her to call me on the lie. If I bundle her home, Ingram'll have something to say about it.

Instead, she says, "I don't want to fight with you."

"You have an odd way of showing that."

"I'm here to learn," she says. "I want to see how you run things."

"You go on telling yourself that," I say, matching her tone from earlier.

She squares her shoulders. "So you're afraid of showing me how the Fishtown Boys work?"

"I just took you on the milk run."

She purses her lips, puffing out a sigh of dismissal. "You let me see your marks. Some of them. Not even half, I'm guessing. I want to see your men. That is, if you aren't afraid to show me."

"Nothing about you frightens me, Fiona."

"I've killed four men."

"Closer to seven from what I've heard."

She doesn't like that. Some of her kills leave her ashamed. That's good leverage to have. I need more details.

But she isn't through yet. "If you're not afraid, Kelly, then let me meet your Council."

"I've nothing to hide. You can meet every one of my made men."

"Fine," she says, those feckin' lips curling into a smile.

"Fine," I repeat.

And that's how I end up telling Fairfax we're having two dozen for dinner on Friday night.

11

SAMANTHA

I've been to plenty of black-tie events. The freeport has them all the time, at least once a quarter. That's what our clients expect.

I know how to twist my hair in a sophisticated up-do. I can paint on everything from a full smokey eye to subtle lash-lengthening mascara, from statement lips to a bare sheen of gloss. I'm able to apply three coats of nail polish without a single smear, on my fingers and my toes.

The first fancy event I ever attended was my parents' tenth wedding anniversary. I was five years old, and my party-dress was Barbie pink, with layers of lace from my chin to my knees.

After That Night, I knew I'd never wear frills or flowers again. I dressed in classic black. Strapless or over one shoulder. Maybe a sweetheart neckline. The fabrics were always sleek. Always severe.

But this is the first formal event I've attended since Braiden and I said our vows. This is the first where I'm bound by house rules.

The hem of my skirt sweeps the floor. Laid out on my bed in the pool house, it covered a generous half-circle. The background silk is black, setting off a riot of huge, blowsy flowers—peonies and chrysanthemums and tulips in a dozen shades of pink and purple and gold. My top is all black, which might violate Braiden's requirements, except the sleeves and back are so sheer I look naked. A fuchsia belt cinches my waist, as wide as my hand. Best of all, the skirt has pockets—like my wedding gown. Like all the clothes I love.

I wait to leave the pool house until I know the party is in full swing. Braiden is entertaining in the ballroom, where the parquet floor covers half a wing on Thornfield's ground floor. I've walked by it before; the doors are kept open year-round. Smoked mirrors line one wall. A fireplace large enough to roast an ox fills another.

Tonight, the room swarms with tuxedos. Starched white shirts. Slim black pants with shiny stripes. Shoes that gleam like molten glass. Emerald cummerbunds, emerald waistcoats, emerald neckties—some straight and more pulled into bows.

Braiden told me he was inviting all his made men, every one of the Fishtown Boys who's sworn a loyalty oath. This is Braiden's true family, more than Madden is, more than Birte and Aiofe. Far more than I, the woman he shacked up with after a sham priest told a few lies.

I pluck a champagne flute from a nearby waiter's tray. For just a moment, my stomach twists into a painful knot. Less than a week ago, Braiden and I were at that other party, the one where I was attacked by a man pretending to be a waiter. We still don't know who put out the hit.

The champagne is sour, but I drink it down like medicine. This ballroom is the one place in the world where I know I'm absolutely safe. No killers are getting into Thornfield. Even the men carrying trays are Braiden's runners, Fishtown Boys, safe and secure. Not an assassin among them.

I swap my empty glass for a full one.

I'm the only woman in the room. The testosterone is so thick in the air, it feels like sunscreen. Each man takes up more space than the laws of physics allow—with their height, their wide shoulders, their hearty laughs and catcalls.

Wait.

There *is* another woman.

Fiona Ingram is in the far corner. I missed her at first because she's wearing a tuxedo like the men. Like their trousers, at least. She hasn't bothered with a jacket. Her backless shirt has a halter collar, drawing attention to her long neck and bare shoulders. She's wearing four-inch heels, and she's holding a champagne glass as if it's a scepter.

The men swarm around her like ants on honeycomb. Fiona throws back her head and laughs at someone's joke. She traces a finger down one lucky man's chest. She looks across the room, measuring whether her game is working.

She's staring straight at Braiden.

He's deep in conversation with Madden—standing a little too close, looking a little too tense. Braiden's hair is ruffled, which means he's been running his fingers through it. He raises a glass of amber liquid and tosses off half his drink, sucking air through his teeth before he dives back in to whatever point he's been making. He doesn't seem to be aware of Fiona at all.

But Madden is. His eyes dart toward her like he's a starving dog, and she's a meaty bone.

My glass is empty again. A nervous boy with acne scars on his cheeks walks by with a tray. I trade for a new, full flute and go back to my survey.

All right. I'm not the only woman here. But I'm willing to bet I'm the only civilian in the room. And the only Italian too. The men here know me as Samantha Kelly. Some of them met me as Sam Mott. But the name on my birth certificate is

Giovanna Canna, and I learned Italian from my *nonna* before I learned English.

As long as I'm tallying up differences, I'm pretty sure I'm the only lawyer here too. One man near the windows is showing another his wristwatch, and I'm willing to bet a year of my freeport salary he's telling a story about how it fell off the back of a truck. A tall man with wavy red hair takes a money clip out of his pocket. He counts out a dozen bills, and I catch the light glinting off Ben Franklin's high forehead as he hands the money to a colleague.

I'm General Counsel at Diamond Freeport. I know how the law can bend around facts. I've spent years stretching obscure legal theories to the breaking point. But this is the first time I've been in a room where I'm *certain* every other person has committed enough felonies to go away for life.

I'm guilty myself. I've taken three lives.

Once more, my glass is dry. It's only champagne. I'm used to handling much stronger alcohol.

I swap glasses again, but better safe than sorry. I'll get some food in my stomach. Make sure my drinks don't go to my head.

I cross the room to a table filled with Fairfax's most delicate offerings, arrayed on serving platters like intricate mosaics. There are miniature lamb chops finished with a perfect mince of mint. Crisped rounds of potato topped with gleaming caviar. A charcuterie tray crowded with ten types of cheese and a stunning array of paper-thin meats.

I'm swallowing a stuffed zucchini blossom when someone comes up behind me. Too close for comfort, he leans into my back. His whisper feels like rancid oil poured into my ear. "Of course you go for the guinea food."

"Madden."

He leans across me, reaching for one of the caviar potatoes. I can either take a step back or let his head brush my chest. I move, which angles me into a corner of the room. I'm trapped by the table, cut off from the crowd.

Madden chews and swallows without shifting his weight, without opening a path for my escape. He wipes his greasy lips with the back of his hand.

I clutch my champagne glass tightly. I've seen Braiden use a flute as a weapon. I can shatter the crystal against the wall and bring it up in one smooth arc, bury it in Madden's throat and watch him bleed out on the ballroom floor.

Jesus. I really *am* a killer.

Madden says, "I'll give you one thing. You're not wearing a wire for your goombah pimp."

He eyes the sheer sleeves of my top. I'm queasy at the thought of him staring at my near-naked back. How long was he behind me before he spoke?

Madden says, "You'll just have to remember everything you hear. All the Fishtown plans you'll pass him while he takes you up the arse."

"You're drunk," I say.

"Not even close."

"Then you're insane."

He eyes me like I haven't said a word. "Maybe you *are* wired. What have you got beneath that skirt? What's strapped to your leg?" He makes a move, like he's going to reach beneath my hem.

I wish I had a pistol strapped to my leg—maybe the nine millimeter I bought to defend myself when I lived alone in Dover. But I'm supposedly safe in Thornfield now, my handgun nowhere close. So I lower my voice like I'm issuing orders to a mad dog. "Touch me and I'll scream."

"So little brother Braiden can come save you?" He twists the words into a child's taunt.

I'm a civilian, not a gangster. I grew up in the Mafia, not the Mob. I'm a lawyer, not a criminal. But I know exactly how to castrate a man like Madden Kelly.

"He's your *Captain*, asshole. Because your father thought your mother was only good for a fuck, not for a family."

Madden surges toward me like a pit-bull on an iron chain. The wall feels like a sheet of ice against my spine, as if my sheer top has been dissolved by my spiking pulse.

I smell whiskey on his breath. His cologne stinks of sandalwood and something else, something sharper, something rank: Fear.

Madden's afraid of me. Or he's afraid of what I've said. Or he's afraid of what he's doing, cornering me on the edge of a crowd, where Braiden is only a shout away.

He growls: "Someone needs to teach you some respect, bitch. Put you on your knees and give you something real to gag on."

"You're such a big man, aren't you? Threatening to rape your brother's wife."

"I wouldn't fuck your scabby cunt if—"

A high laugh trills in the air, the sound of honest amusement, of humor and flirtation. Madden jerks back like someone tased his crotch. I look over his shoulder and see Fiona in the precise center of the room.

She strikes a pose, jutting out one hip and raising her glass to the chandelier. "I'll see your limerick, Declan Fitzgerald. And I'll raise you another." She folds both hands around her whiskey, her schoolgirl pose ruined by her bare shoulders. "There was a young fellow named Tucker…"

Before she can finish her rhyme, Braiden looms behind Madden. "Not walking into another wall are you, *dearthàir?*"

Madden glares, but he doesn't try to answer. Fiona finishes her filthy poem, and the room explodes with laughter.

Braiden extends his hand to me, like he's asking me to dance. Or maybe he's helping me across a yawning chasm. "Mrs. Kelly?" he says.

I want to tell him that's not my name. I didn't agree to take his, even when I thought we were legally married. But under the current circumstances, I won't place even the smallest wedge between us.

Madden's a liar. Madden's a jerk. Madden's a paranoid, delusional moron with a fixation on my being Russo's tool.

But Madden is also Braiden's Clan Chief, his second in command. Whatever squabbling the brothers have done for thirty-five years, they've figured out how to make things work. I disrupt that balance at my own peril.

Fiona calls out from her circle of admirers, "Sam! Come on! It's your turn now. Let's hear your dirtiest limerick!"

I've left Braiden waiting all this time—too long. And now every man in the room is staring at me, waiting for me to join in the fun.

12

BRAIDEN

❧

Samantha looks like a child lost in the middle of a county fair. Staring at my hand, she shakes her head, wiping her palm on her skirt instead.

And that skirt...

She looks like some sort of fertility goddess done up in flowers. There's enough cloth that a man could hide under there—and I've given it some thought since I saw her walk through the doorway.

My fingers itch to back her into the same corner where Madden had her. But I wouldn't waste my time talking to her. I'd get a hand under those flowers and tease her till she's soaking wet. Then I'd finger-fuck her till she hides her face against my shoulder to scream.

"Come on, Sam," Fiona calls. "One quick limerick. Prove you're one of the Boys."

The crowd parts. Samantha stumbles forward as if Fiona's got her in a trance.

I reach over and slap Madden's head. "I catch you bullying her again, and we'll settle it with fists."

He scowls. "Not bullying, *deartháir*. Keeping an eye out for my Captain."

The thing is, he might truly believe that's what he's doing. From *his* perspective, Samantha's just a quick fuck I dragged to the church after knowing her for less than a week.

He's never seen the work she does at the freeport. He wasn't there the morning Russo bulled his way into her apartment, saying he'd have her wed by sunset. Madden doesn't know I love her.

Truth be told, Samantha doesn't know that last bit either. I didn't realize it myself, until my arm was torn open by that bullet at the freeport.

It still feels too raw, saying those words out loud. Now that Samantha knows about Birte, it'll sound like I'm trying to manipulate her: *Sure, I've got a first wife, an Irish virgin I'll never take to bed. But you're the one I truly love. Drop those knickers, piscín, and let me fuck you blind.*

Right. Sure. She'd be a fool to believe a line like that.

But I'll tell her. In a way she'll believe. Soon.

Fiona's leading the lads in a chant, slicing the air with the edge of her hand like she's holding a conductor's baton. Half the boys in the room are drooling so hard they can hardly shout: "Sam! Sam! Sam!"

Fiona gulps from her glass of whiskey, leaving a ring of scarlet lipstick on the rim. When she passes the glass to Samantha, her eyes spark with a devilish challenge.

Samantha takes the whiskey. Downs it all. Swallows hard and looks around at the men hooting her name.

She takes a deep breath and says, "Jack and Jane went down the lane—"

The boys start booing before she finishes the line. Fiona makes the sound of a game show buzzer. "Wrong meter. Time to drink!"

One of the lads passes up a full glass. Samantha takes it automatically.

Fiona says, "Drink it down and try again."

Samantha seems as dazed by Fiona Ingram as my men are. She downs the whiskey like it's a requirement for getting paid.

The crowd settles to an unruly hush. Samantha closes her eyes and recites, "Mary, Mary, quite contrary—"

Groans drown her out. Fiona calls over to Cormac, who's closest to the bar. "Pass us the bottle, will you? Sounds like she'll need it!"

Samantha flushes—from the alcohol or from embarrassment I can't be sure. She tries to step out of the circle, but Fiona grabs her arm. "Not so fast!"

Samantha says something, but her protest gets lost in the boys' roar. She looks around, confused, with just enough fear in her eyes that I know she's hopeless as a poet.

She needs me.

And it's easy enough to oblige.

I shoulder through the crowd and take the bottle Cormac's handed over. The room falls dead silent as I raise it overhead.

"There was a young couple named Kelly,
Who met on the steps of a deli.
He fed her his cock,
Till she couldn't walk,
And now she has twins in her belly."

I suspect Kieran Ingram hears the cheers up in Boston. Fiona spins toward me, closing her hand over mine, where I grip the bottle. She raises the Jameson to my lips and sees to it that I down a shot or three.

When I wrestle back control, she laughs and tumbles into my arms. Her mouth lands on mine, hot and ready, her tongue taking advantage of my surprise to go deep. I find her hips and push her away, swiping the back of my hand across my mouth to clear away her lipstick.

Laughing, she takes the bottle and raises a toast: "To Himself!" My men echo her words, hooting and hollering like a flock of feckin' jackdaws.

I finally manage to turn toward Samantha.

She's staring at me like she's the queen of England. Her spine is stiffer than I've ever seen it before. Her jaw is frozen in marble.

Her chin quivers just a little, not enough that any man would see it who hasn't already carved her face on his heart. Her eyes gleam like the bottom of a whiskey bottle, unshed tears trembling.

"Come on, *piscín*," I say, pitching my voice just for her. "It's a joke."

She turns and flees the room, pushing her way through the crowd of my astonished men.

I take two steps, but that's all I can give her. I can't leave Fiona here, can't trust whatever game she's playing. There's Madden, too—the fecker's on my last nerve, and I don't like the way he stared daggers when I caught him taking the piss out of Samantha.

That flower-covered skirt disappears upstairs. I stop short of calling after her just before she clears the landing. Instead, I shove the whiskey bottle toward my brother. "You're up," I say.

Fiona barely hesitates before she starts a new chant: "Madden! Madden!"

In the midst of the chaos, Fairfax is scoping out the food table. He's brought out another platter of those yellow flower things, the fried ones stuffed with cheese. I catch him before he heads back to the kitchen.

"Could you do me a favor?"

He looks like I've just spoken in Swahili. I realize I don't ask him many questions; I'm far more accustomed to issuing orders.

"Samantha's upstairs. Can you check on her? Make sure she's all right?"

"Of course," he says. He was in the kitchen for my bit of poetry, but he's too professional to ask why she wouldn't be just grand.

I wish there was something I could give him to take to her. My ring, but she already has two of mine. A glass of whiskey, but she's had enough of that. One of those flower things Fairfax just set out, but I suspect she's too hepped up to eat.

Fairfax is my chief of staff. He cleans up my messes, day in and day out. I have to trust he'll do his usual fine job tonight.

So I turn back to the crowd that's cheering Madden's limerick. I watch the bottle go to the next man. I see how Fiona has every lad in the room eating out of the palm of her hand. And I cheer my Fishtown Boys because I'm their Captain and they're my men, and we'll gladly give our lives to save each other, come whatever, fair or foul.

13

SAMANTHA

I stand in the bedroom—Braiden's bedroom now—in front of the open dresser. The velvet box sits alone in the top drawer, like it's on display in a museum. Like it's something precious.

My hands shake as I open it. Framed against the jet-black background, the emerald is even darker than I remember—a gateway to a secret world, a door to a hidden dimension.

What is my collar worth? Twenty thousand dollars? Thirty?

If I sell this necklace, I can use the money to escape. I can travel all the way across country, safe in the anonymity of cash. I'm sure I can find a forger in California, same as I did years ago in New York.

A new name. A new identity. One without paparazzi following me like velociraptors. One where I'll never practice law, never have to worry about my license being revoked. A new life, where I'll never have to figure out who tried to kill me at the freeport.

Where I'll never have to be chained to a man like Braiden Kelly, just to survive.

Because there's one thing I just learned, downstairs in the ballroom: I will *never* belong in Braiden's life.

My heart knew it, even before my brain caught up. That's why I was so uneasy, walking into the party in the first place. That's why I downed three glasses of champagne before saying a word to a single guest. That's why I drank Fiona's whiskey.

Madden's a deluded ass, but he's succeeded in making me understand one thing. He'll never trust me. I could stay at Thornfield for a hundred years, mastermind a thousand illegal deals for Braiden, endure a million drunken parties with the Fishtown Boys.

But I can never erase the fact that I was born Giovanna Canna. That Russo claimed me before Braiden ever could. That my family was Cosa Nostra, my blood is Mafia, drenched in the citrus-and-wood Acqua di Parma cologne all of Russo's lieutenants wear to imitate their don.

I'll always be the enemy.

I could go to Braiden with Madden's threats. Braiden's still enough my husband that he would defend me, same as he rescued me from the freeport shooter.

But every night when I try to fall asleep, I see that waiter's blood. I hear the explosion as the gun takes off the back of his head.

I don't want to be the reason another man dies. Even a man as infuriating, as disgusting, as downright unhinged as Madden Fucking Kelly.

A roar of laughter billows up the stairs. The men in the ballroom are howling some chant, joining in another bonding ritual.

Why couldn't I come up with a stupid limerick?

It's easy to blame the alcohol. Champagne blurred all the edges, made it hard to pretend, impossible to think.

When I stood in the center of the room, in front of Fiona, surrounded by men, I could barely remember my own name. A million words scrambled in my head—nursery rhymes and Christmas carols and every poem I ever had to memorize in school.

Fighting for a limerick was like trying to net a goldfish in a pond. The words just floated away.

I panicked.

But Braiden didn't. He stepped up to save me with a grin and a filthy rhyme.

Even then, I could have laughed. I could have teased him, in front of all his men. I could have kissed him—like Fiona did.

I'm not made for this life. Not the heavy drinking. Not the raunchy humor. Not the raw, male power of it all.

Not the Irish Mob.

I pluck my collar from its velvet bed and shove it in my pocket. It's mine. I've earned it.

Turning to escape, I find Aiofe standing in the doorway. She's wearing her pajamas—soft pink fleece with a pattern of turquoise puppies. The slippers on her feet are huge lumps of purple fur that make her look like a baby sasquatch. She's carrying a worn stuffed animal, a bunny with one ear permanently crimped into a fold.

"Hey there, little one," I say. My hand is still in my pocket. I close it around the necklace, like I'm afraid she'll try to take it away.

She comes into the room cautiously, as if the Big Bad Wolf might leap out from any corner. When she reaches me, she studies my skirt. She finds one of the tulips—brilliant pink against the black silk background—and she folds her hand around it.

"That's right," I say, when she looks up at me. "Just like the flowers you brought me."

She smiles. Her teeth are tiny and perfect, like the "after" picture from an ad for orthodontia. Her grin lights up her entire face, and she finds other tulips on my skirt—purple ones and gold ones and more deep pink, scattered across the cloth.

"There you are!" We're both surprised by the voice in the doorway. I don't know what Aiofe thinks, but my mind automatically registers that it's wrong. It's too high, too English, too not-Braiden.

Fairfax claps his hands, as if he's just discovered an overlooked present under his own private Christmas tree. "My two favorite girls, both in one place."

Aiofe beams again. I try not to look like a thief as I drag my hand out of my pocket.

The noise from the party surges again. Fairfax glances over his shoulder before he shakes his head. "I hope you two can help me out." He lowers his voice so we have to step closer, have to become part of his conspiracy. "I made too much food for the party downstairs. I have a pot of tea left over, and a plate of biscuits that will just go to waste. Will you let me bring them to you? A bedtime snack in the nursery?"

Aiofe claps her hands, her whole body wriggling with excitement. When she looks at me, her face is full of hope, as if I'm the only person in the world who can grant her fondest wish.

Fairfax is looking at me too. "Himself would be pleased if you stay," he says.

He isn't talking about tea and cookies.

"I don't think I can do that," I say.

Aiofe's face crumples. Fairfax says, "Have a cuppa, and then make your decision."

"I don't like tea."

"It's chamomile," he says. "Soothes the soul."

Aiofe doesn't need words to plead with me. Every line of her body is a breathless, desperate prayer.

"My soul is fine," I lie to Fairfax.

"Of course it is."

Another shout rises from the party. Fiona distinctly says, "You Fishtown Boys—" I can't make out the rest of her declaration but the roar of male approval billows up the stairs like sewer gas.

Aiofe's shoulders slump. So I say to Fairfax, "One cup."

"And a couple of biscuits," he urges.

I nod.

"I'll be back in a tick."

Aiofe positively dances as she leads me down to the nursery. There's a table in the corner, where I know she does her school-work. The chairs are sized for a child. I take the one closest to the window. Aiofe sits with her back to the door.

She sets her stuffed rabbit on the edge of the table, taking care to arrange his head over his floppy paws. "Does the rabbit have a name?" I ask.

Her eyebrows meet in a frown. I can practically see the gears turning inside her head as she fights to make herself under-stood. I think about the child I met three months ago, the one who simply stared at me when I greeted her, seemingly deaf as well as mute.

She reaches under the table and slides open a drawer. Her sketchpad is inside, along with a box of crayons. She turns to a blank page and prints her letters with care: C-O-I-N-Í-N.

"The rabbit's name is Coinín?" I pronounce it like it looks—coin-in.

Aiofe's lips twist in a frown, but she gives a nod. That must be her way of saying I'm close enough.

I think about Braiden's pet name for me—*piscín*. Kitten. The name he called me as I fled the party. It has the same ending as Aiofe's word. "What does it mean?" I ask. "Coinín?"

She taps the rabbit.

"I know it's his name. But does it have a meaning?"

She taps the rabbit more emphatically, raising her eyebrows as if I'm a very slow student. "Oh!" I finally say. "It means rabbit?"

She nods happily, and then she starts to draw on the page above her precise letters. Coinín's round body quickly takes shape, along with his four legs. It only takes me a moment to realize she's making a portrait. She pays extra attention to the ears, capturing the folded one perfectly.

When she's finished, she catches her bottom lip between her teeth. She leans over the sketchbook like she's peering into a microscope. Her fingers move very carefully, separating the page from the book. When she's done, she hands me the picture.

"It's mine?" I ask, surprised and truly touched.

She nods vigorously.

"Will you sign it for me? Like it's a painting in a museum?"

I'm pretty sure she's never seen a painting in a museum, but she takes the picture back and adds her name to the lower right corner: Aiofe Máiréad Mason.

"Thank you," I say. "Thank you very much."

Fairfax clears his throat from the doorway, and I wonder how long he's been standing there with his tray. "Here you go," he says. "Tea and biscuits."

He's rounded up formal china and delicate lace napkins. He pours for us like he's a butler, placing a silver strainer across Aiofe's cup first, then mine. The tea is a grassy yellow, and it smells like apples rolled in straw.

The delicate cookies are homemade—shortbread and lemon snaps and ginger cakes. I can't imagine him serving any of them to the brutes downstairs.

As if my thought has summoned them, there's a shout from the ballroom. The chant of "Drink, drink, drink!" trembles through the floor.

"What do you have there?" Fairfax asks, as he steps back from his pouring duty.

"A picture of Coinín," I say. "Aiofe drew it for me."

"You're a lucky one," Fairfax says. "It's not everyone who gets a signed portrait of Coinín."

Cuh-neen. Swallowing half the first syllable. Lesson delivered without a fuss, without a hint of condescension.

"It's not everyone who gets a Fairfax, watching out for her," I say.

He simply nods, then says to Aiofe. "Finish your tea, love. Then brush your teeth. I'll be up to tuck you in in half an hour."

She shakes her head and sets her face in a dull frown, a remarkably accurate portrait of Grace Poole.

Fairfax says, "Grace is with Miss Birte tonight. They're upstairs, away from the noise of the party. You're stuck with me, lass. Now, drink up."

Aiofe starts to nibble on one of the ginger cakes.

I take a sip of my steaming tea. It looks like a melted jewel, but it tastes revolting.

I look up to find Fairfax staring at me expectantly. I shake my head, just a little. "Nope," I say. "Still tastes like dirt."

He shrugs. "Can't blame a lad for trying."

Lad.

He's not talking about himself. He's talking about Braiden. He's asking if I can make room in my heart for a man with good intentions.

The collar is heavy in my pocket. I could get so far… I could build such a new life…

"Maybe tomorrow," I say. "You might find a tea I'll drink tomorrow. Or the next day. Or the one after that."

"Himself will be pleased you're trying."

"I'm not doing it for Braiden."

I'm doing it for me. For me, and for Aiofe, who's eyeing *my* ginger cake, having polished off her own.

"Of course not," Fairfax agrees. Then he says to Aiofe, "Half an hour now. I'll be back."

I return the collar to its velvet case before I sneak back to the pool house.

14

BRAIDEN

S amantha follows my rules to the letter.

She's at breakfast Saturday morning, even though she's clearly nursing a headache and a dodgy stomach. Fiona doesn't make it at all, which is just as well, given Birte's decision to recite her rosary at the table, increasing her volume with each repetition.

I'm not sure why Birte thinks she needs Mary's intervention. Maybe it's Father Regis's influence. The priest has been round to talk with her three times already.

By the time Birte reaches her third decade on the beads, my own head is pounding. I push back from the table and lock myself in my office for the rest of the day.

I owe Samantha an apology. Not for Fiona kissing me—that was nothing I asked for and nothing I gave back.

But I do regret the limerick I tossed off. I honestly meant to save her from the boys' scrutiny. I figured I'd recite a poem, and the game would be over. I forgot my bride wasn't raised around a bunch of braying jackeens, as I was.

Sunday morning's the same. Coffee for Samantha and tea for the rest of us. It's Fairfax's well-deserved day off so I man the stove, but Aiofe's the only taker. I make her usual—one egg sunny side up and toast soldiers.

Samantha sticks with coffee and cold cereal. Fiona can't still be hung over from Friday night, but from the green tinge to her face, she clearly celebrated her Limerick Queen status last night as well. I'm not sure which of my men was fool enough to join her. Now, she's nursing a cup of coffee and eyeing my omelet as if it's a tripwire ready to send her sprawling.

Aiofe eats the white of her egg in tiny bites, edging closer and closer to the yolk with the tines of her fork. When she's left with only the center, she stabs it with her toast.

Yolk oozes over the plate like bright yellow blood. Fiona sprints for the jacks. Aiofe giggles and finishes her meal, unrepentant even when I tell her she's a fiend.

Samantha waits wordlessly for me to finish eating, then heads back to the pool house.

By mid-afternoon, I've had enough. She's had a chance to lick her wounds. Time to kiss and make up.

A new lock gleams on the pool house door.

I could grab a chair from the deck and crash through one of the windows. Kick in the door with a few well-placed blows. Stand outside and ring her phone until she gets sick of the noise or blocks me.

Instead, I sulk in my office for the rest of the day. I send a text to Fairfax, telling him if he ever installs another lock on Thornfield grounds without my express permission, he's fired. He responds with an immediate thumbs-up—pure proof he's read my ultimatum even though he's off the clock. Pure proof he doesn't give a shite about my threat.

Monday morning, Samantha texts that she'll miss breakfast because she has to leave early, to prepare for an 11:00 meeting at the freeport. I know she has an 11:00. I'm the one who requested the meeting.

Liam drives her down in the Bentley, which lights my fuse, because I planned to take her in the Jaguar. I don't like the thought of her on freeport property without me, even if Liam is one of my best men. Not when it's only been a week since the Diamond Ring meeting with the rogue waiter, a week since I almost lost her forever.

We still don't know who sent the gobshite I killed. I want to believe it was Russo, because then I'd have an excuse to go after the guinea arsehole, to take him out once and for all.

But Russo would have hit back by now, taking revenge for the jackeen I blew away. And if the waiter wasn't sent by the Mafia don, I have no idea who wants Samantha dead.

Which means I'm half-mad with worry when I get to the conference room fifteen minutes before our scheduled time.

Liam's standing by the closed door, face blank as a stone wall. "Boss," he says, and just from the one word, I know he's heard the whole story—the party, the dirty limericks, Fiona pressed against me like a bitch in heat.

"Get back home," I snarl, even though none of this is his fault.

"Boss?" He's staring at a point on the far wall. From the way his shoulders tense, I'm pretty sure he expects a sharp jab to the gut.

"I'll see Herself safely home. Take the Bentley and go."

"Boss," he says.

I remember when Liam was one of my most articulate men. That's why I assigned him to Samantha in the first place. I thought she'd appreciate a bloke who could talk about something beyond football and the price of Guinness. Now Liam's vocabulary is reduced to a single word. And if I hear it one more time, I might tear his feckin' head off.

When he opens the door to the conference room, Samantha looks up from the head of the table. She's typing at her computer, which is projecting a map of Ireland onto the screen behind her. "Do you need me, Liam?" she asks.

"Boss is here," he answers, as if I'm not standing right behind him, hearing every word. "Says he'll take you home. I want to make sure that works with your plans."

I should gut the gobshite right here, let him bleed out in the freeport hallway.

But Samantha sounds grateful. "Thank you for asking. I'll be fine."

"If anything changes," he says. "You have my number. I don't mind coming back. Any time of the day or night."

"Thank you, Liam. I appreciate it."

He tips an imaginary cap to her and closes the conference room door. His face turns back to stone as he says to me, "Boss." He walks out without looking back.

I should kill him. Or throw him out of the Boys. Or thank him for giving Samantha what she needs and slip him a few thousand bucks for his good work today. One of those three. I just don't know which.

I wait in the hallway, because this isn't my territory. I have plenty of time to study the carpet on the floor, the paint on the walls, and a signed and numbered print of a can of tomato soup, floating in a jet-black frame.

At one minute to eleven, Alix Key shows up. She has a computer tucked into the crook of her arm and a professional smile on her face. She's the freeport's auctioneer, still handling sales even as she takes on more and more of the tax haven's day-to-day operations.

"Braiden!" she says, as if I'm Diamond Freeport's most important client. "Is the room locked?"

"Samantha's just getting ready," I say.

Alix looks surprised. Trap has surely told her what happened at the last Diamond Ring meeting. She knows what I did for Samantha. There's no good reason for me to be admiring what passes for artwork instead of sitting with the woman I love.

But Alix is professional enough to ignore the disconnect. "I'm sure everything's set up now." She turns the knob and gestures for me to go in before her.

She's right, of course. Everything's ready. Samantha has a slide deck up and running, with my name, the date, and a snap she grabbed somewhere of a Celtic knot. I can't keep my gaze from going to her hand, to the ring I gave her the day I proposed. It has a knot, too. It's the symbol of the Fishtown Boys, of a family joined together for eternity.

I can't hide my sigh of relief that she's still wearing it—my signet, along with her wedding ring. There are words inside the gold band: *Is liomsa tú.* You are mine.

I need to remind her of that.

We're joined by other freeport staff—a metallurgist who specializes in oxidation, a conservationist who works with manuscripts, and an intern from Sherman University who's been tasked with a wide range of research.

The presentation starts off rough. I don't know if Samantha's flustered because I'm in the room, or if she hasn't gone over the material enough, or if there's something else going on. She's distracted. She loses her place three times. She repeats an entire slide, without seeming to notice.

Alix interrupts before things get too out of hand. "Thanks, Sam. Maybe we could move on to an overview of the laws and regulations?"

Samantha blushes. She knows she's making a dog's breakfast of the meeting.

After closing her eyes and taking a deep breath, she closes her computer. She studies her hands for a moment. And when she starts again, she's *talking* to me, telling me all I need to know.

As Alix suggested, she starts with a summary of the new Irish law on antiquities, explaining that anyone who comes into possession of any archeological object is required to report it to the National Museum of Ireland within ninety-six hours. She presents the penalties—fines of more than 100,000 pounds and five years of prison.

She doesn't wait for me to say I'm ignoring the law. Instead, she calls on the freeport experts to summarize the book I'm bringing in. Everyone uses careful language; they haven't seen the actual item yet, and it may turn out to be a fake. But we're all pretty sure the Book of Skreen is worth several million dollars.

At Samantha's gesture, Alix reviews the auction procedure. We'll set a reserve value before I consign the book to the freeport. "If the auction doesn't get to that level," Alix says. "The book goes back to you. But I don't anticipate any problem meeting the reserve. Even without a perfect record of ownership, finds like this attract a lot of interest."

I need a lot of interest. I'm millions in the hole for the year, with the truck of cocaine that ended up in Russo's hands. And it's just turned April.

Alix goes on. "As a matter of course, we advise our consignors, um, *you*, to be certain you want to put the goods up for auction. No consignor can bid on his own property."

The restriction makes sense—fair play says an owner shouldn't be allowed to bid up the price for his own possession. I gesture for her to go on.

"Auction houses schedule their blockbusters for May and November. You're one of the freeport's best clients, and you remain one of my absolute priorities. But I don't think we can do justice to a treasure like the Book of Skreen, pulling something together in a mere six weeks. I advise you to wait until November."

That sounds like a century or more. But I've come to the freeport because they're experts on this type of thing. If Alix says we should wait six months, I have to trust her. Even if the delay will make my cash flow issues more…intense.

"November," I finally agree, already calculating where I can cut corners with Kelly Construction.

There's more—talk about catalogs, commissions, deadlines for printing and distribution. Samantha wraps up with a review of legal issues—the challenge of proving the book's origin, taxation if it leaves the freeport, and dozens more details that leave my head spinning.

Samantha is calm. She's professional. She's brilliant at her job, and I could listen to her talk till sunset, even if I wasn't thinking about fifteen different ways to make her come.

"Do you have any questions?" Alix finally asks.

"You'll be the first to know, when I do," I say. Then, looking pointedly at Samantha, I correct myself. "Or, more likely, the second."

Alix laughs. Samantha doesn't.

Alix collects her computer and I stand to shake her hand. "Thank you for trusting us with this," she says. "I can't wait to see the book in person." It seems to take forever, but she finally leaves the room with the other freeport staff, who all wish me the very best of luck.

"Samantha," I say, the instant the door is closed.

"Don't."

I cross to the head of the table. "I'm a feckin' eejit," I say.

It takes all her concentration to find the power button on her computer.

"I wanted to help you," I say. "I thought I'd be funny. I thought you would laugh."

"They think I'm your whore!"

"Any fecker who says that'll answer straight to me. Fists or knives. And he'll be out of the Boys for life, made man or not." My old scar pulses. This is a promise I can keep.

But Samantha says, "You can't do that."

"I'm the Captain. I can do whatever I want."

"Then send Fiona home."

Christ. I'm the Captain of the Fishtown Boys. But Kieran Ingram is General of the GIU. I hedge: "She means nothing to me."

"Get rid of her."

"I can't," I have to admit.

"Can't?" Samantha challenges. "Or won't?"

"Her da has my bollocks in his back pocket."

"And what are you doing to change that?"

I don't have an answer for her. I'm waiting for Fiona to get bored. I'm hoping Kieran'll find another Clan to persecute. I'm thinking a man who smokes three packs a day and sounds like every breath's his last can't hang on forever.

"If she doesn't leave of her own accord, I'll send her packing after Easter."

"Easter!"

"Less than a month, *piscín*."

She leaves my excuse hanging there for what seems like forever. But finally, she whispers, "Promise?"

I reach for her hand. Pull it close to my heart. Cover it with my other fingers, like I'm trapping a frightened bird. "I promise."

Come Easter, Fiona will have learned all she can about the Fishtown Boys. Come Easter, I'll have a fair argument for sending her home. I hope. I pray.

Samantha finally nods. "Easter," she says.

I can't stop myself from from kissing her. Releasing her head, I tangle my fingers in her hair. She moans a little, into my mouth, and my cock turns to steel.

I want to lay her out on the table. I want to shove her narrow black skirt up to her hips. I want to yank down whatever panties she's wearing—black or white or gray, I don't give a holy fuck—and I want to bury my face between her thighs and suck her clit until she screams. And when she's dissolved like wet candy floss, when her legs hang limp over the edge of the table, then I want to sink my cock deep inside that pool of sweetness and bring her back for another round or three.

My fingers are going for her hem when the conference room door opens.

15

SAMANTHA

The sounds coming out of me aren't human. They're the whistling grunt of a hungry guinea pig and the whine of a lonely dog and the purr of a cat being scratched in the perfect place behind her ear. I've hooked one foot behind Braiden's knee, holding him close, framing the heat of his heavy erection between my thighs.

He's caught my lip between his teeth, and I'm pinned just short of pain. His fingers rake my hair like low-hanging branches of a tree. I'm melting beneath him, losing my thoughts, losing my bones.

"Excuse me!"

Alix's voice cuts through the boiling sap that's taken the place of my brain.

I squeak as Braiden pulls away from me. My skirt is hiked halfway to my hips. My top has slipped from my waistband, and my nipples stand out against the silk like searchlights in a storm.

I'm breathing like I've just run the bases for an inside-the-park home run, and I'm not entirely sure I remember my name.

"I'm so sorry," Alix says, as Braiden steps between us, giving me a chance to tug my clothes back in order.

I catch a glimpse of Alix's face. She's blushed the color of a good rosé. Her eyes are locked on Braiden's face, as if the world will end if she notices anything below his belt.

"I'm so sorry," she says again. "I realized I didn't show you a prototype of the auction catalog. We had one last month that's a good example…"

Apparently she realizes her computer offers good cover, because she opens the laptop with enough force that the screen nearly sails across the room. Balancing the device on one hand, she starts typing with the other. "I've got it here somewhere," she says. "Just a second… No, that's not the right file…"

My skirt is back where it belongs. My top is tucked in, its pearl buttons all in a line. My breasts aren't cooperating entirely, but I remind myself of warm summer breezes and lazy days in the sun. My heart still pounds, but I no longer sound like I'm about to hyperventilate.

I turn around and move to Braiden's side, brushing my hand against his sleeve as a silent thank you for his gallantry. A quick glance shows he's tamed his erection either with his own guided imagery or the sheer embarrassment of our being caught necking like two horny teenagers.

Braiden clears his throat. "Why don't you just send me the file?" he says to Alix. "I need to check something in my gallery." And then he asks, "Samantha? I'll meet you at the car in half an hour?"

"Perfect!" I say, wincing as my voice comes out in the too-bright tone of the weather forecaster on the nightly news.

I wait until he closes the door before I slump into one of the chairs at the table. Covering my eyes with one hand, I try to smother an embarrassed giggle. "Sorry about that," I say.

Alix sits beside me. "*Please*," she says. "I've seen worse."

"God, I hope not."

"I was just coming back to make sure you're okay. Things seemed off at the start of the meeting."

"They were," I say. "I got some bad news as I came down to the freeport this morning."

"Bad news?"

A detective—Tarrant, he said his name was—called from the Philadelphia police department. He wants me to come down to the Broad Street station. Just a conversation. Just a chance to go over facts.

Facts about how I killed three people and did my best for eleven years to cover it up.

I've known for weeks that there will be some sort of formal investigation into the three bodies I left on that mountaintop. But I've been so focused on the ethics proceeding and the potential loss of my law license that I wasn't prepared to hear from the actual police this morning.

I can't imagine what I'll say when I stop in at the station. How I'll defend myself. How I can ever justify what I did.

The instant I got off the phone with Detective Tarrant, I called Sonja, my lawyer. She said I should find someone else to represent me in "the fucking criminal matter." Sonja's strong suit is ethics. Not crime.

But she administered another dose of disaster before she ended the call: "I spoke with Alyssa Lopez this morning."

"Alyssa Lopez?" The name is familiar, but I can't put my finger on why.

"She's the one with the Mousetrap podcast. *True crime in real time.*"

"Jesus," I said, remembering the motto.

"They're turning your story into a ten-part serial. She's sending over the first episode as a courtesy. It's set to air a week from today."

Seven days before my name is smeared by the most popular podcast in the country. But I can't burden Alix with all of that now. So I sigh and tell her a different truth: "Braiden and I had a rough weekend. But, um, we just talked it out."

"So I gather." Her voice is as dry as a silica pouch in the bottom of a new purse.

I lean my head back against my chair. "Do you ever feel overwhelmed?"

"Every single day," she says.

I wave a limp hand at the room. "Not by this. Not by work. I mean..." But then I chicken out and shake my head. "Forget it."

"No," she says. "Go on. What were you going to say?"

"I have no business prying into your personal life."

"Pry away. I'll let you know when you get too close to home."

I still can't say the words.

"Sam," she says. "You look like you need a friend. You can trust me. I promise."

I take the leap. "Do you ever find yourself doing things you never thought you'd do? Accepting situations you never believed you could? Do you ever feel like you're drowning in a sea of testosterone? Like you've slipped a leash onto an alpha wolf, and you might not survive the ride?"

"Every single day," she says. And then, after barely a hesitation, "Every night." Then: "You've met Trap."

I nod. I *have* met Trap. He's my boss. The man who hired me. The man who cuts my paycheck. And I've seen the way he looks at Alix—with the same calm mastery that scares the shit out of me when I see it in Braiden's eyes.

"I'm a strong woman," I say. "I put myself through law school. I've built a career. I don't need a man to run my life."

"Of course you don't *need* one. But it can be a hell of a lot more fun to have one."

I laugh, because something swells in my throat. If I don't

pretend to be amused, I might burst into tears. "I just don't know if I can do what he wants me to do," I say.

She stiffens. "Does he hurt you?"

I don't answer right away, because I'm ashamed of my reply.

"Sam," Alix says. "This is important. Does he make you do things you don't want to do?"

I shake my head. It's easier to answer with my eyes closed. "I want it. All of it. He's never forced me to do anything."

Her exhale is long and low and tells me more about her past than I think even she realizes. "What are you afraid of?" she finally asks.

I'm afraid Braiden's life and my life are too tangled to ever pull straight. His marriage to Birte. His responsibility to watch over Aiofe. His running the Fishtown Boys, and whatever pull Fiona has over him, and Madden's fucking lies.

I'm afraid he'll find someone braver than I am to wear his collar.

I'm afraid he'll get tired of me.

But I say out loud: "I'm afraid he doesn't need me as much as I need him."

Alix's smile is soft. "What can you do for him that no other woman can do? That no other *person* can do?"

The question takes me by surprise.

Braiden has all the money in the world. He has loyal men who'll put their lives on the line without question. He has power and glory and prestige. There is literally nothing he can't buy.

That leaves my body.

The only thing I have that Braiden might want is my physical body. The one he puts in a collar. The one he uses until I ache, in my heart and in my flesh. The one I give to him, over and over and over again, because I can't imagine a life without the release he gives me in exchange.

I don't know if Alix reads my answer on my face. But she

puts her hand over mine and says, "Think about it." Squeezing my fingers, she climbs to her feet. "And if you need another place to make out, be sure to reserve the room on the master calendar."

My laugh is only a little shaky as I follow her out of the conference room.

16

SAMANTHA

~

Since my talk with Alix, I've been in the strangest mood.

Alix's question—*what can you do for him that no other woman can do?*—drives me more than a little wild. A pulse beats between my thighs, reminding me of every orgasm Braiden has ever delivered.

It's devastating to think I have no currency other than my own flesh. My worth is sculpted down to a single bare essential.

But I have to admit, it's exciting too. As Braiden drives us home from the freeport, I want to grab the steering wheel. I want to jam his foot down on the gas pedal. I want to drive to Thornfield, blow past the gate, and fuck Braiden on the hood of his car.

I'm drunk on the mere thought of sex.

This drive is so different from my trip to the freeport this morning. Then, I took the call from Detective Tarrant. Then, Sonja told me I needed more legal counsel. Then, I learned my life will be splayed for the public on Mousetrap.

But right now, in the midst of my madness, all those complications seem like a distant nightmare. No. Not a nightmare.
Nightmares aren't real.

The police investigation and the ethics hearing—even the
paparazzi who will swarm the Thornfield gate when we get
home—none of them matter in the confines of this car tonight.
They're waiting for me. I can't avoid them. But I can pick them
up in the morning, after Braiden quenches the crazy drunken-
ness inside me.

The April air smells sweeter than it ever has before. Colors
are brighter. I can hear individual blades of grass growing.

When we finally arrive at Thornfield, Braiden heads for his
office. I know he's reaching out to Patrick Moran, making final
arrangements for the transport of the illuminated manuscript.
He's applying all the facts I gave him today. He's working. He's a
machine.

I go to the pool house.

I plug in my computer so it can recharge after the day's work
at the freeport. I skim through social media, but I can't concentrate. All the colors are too bright. All the words shift together.

There's too much space here for one person. I rack the balls
on the pool table, and I select a cue from the rack. My break is
decent, but I scratch on my second shot, hitting the ball too
hard, without enough control.

I decide to take a shower, trying to drown the crazed restless-
ness that shimmers through my body. I'm not afraid to use the
hand-held shower-head, focusing on my clit. I run myself to an
orgasm in less than a minute, but my pussy's mechanical clutch-
and-release leaves me even more needy than before.

Braiden's ruined me. All the things he's ever done to me. All
the things he was going to do this afternoon, before Alix came
back to the conference room.

I need his fingers. I need his mouth. I need his cock,
stretching me, filling me.

I need him.

I towel dry and dress for dinner. House rules. My shortest skirt is a riot of crimson roses and shiny green leaves that cuts off halfway down my thighs. I don't have a top to do it justice, so I choose a black cami—soft silk with spaghetti straps. I don't bother with panties.

When I look in the bathroom mirror, I see a stranger.

There's something missing. Something gone astray.

I towel-dry my hair so that it falls in waves over my shoulders. That's not it.

I add eyeliner and mascara until I look like a raging rock musician. That's not it.

I slash lipstick across my mouth, the same deep red as the flowers on my skirt. That's not it.

I go to my closet for the tallest heels I own—four-inch stilettos with a cuff around each ankle. That's not it either.

But the cuffs feed the fire snapping deep inside me. They tell me what I really do need.

The air is cool as I walk to the main house. It's only the beginning of April, and the sun glows scarlet in the west. I should have goosebumps. I should be chilled.

But there's a furnace burning in me now.

I smell dinner cooking when I enter the house—grilled meat and fresh baked bread and something that might be melted butter. But I'm not hungry for food.

My legs flex as I climb the stairs. My shoes force my toes to grip, to anchor me, to dig in with every step I take.

I hear voices from Braiden's office—Fiona, saying something low and urgent. Madden, cutting her off to make his own insistent point.

But I don't go toward the office. I go toward the master bedroom.

How many times have I looked at that emerald? How many times have I put the collar around my neck?

This is the first time I've turned the platinum key. The first time I've sealed the lock myself.

A circuit closes, firing every nerve in my body. I can see more, hear more, taste more. My fingertips come alive, and when I press them to the pulse beneath my ear, I whine like an animal is chewing its way out of my heart.

The emerald pulls me down the hall. It drags me to Braiden's office. It pins me in the doorway.

Braiden is showing Fiona and Madden something on his computer screen. He's leaning forward, making a point with his index finger.

He doesn't know it yet, but I'm about to make my own point. I'm going to show Fiona how to get a man like Braiden, and how to keep him. I'm going to prove to Madden once and for all that his backstabbing and his lies mean nothing.

Braiden glances toward the doorway, barely shifting his eyes. "Samantha," he says. "Great. You'll do a better job explaining this than I can."

I don't answer him. I don't remember how words work.

Instead, I cross the room, my cuffed ankles steady in their wicked shoes. I turn Braiden's chair so he can't watch his screen. I straddle his legs with mine, and I sit on his lap.

His fingers close around my waist, more by reflex than intention. His head tilts up. He doesn't understand, not yet. His mouth opens in surprise.

I need that mouth. I need his tongue. I need his breath, pushing its way past mine.

I kiss him, drink him, eat him, drown. I can never get enough.

But my body is still human. It needs air. When I finally push back to steal a breath, my vision is clouded, as if I'm falling through miles of coal-black clouds.

Braiden holds me steady as I sway. His eyes are narrowed, and I can't tell if his smile is amused or cruel. "That's not the way this works, *piscín*."

"It is now," I say. And because I'm a foolish woman, or

maybe just naive, I dangle the key to my collar in front of his lips.

I mean to snatch it back. I'm going to fold it in my fingers, hold it tight until I've got what I really want.

But Braiden's bigger than I am and stronger and he's not about to let me change the rules. Faster than my eyes can follow, he catches my right wrist. He twists, putting his weight behind the rotation, and I'm suddenly on my knees before him, my face pressed into his crotch.

I feel the pulse of his erection against my cheek, matching the throb between my legs.

His fingers find the pressure points in my wrist. I can't keep my fingers closed. I drop the key into his palm.

"Let's try this again," he says, slipping the key into his breast pocket. And then he looks over my head. "Madden," he says. "Fiona. We'll pick this up tomorrow."

No.

He can't do that. He can't send them away.

But I don't want them watching whatever happens next.

I'm confused.

I don't want to be used like a toy, put on display, stripped and savaged in full view of the world.

But I want Fiona to know that *I* have Braiden. She doesn't, and she never will. I want Madden to know his brother is the man who drives me wild.

Fiona is already at the door. Her lips curl into a secret smile, as if she read all my thoughts in a hidden diary, and now she's memorized them for all time.

Madden doesn't bother with secrets. He just pushes out of his chair with a sneer on his face. He sniffs like a cocaine addict, or a man breathing in something rotten. "Use a johnny with that one," he says from the doorway. "You can't know where she's been."

The shout that rips from my throat has no words. It's woven

of pure fury, of weeks of baseless shame. But it's fed by the fact that I can smell myself when I stand. I breathe in the scent between my bare thighs, the honey I've left on Braiden's trousers.

I'm mortified.

I throw myself at Madden, wanting to scratch the sly grin from his face. But when he steps out of the way, I just keep going, too embarrassed to turn back.

I hear Braiden behind me and the smack of a fist against the meat of a body. There's grunting and the hiss of air between teeth and the scuffle of feet fighting for a purchase.

But I don't look. I don't watch.

I push past Fiona in the hall. I tear down the stairs and sprint across the patio. I throw myself into the refuge of the pool house, locking the door behind me.

I'm not brave.

I'm not sexy.

I'm not the type of woman any man would claim.

I'm cheap and I'm painted and I've broken one of my stiletto heels. I crash against the footboard of my bed, trying to pry off the emerald, trying to break my collar. When I can't get a purchase, I scratch at my neck, clawing helplessly at my skin.

And when that hurts too much, I drop my head to my knees. I pound the heels of my hands into the floor. I scream until my throat feels like shredded tissue.

Madden's ruined everything.

17

BRAIDEN

I leave Madden in my office, nursing a broken jaw and some kicked-in ribs. It's no more than I gave him when we were lads, and less than he deserves, but I don't have time to pay the full bill now.

Fiona's pressed against the wall in the hallway, like she was blown there in a storm. She cocks her hip and starts to say something, and I don't trust she can get it out without my needing to kill her. "Don't start," I say, wagging a finger in her face. She's smart enough to shut her feckin' gob.

Before I've caught my breath, I'm pounding on the pool house door, hard enough to make the glass rattle in its frame. "Open up, Samantha!"

Of course, she doesn't do it.

I kick at the lock, but the bolt is better than it looks. The wood around it shudders but holds fast. "I'm coming in, Samantha. Make this easy on yourself."

Nothing.

She told me once that I wasn't allowed in the pool house without her express permission. But that was pretty much an engraved invitation she just left on my lap.

Besides, I'm her Dom. I decide when I get to enter.

I whirl to the pool deck behind me. There's seating all around—chaise lounges framed in metal with matching chairs and tables. The three-legged tables are light for my needs, but one of those chairs will work a wonder.

It helps that all the momentum of my swing is focused on one metal leg. The glass door cracks on the first blow. I swing again, and a fist-size web of tempered squares breaks away. One more arc, and the entire door falls inside, shattering into a million jagged pieces.

The window shade sways crazily as I barge in, not bothering with lock or knob. I wade through the crumpled remains of the glass, ignoring its crunch underfoot.

She's crouching at the foot of the bed. As I crash over to her, she scrambles like a crab, trying to flee sideways. I get one hand over her biceps and haul her to her feet.

"No," she's chanting. "No, no, no."

But she's not looking at me. She doesn't seem to know I'm leaving a perfect ring of bruises on her arm.

She's staring at the glass.

It's spread like a fan across the floor, turning to crystal fire in the light above the sink. There's more of it than I thought there would be. One door shouldn't fill the room.

"No," she cries. "No, please, no." Her palm is pressed against her temple, sealed to the line where her hair meets her face.

For just a moment, I think she's bleeding. But then I realize I've trapped her in her past.

She stood at a window and watched her parents' car explode. She was caught in a shower of glass that night. She still bears the scars today, the web of white worms she's covering now.

"You're not Giovanna," I growl, pulling her hand from her face. "You're Samantha Kelly."

She stares at me like I'm shining with the fire of Pentecost.

"You're Samantha Kelly," I repeat, and I press her collar into her throat with the weight of my thumb. "And you're fucking mine. Say it."

She stares.

I shake her. Hard. "Say it, *piscín*,"

Her teeth chatter. "I— I'm Samantha Kelly."

"And?"

"I'm fucking yours."

I clutch her hair and use it to pull her close enough to kiss. Her lips move like a drowning woman's. She's hot and she's wet and I could drink her for hours if I didn't have another point to make.

Pushing her onto the bed, I reach for her computer. Its cord isn't long enough to do what I want, but it will give me a chance to find what I need. I loop the white line around her wrists, tight enough to keep her hands from moving, and then I lash her to the headboard.

"Say *red*," I tell her. "*Red*, and I'll stop."

She doesn't say a word. Instead, she thrashes like a marlin as I stomp into the bathroom. The towels are too heavy. The flannels too small. I find one of the flat sheets she uses for the bed— a waste of good linen when all she needs is a duvet. It takes her nail scissors to get the job started, but then I tear it into strips.

"Braiden," she says as I carry my bonds out to the main room. She's past her panic now, back to a grown woman instead of a lost little girl. Her voice is measured, like she's talking to a judge in a courtroom. "We can talk about this."

"The time for talking's past."

"I didn't mean—"

"You meant exactly what you did."

"Please," she begs, and she's pitiful enough that I stop while I'm tying her ankle to the footboard. "The door," she says, jutting her chin toward the shade I mangled when I broke in. "Anyone can see what you're doing. Anyone can see us. See me."

"You should have thought about that, *piscín*, before you started this game."

I swap out the rubberized computer cord for my torn sheets. That lets me spread her arms to the edges of the headboard.

She's splayed on the mattress, arms and legs wide. Her skirt's rucked up around her hips, giving me a clear view of her cunt. That barely-there excuse for a shirt has twisted around her chest until it frames her right tit.

Her collar gleams, the emerald gathering all the light in the dim room and throwing it back in a thousand shades of green.

"Let me go, you motherfucker," she says.

I laugh.

Now that she's secured, I take my time getting undressed. I toe off my shoes and socks, covering them with my suit jacket. I strip the knot of my tie and run it through my hands, wondering how I'll make her wear it.

I undo the top three buttons on my shirt. That's enough to pull it over my head and drop it on the floor, where it's quickly covered by my pants and boxers.

She got me hot and bothered this morning, when I nearly had her screaming my name in the conference room. My cock took quick notice of her riding me just now, when she broke into my office with her slutty makeup and her urgent need.

I'm hard enough to fuck her now, to plow hard, to stroke deep.

But she has a lesson to learn. Too many times, she's tried to top from the bottom. She tells me what she wants, tells me what to do, how to do it, when, and no Dom in the world will put up with that, even from his sweetest little sub.

So my cock will have to wait.

And so will Samantha.

I start with her electric toothbrush. It stands on the bathroom counter like a brave little soldier, charged and ready to go into battle. I toss the brush attachment into the sink and go after her with the handle.

My little *piscín* may protest the open door. She may fight to break free of her bonds. She may call me names no smart sub would dare.

But she's ready to come in less than a minute.

I bring her to the edge three times before I drop the handle on the floor.

She's got ice in the mini-fridge.

Her cunt's so hot the first cube melts to nothing while I'm pushing it in. I rub her clit with the second one, and then she takes four in her snatch.

I put a cube in my mouth and go after her tits. Her nipples are hard when I start, and they double in size as I play. I suck hard enough to leave marks and then I bite, layering the heat of my tongue with the chill of the ice until the cube melts to a single useless sliver.

"Please," she begs. "Sir. Master. You're right. You always are. I never should have come to your office. I had no right."

"Oh, *piscín*, you still don't understand." I work her clit with my fingers, alternately stroking and tapping, tugging just enough to hurt. "You're allowed in my office." Stroke, tap, tug. "You're allowed anywhere in my home." Stroke, tap, tug. "You're my wife." Stroke, tap, tug. "Everything." Stroke. "I." Tap. "Have." Tug. "Is."

Her legs are shaking so hard, the bed is rocking. Tears stream from her eyes. Her mouth is stretched in a perfect O, and she's holding her breath, ready to break. Ready for me to say: "Yours."

I walk away from the bed.

She screams in frustration.

"Wrong answer," I say from across the room. "Your job is to thank me. To accept whatever I do to you. Whatever I decide not to do."

I pick up one of the pool cues and balance it in my hands.

"By the way," I say, as if we're talking about the weather. "The mistake you made in my office was not coming into the room. Not showing off your body to Madden and Fiona. Not even riding my cock. You could have done all that...if you left your collar in its case."

"I wanted—" she starts, and thinks better of it.

"I thought—" she tries again, but recognizes her mistake. "Yes, Master."

I look up sharply, to see if she's mocking me. But her face is clear. Her eyes are wide. She's honestly, finally, conceding.

I raise my knee and shatter the pool cue. Tossing the tapered tip to the floor, I'm left with the butt end. It's as long as my forearm, the maple shaft polished to a mirror-like gleam.

She eyes it like it's a live cobra. Her fingers curl around the torn sheet, as if she can shatter the headboard. As if she can escape.

I run my thumb along the inside of her thigh. She rises by reflex, hips leaving the bed in a silent plea. I sink three fingers into her cunt.

She's soaked, from melted ice and her own sweet juices. She can take this. She can do everything I require her to do.

"Please don't..." she whispers. "I can't... I'll tear... I won't..."

But she doesn't say *red*.

As I slip the rounded end of the cue past her folds, she starts to sob. It's hard for her to give up absolute control. I know that. That's why I love her.

Once she's holding the cue, I find the necktie I set aside. I slip it over her head so it dangles between her tits. The silk brands her as mine.

"Who are you?" I ask as I slowly pump the wood between her thighs.

She closes her eyes. "Samantha Kelly."

"Who do you belong to?"

"You," she whispers. And then, as the friction builds, she says it faster. "You. Always you. Only you. Oh God, please, God, you."

I stop one stroke shy of setting her free. This time, when she's stranded, she's silent except for her heavy breathing. Tears leak from beneath her closed eyes.

But she doesn't beg.

Doesn't issue orders.

Doesn't even offer up a suggestion.

I pull the cue out of her snatch and roll it over her lips. She doesn't understand for a moment. Then she shapes those lips into a perfect O. She arches her throat. She sucks her juices from the wood as I fuck her mouth.

The sound of her sucking is a battle hymn to my cock. My balls are as hard as granite. One good pull, and I could spill all over her pretty face.

I make myself slip the knots on her arms. I free her legs. I take the cue from her lips and force her over to the pool table, half-dragging, half-carrying her.

Her forearms settle on the green felt, my tie splayed in front of her. I kick her legs wide, just as a breeze blows through the shattered door. Her spine goes stiff, and she moans, "They'll see me."

I slap her bare bottom. "Isn't that what you wanted? When you came into my office dressed like a slag?"

She shakes her head like a woman in a dream. "I wanted you. You're the one. The only one. It's you, only you, always, always you."

The shade rustles again, shifted by the breeze. She tries to look over her shoulder. I spank her again, and she groans.

I lean close and whisper in her ear. "Look at you. Bent over the table. Dripping for me. Arse red from my hand."

I smooth my fingers over that hot, flushed skin. Her whole body starts to shake. She flattens her hands on the felt. She grits her teeth as her knees begin to buckle.

And I sink into her from behind—my entire cock, all my weight. She screams my name as she shatters all around me. I keep her on her feet, digging my fingers into her hips, and then I'm as wet as she is, as hot as she is. She's milking me and I'm filling her and neither one of us is fully human as we come and come and come together.

My throat aches when I finally let her go. The April night swirls behind me, cold fingers swiping down my sweaty spine, smacking my bare arse.

Her teeth start to chatter, and I pull her into my heat. We cross the room and collapse onto the bed. I find the duvet and pull it up to our chins, and I wrap her in my arms and legs.

I want to carry her back to the house. I have arnica gel there and a store of the chocolate she loves. I could feed her the dinner Fairfax prepared, make up for the meal we both missed. I could put her in my bed and keep her there forever.

She'd protest. I know she would. She won't sleep in the big house until I atone for Birte.

I could order her to my bedroom. Use my Captain's voice. Take away her choice.

But I want her to *decide* to come back.

So I press her close to my body. I kiss the spiderweb of scars at her temple. I wipe the tears from her cheeks and I stroke her hair and I tell her that she's my *piscín*, that she's magnificent, that I've never known anyone like her in my entire life.

"*Mo chailín maith*," I breathe, so softly I'm not sure she hears. She sighs, though, relaxing against me. Another breeze steals through the ruined door, and I pull the covers close to keep her warm, holding her close as she drifts off to sleep.

18

BRAIDEN

F our days later, the last note of the national anthem carries over Fenway Park. Half the men in the Diamond Ring head back inside our luxury suite. The wind is predictably fierce in Boston on this April Saturday, the first home game for the World Series Champion Red Sox.

But when Prince stays outside, I do too. He takes a long pull from his beer as the first pitch crosses the plate for a strike. The cheering crowd is loud enough to shake the old stadium. I wait for the New York batter to strike out before I start my own sort of pitch.

"Another month, another Diamond Ring event," I say, keeping one eye on the game below.

"Maybe we'll get through this one without a special clean-up."

Without my leaving a body on the ground, he means. "Any complications from that?" I ask.

He shakes his head. "Best does good work."

We both glance inside, where Sawyer Best is deep in conversation with Cole Wolf. Military dark ops and underworld computers. What could possibly go wrong?

The crowd around us cheers another out. I take a sip of whiskey. "About that waiter…" I start.

Prince grunts.

"I assume he wasn't freeport staff."

"Never saw the motherfucker before."

"But he got past freeport security."

Prince eyes me steadily. "What's on your mind, Kelly?"

"I'm not sure you can keep my wife safe."

He gives me a filthy look. "We've updated our procedures."

"So ya've decided not t' let killers past th' front gate now?" I don't mean to let my accent off the hook, but it feels good to say exactly what I'm thinking.

Prince snorts. "The jizzstain you killed came in with the caterers. Near as we can tell, he took out one of *their* guys and got in on his credentials."

"And what are ya doin' t' keep it from happenin' again?"

"Effective last Monday, the freeport uses no outside staff. We've hired all our own waiters, bartenders, busboys, the lot. And every cocksucking one of them clears freeport security before they set foot inside the gates."

Jesus. I can't complain he's ignoring the threat. But I'm not ready to back down completely. "You've had almost two weeks. What do you know about the guy who went after Samantha?"

"Best didn't read you in?"

I shake my head.

Prince says, "I'll have him send you the files. We've got a name—Terrence King. No known address. The shitball was in and out of prison five times after he turned eighteen."

"He's with Russo?"

"Who?"

"Antonio Russo. Philly's Mafia capo."

"That motherfucker at your wedding?"

I grit my teeth. If I'd had my way, Russo wouldn't have been within a hundred miles of St. Columba's that day. "That's the one."

Prince shakes his head. "This guy was local. Dover born and fucking bred."

That doesn't make sense. I don't have enemies in Delaware. No one local to the freeport should be going after Samantha.

Prince's voice is deceptively mild as he says, "Too bad we can't talk to the asshole. Get more information from the horse's fucking mouth."

"Don't start," I warn.

"Don't drop any more bodies at my freeport."

We stare out at the baseball game. They've started the second inning.

"We're okay?" I finally ask, after the pitcher throws a monster curveball. Because Prince has a point. I should have waited before I killed the guy.

"Don't let anything happen to Sam."

"You know I won't."

We shake on it.

After that, I make my rounds, checking in with other members of the Diamond Ring. For most of them, that adds up to a handshake and a couple of questions about how business is going.

But when I get to Connor Boyle, it's time for a more cautious conversation. I want to know if the Grand Irish Union is pushing for control in New York, same as in Philly.

Boyle rolls his shoulders in a massive shrug. "I won't speak ill of the General," he says, which lets me know *ill* is on his mind. But then he adds, "That daughter of his is a real stunner."

I take a chance and say, "Thinks she'll be running Boston before she turns thirty. And the Union a year or two after that."

"From what I hear, she's got her heart set on your corner of the world." Boyle's eyes are sharp over the rim of his glass.

We're not just acting the maggot anymore. This is a serious discussion.

"Then she'll learn to live with disappointment."

"She never has before," Boyle says. "Her da's seen to that."

"First time for everything."

Boyle nods. But he says, "Watch your back."

Before I can respond, Arsene Dubois approaches. Like a concierge at one of his international hotels, the Frenchman is making his own rounds, shaking hands and catching up on business. I ask about his new property in Dubai but don't bother listening to the answer.

If Boyle's warning me, the situation with Fiona is worse than I thought. How many bosses are watching from the sidelines? How many men are placing bets the Fishtown Boys will fall?

When the game reaches the seventh inning stretch, I duck out of the suite. Aoife's birthday is next Wednesday. I have no idea what an eleven-year-old girl wants, but I've seen plenty of lasses in pink Red Sox shirts here at the game. I'll bring one home, and at least she'll know I thought of her.

I'm halfway to the store when I hear my name, slicing through the crowd: "Kelly!"

I recognize the voice before I turn. Kieran Ingram is surrounded by half a dozen of his most powerful lieutenants, as if they've all been conjured by my conversation with Boyle.

The deadliest man in Boston is wearing blue jeans and a weathered navy sweatshirt sporting the team's stylized B. His thinning hair is covered by a cap marked with the same faded logo. It looks like he dug the outfit out of someone's cellar.

He's dropped at least two stone since I saw him last. The loose flesh of his neck droops over his collar like a turkey's wattle. His eyes are bloodshot.

"Boss," I say warily.

"Ya don't call your General before ya come t' town?"

"I'm here on private business."

He doesn't like my answer. He doesn't like *me*. And just like that, the predator rises in him, an old fox snapping at a rabbit's neck just because it can. Eyes narrowed, he says, "Then speakin' o' business, boyo——"

I want to tell him I'm not his boyo, but he's still my boss so I keep my mouth shut.

"—yer tithes've come in light."

I won't stand here in public, talking about my finances. Passing sports fans don't need to hear a word about the cocaine Russo stole. But my General's waiting, so I have to say something. "You get a share of everything I see. Same as ever."

"Chicago turned in more last month than ya sent th' past year."

I make a mental note to send Mickey Reardon my congratulations. But I tell Ingram, "I've been fair with you. Point me toward any man who says otherwise."

"Time t' prove ya mean t' stay in the Union, boyo." He eyes me like he's measuring me for a coffin. And then he hits me with a direct order: "Ya'll marry Fiona by Easter."

"I will, yeah." The words are out of my mouth before I can stop them, and any Irishman in the world would know from my tone they mean the absolute opposite of what I've just said.

Ingram's so surprised I've talked back that he starts to choke. His chest sounds like it's full of tire irons wrapped in wet blankets, and his face turns redder than the B on his chest. Other sports fans cut us a wide margin. No one wants what he has, if it's catching.

Still coughing like a shattered engine, he fumbles for a handkerchief and holds it to his lips. I don't see what he spits into the white cotton, but it can't be good. My stomach turns as he shoves the wad back in his jeans pocket.

When he can finally breathe again, he drills a finger into the center of my chest. He's angry now—at my giving him lip, but also because I've seen how weak his body is. "By Easter, boyo."

I want to break his feckin' wrist, but there'd be holy hell to pay if I did that to my boss. Besides, I've been told since I was a wee lad I could never marry for love. Weddings build empires. That's why I skulked around County Cork in the first place, tying the knot with Birte where no one could stop me.

All my life, I've been groomed to take a wife like Fiona Ingram. If Da were still alive, he'd be toasting Ingram's command with the Jameson 21. Hell, if Da were still alive, he'd angle for the girl himself.

But Da is gone, and Ingram's repeating his order: "By Easter. Or I'll put a man I can trust in charge of the Fishtown Boys."

He doesn't get to choose who runs the Boys. But with the weight of the Union behind him, he might be able to push me out.

I remind him, "That's three weeks away."

"Then ya better take out yer checkbook, boyo. I hear ya have some complications t' work out before ya take yer vows."

Money would take care of Birte. I can buy an annulment in Ireland—rebuild a few churches, pad a few pockets from priest all the way up to bishop. It would cost a fortune on such short order, but I could do it.

But Samantha's another matter. I'm not setting her aside, for Fiona or anyone else. To buy time, though, I say, "It'll take a while to run things up the chain in Philadelphia."

"Ya don't need a chain, boyo. Ya bought yerself a dirty priest before ya took yer dago skirt."

My fingers curl into fists, but I can't take a run at my General. Besides, once I get past the slur, I have to admit he's right. It's child's play to annul my marriage to Samantha. I made sure of that when I ducked the bigamist noose.

I shoot in the dark, same as I did when Ingram told me Fiona was coming to stay a while. "What will your daughter say about this?"

"Fiona'll do as she's told. Before I sent her t' ya, I gave her a month in Dublin. Let her sow her wild oats, same as any son.

Now ya'll marry Fiona by Easter or ya'll regret it from six feet under."

I can't let that threat go unanswered. But I can't start a fight in the middle of a baseball stadium either, same as I can't take a swing at a wheezing old codger.

Choosing the best of my shite options, I retreat toward Prince's suite.

"Hey, boyo!" One of Ingram's thugs slaps the back of my head. "Don't turn yer back on yer boss."

I swing before I think out the consequences. It's a sucker move, because it's six against one. Ingram's men aren't armed; the metal detectors outside the stadium have seen to that. But one grabs my hand in a professional wrist lock, and another gets his arm around my throat. Someone shoots a fist into my kidney, sharp enough that I see actual stars. Another fist lands by my right eye, a blow that vibrates down my spine.

"Hey! Why don't you try a fair fight?" The shout is backed up by someone wading in next to me. The hold around my neck breaks, and I turn to find Gage Rider grinning like a Viking raider. The former hockey player is landing short, sharp jabs to the ear of the guy who still has me pinned by the wrist. Rider takes a break for long enough to throw an elbow at another one of Ingram's men, and the crunch of nose cartilage is audible over my rasping breath.

I finally manage to kick the knee of the guy who has my arm, breaking free. Rider and I instinctively line up back-to-back, holding our fists at chest level.

But before either of us can get in another blow, a pair of security guards runs up. They're gripping weapons that can do a lot more harm than Tasers, and one squawks into a radio pinned to his shoulder.

Ingram calls his men off with a single bark that brings on another coughing fit. As his crew gathers round, Radio Cop asks for any available EMT to come to the luxury suite lobby.

"You okay?" I ask Rider, who's working his fist like it hurts.

"Never better." He grins like a Labrador retriever set free on a beach.

"How—"

Did you know I needed help is the rest of that question. But Rider interrupts. "Boyle said you might need a hand."

Connor Boyle must have taken his own stroll from the suite. But rather than fight his General directly, he sent the next best thing—a man who built a professional career fighting on ice.

Before I can thank Rider, Trap Prince pushes his way through the crowd of gawking baseball fans. "Jesus fucking Christ! You cocksuckers can't be left on your own for one motherfucking minute!"

Parents cover their kids' ears, and smart folks scurry back to their seats. The rent-a-cops send Gage and me to one corner, and Ingram's men to an alcove across the way.

Prince talks to Radio Cop, and then to someone more senior in uniform, and then to a man with a size-twenty neck in a cheap suit and a name tag that says he's the Director of Security. I don't know if money changes hands or if cooler heads prevail, but we're finally told no charges will be filed.

All of us have to leave the park, but the security guys send Ingram's men out first. That's a wise choice, because the General of the Grand Irish Union is the color of a wet baseball, barely able to stand without assistance. He refuses treatment, though. The ballpark EMT strongly suggests he see his own doctor for attention to that cough.

By the time the Boston group has left, the baseball game is over. Prince collects the rest of the Diamond Ring, and we all make our way to our waiting limousines and our rooms at the Mandarin Oriental.

Connor Boyle avoids me at the after-party, and I can't really blame him. He risked enough for one day. Rider and I do our best to keep our distance from Prince. Best shakes his head on the sidelines, like he's grateful he didn't have to call in a clean-up crew.

I'm the first man to call it a night. A hot shower doesn't make a dent in the ache of a bruised kidney. But it isn't the pain that keeps me awake.

I have three short weeks till Easter—twenty-one days to take a stand for Samantha and the Fishtown Boys. And Fiona Ingram's still living in my feckin' house.

19

SAMANTHA

I'm curled up on the sofa in the den, reading a Tana French mystery I took from the shelves by the safe room, when Braiden returns from his Diamond Ring meeting. "How was Bos—" I start to ask, marking my place in the book. But then I take in his black eye and the hitch in his step as he makes his way across the room. "What the hell happened to you?"

"Ingram was there."

"At the Diamond Ring meeting?" I'm astonished. Those monthly getaways are sacred. Only the freeport's top billionaires attend Trap's events.

"At the stadium." Braiden lowers himself to the couch with enough care that I wonder if I should call Dr. Kelleher.

Braiden picks up the book I've been reading and returns it to my side. He picks at the fringe on a throw pillow. He looks out the window, as if he's heard a car come down the driveway, and then he studies the bruises on his knuckles.

"What?" I finally ask. "What are you trying so hard not to tell me?"

He's strong enough to look me in the eye. "Ingram gave me an ultimatum."

My stomach swoops with a sickening twist. There's nothing that old man could say that I want to hear.

Braiden holds my gaze. "I'm to marry Fiona by Easter."

I answer without thinking. "Fuck Ingram. And fuck his ultimatum. What did you tell him?"

Braiden actually manages an exhausted smile. "Not that. But he knows I'll not go along with his plan."

I have a thousand questions. I want to know what Braiden *did* say. I want to know who he fought. I want to know what happens to me when Ingram pushes back, because the old man will fight insubordination, tooth and nail.

And I want to know if Fiona's known this was the plan all along.

But I settle for asking, "So what do we do?"

"Nothing, for now. Nothing till Easter."

"And then?"

His hand cups my cheek. I want to lean into it, but I can't allow myself that weakness.

"What happens then, Braiden?"

"Don't worry about it, *piscín*."

"I have to worry about it!"

But worry won't change a thing. And there's nothing *I* can do. I can't file a complaint in federal district court, demanding Ingram back off his claim. I can't write a brief about Fiona, about all the ways she turns the Fishtown Boys upside down. There aren't any statutes to apply or regulations to parse.

I'm helpless.

But I can turn my head, so my lips brush Braiden's palm. I can stand beside the couch and wrap my fingers around his. I can lead him down the hall to his bedroom and find the arnica in the nightstand and rub some gel into the bruise around his eye. When he hisses, I can tell him not to be a baby, and when he growls, I can laugh, because we both know he's in no shape to make me stop.

I help him out of his clothes, and I pull the comforter up to his chin, same as he did with the duvet in the pool house. I tell him I'll bring him something to eat, because it's Sunday, and Fairfax has the day off. In the kitchen, I make a cup of tea, and I add extra butter to thick slices of toast, because I know he thinks toast and tea can make everything right.

But he's sound asleep when I get back to our bedroom. I leave the food on his nightstand, even though it will be stone cold before he wakes to eat it. And then I go back to my murder mystery, wondering how long it will be before bodies start falling here at Thornfield.

20

SAMANTHA

⌇

M eals become fraught at Thornfield.

Fiona's at breakfast every morning, glorying in a cup of coffee, refusing the food Braiden requires the rest of us to eat. It's like she doesn't hear Birte chanting her little rhymes. She doesn't see Aiofe's suspicious frowns. Fiona borrows sections from Braiden's newspapers, turning pages too quickly to actually be reading. More than once, I catch her staring at me over the rim of her mug, eyebrows raised in silent study.

I miss lunch for an entire week.

On Monday, I'm down in Dover, working with Sonja Heller. The ethics board has issued another round of questions, focusing on my application to law school and my activities while taking classes in New York. After scorching my ears with a thorough dissection of the board members' preferred sexual acts, Sonja fires off a letter of protest, saying the board has overstepped its bounds. She says we'll likely lose that argument—the board has virtually unlimited power to ask about my past. But at least we've delayed the process for a short while.

On Tuesday, Liam drives me to an office tower in downtown Philadelphia. I meet Teddy Newland, the criminal attorney Sonja recommended to assist me with the police inquiry into That Night. Teddy looks like somebody's absent-minded grandfather—he has a fringe of gray hair and glasses that slip down his nose, and there's a stain on his Harvard tie.

Looks are deceiving. He grills me like he's paid by the Spanish Inquisition, going over every detail of That Night once, twice, three times, four. Only after he's convinced my story won't change does he call Detective Tarrant to schedule a meeting for Friday.

On Wednesday, I take online meetings at home from ten in the morning till six at night, trying desperately to catch up with my work for the freeport.

On Thursday, I meet Alix and Trap in New York, delivering a new-client orientation for a reclusive billionaire who hasn't left her Upper East Side condo in twenty-seven years, not even to see museum exhibits of the German Expressionist paintings she collects.

On Friday, the first episode of Mousetrap airs.

I told Sonja I didn't want to listen to the podcast. She said I didn't have a fucking choice—the details will become the basis for yet more questions from the ethics board, from Detective Tarrant, from the world at large.

So I listen to it, every word. I learn more about my father's career as one of Antonio Russo's lieutenants than I ever cared to know. I begin to understand why Zia Sara and Zio Matteo were always so cold to me, how they had to answer to Russo for taking in the daughter of an executed traitor. The nun who taught me catechism says I fell asleep in class. Former teachers —at least the ones featured in the recording—remember me as lazy, shifty, untrustworthy.

The podcasters are experts at foreshadowing. They bring my

cousins Elisabetta and Giorgia and Gianni to life. They make a long-forgotten parking ticket sound like proof that I was a reckless driver from the instant I got my license.

And the podcast finds its audience.

By Friday night, a group of protesters sets up camp outside Thornfield's gates. The group of podcast fanatics holds up signs: *Pay the Price. Justice for Giorgia* and *Gianni. A Murderer Lives Here. Shame, Shame, Shame!*

The reinvigorated paparazzi have a field day. They conduct interviews and they film protests, gaining valuable footage even when I don't set foot outside the gate.

Birte seems oblivious to the changes outside her home. But Aiofe glances at the windows often, and more than once I catch a worried frown creasing her forehead. Braiden swears and calls a local official on his payroll. Sadly, every time the crowds are dispersed they return within an hour.

Fiona has a field day.

She comes to dinner late three nights in a row, shrugging and saying she couldn't get her Cooper Mini through the throng. She laughs when she finds an online article with the headline *Known Mobster's Daughter Holing Up at Murder Mansion.*

She offers to address the press on my behalf: "I'll be your surrogate," she says, all the while eyeing Braiden. When I clench my fist around my wedding band and coldly refuse, she laughs.

Braiden puts me in my collar on Tuesday, and on Thursday, and again on Friday night. He measures out my punishment with a fierce determination. He leaves me aching and breathless, a soaked cloth wrung out so thoroughly that each individual fiber threatens to fray. He comes as hard as I do, calling me his *piscín*, insisting I'm his *chailín maith.*

And every night, I go back to the pool house, where my angry, frustrated tears can leak silently into my pillow.

After a week of hell, another Sunday morning dawns cool, like the middle of April should. The sky is a piercing blue, without a cloud in sight. House rules be damned, I have stacks

of work to do for the freeport, and I'm hoping my piles of corre-
spondence will distract me from all the things I can't control.
I've just pulled on yoga pants and an ancient cashmere pullover
when I'm startled by a sharp knock at the pool house door.

I open it to discover a yellow chick and a snow-white rabbit.
Or, rather, to find Aiofe and Birte, with brightly colored Easter
masks strapped to their heads and wicker baskets gripped in
their hands. Grace Poole stands behind them, holding a third
mask—a curly haired lamb—along with a headband sporting
bunny ears.

"Ya've got a choice," she says. "Lamb or rabbit."

I smile, even though it sounds like she's reading from a
menu. "Sorry, ladies," I say. "I have work to do."

Aiofe shakes her bright yellow mask so vigorously her hair
billows around the elastic strap. With her free hand, she points
to Grace's hands and then to me. Someone has to complete the
happy foursome.

I make my words gentle. "I wish I could, Aiofe. But I have to
finish my assignment. Same as when you do schoolwork for Mr.
Bell."

But Aiofe just digs in her wicker basket until she produces an
Easter egg decorating kit. I haven't used one since I was her age.
Maybe younger.

"Colored eggs," Birte says suddenly, like she's just awakened
from a restful nap. "Move your legs. Aiofe begs."

Taking her cue from her aunt, Aiofe clasps her hands in
front of her heart. She turns her masked face up to me as if I'm
the sun, the moon, and the stars in her little world.

The freeport work can wait until tomorrow.

"Okay," I say. "Easter eggs it is. I'll be the bunny."

Birte claps. Aiofe lets out a high-pitched squeal of excitement, the first sound I've ever heard her make. Grace hands me
the bunny-ear headband and leads the way to the kitchen in the
main house.

Aiofe turns out to be a vicious little general. Fairfax has left us three dozen eggs, already hard boiled. Even without words, Aiofe makes it perfectly clear that we're supposed to start with solid colors, then we'll do a batch that are part one color and part another.

Halfway through the second dozen, Aiofe picks up a white wax crayon. She labors over an egg with intense concentration, drawing something on the surface. When she finishes, Grace dips the egg in green dye.

While we're waiting for the color to set, Birte reaches for the crayon. She folds her fingers around it and holds it in front of her, as if it's a candle. Bowing her head, she mutters a long prayer in Irish, ending with *amen*.

Did she say a prayer when she lit the candles she placed against Braiden's office door? Did she call on God when she tried to burn him alive?

"What were you thinking, Birte?" I ask, not truly expecting an answer. "The day of the fire?"

She continues to finger the crayon without looking at me. But her humming changes to a soft sing-song. "Day of the fire," she says. "Song of the choir. Punish the liar." She seals her lips and goes back to her hymn for a few bars before she chants, "Punish the liar, punish the liar, punish the liar..."

Her soft voice raises goosebumps on my arms. I glance at Aiofe and Grace, but they're intent on the masterpiece Grace is fishing out of the green dye. It's a portrait of Coinín the rabbit, bright white against a grassy field.

"Fire," Birte says, loud enough to make me jump. "Choir. Liar."

Braiden has to be the liar. He's the one who said he'd always love her and honor her, protect her and cherish her.

Aiofe looks up from her eggs, her lips trembling inside the cut-away of her plastic yellow-chick mask.

"Fire!" Birte shouts again.

Aiofe covers her ears, striping her masked cheeks with blue and green food coloring.

"*Fire!*" Birte hollers.

Aiofe folds her arms around her waist and rocks back and forth, sending the nearest flat of eggs flying. Bits of colored shell scatter from the stove to the window, and her clothes are streaked with bright dye.

"*Fi—*" Birte starts again, loud enough to hurt my ears.

"What the hell?" Braiden shouts from the doorway.

Fiona's behind him, looking like a refugee from a fashion shoot. She's wearing black leather pants and a scarlet corset that matches her slick lips, every hair perfect in her sleek black bob.

I wonder what the two of them were doing, why they've arrived in the kitchen at the exact same time. I wonder if house rules apply to Fiona, if she's forbidden from working because it's Sunday. I wonder if I'll be able to draw a full breath against the spike of jealousy piercing my lungs.

Aiofe runs to Braiden, burying her face against his side. He smooths her hair automatically, apparently oblivious to the streaks of color she smears on his crisp white shirt. Birte falls silent mid-shout, like someone pulled the plug that animates her. Grace mutters over the broken eggs, as if she's casting some wicked spell in words that might be English, might be Irish, might be known only to her.

"Samantha?" Braiden asks, bewildered.

"We were dyeing Easter eggs," I say, as if that's any explanation at all.

Braiden's large hand settles on Aiofe's head, soothing, calming. Birte starts a new chant: "Liar. Liar. Liar."

Braiden scowls. "Grace," he says, without raising his voice. "Birte is obviously overtired. Get her upstairs for a kip."

Grace takes Birte's hand, more gentle than I could ever be. She leads the chanting woman out of the kitchen, trying to avoid the larger pieces of boiled egg.

Braiden waits until they're gone before he produces a snowy

linen handkerchief from his pocket. Pushing Aiofe's yellow mask up to her forehead, he wipes tears from her cheeks. Then he holds the cloth to her nose and waits for her to blow. "There's my girl," he says in a soothing voice. "Now upstairs with you, and change into clean clothes."

She obeys him without looking back.

Only then does Braiden grimace at the mess left behind— eggs and cups and brightly colored water all over the counter and floor and cabinets. Fiona follows his gaze, but she steps back as if her Manolo Blahniks might catch fire.

"It's half past three," she says. "Da will be done with his Sunday roast and expecting me to call."

"Call, then," Braiden says, already rolling up his sleeves.

Fiona glances at me. Her thoughts might as well be written in letters ten feet tall: *Samantha can clean this mess.*

"Don't let us keep you from your da," Braiden says.

Fiona opens her mouth. Closes it. Judging by her outfit, the afternoon has just taken a dramatic turn from whatever activity she was doing—or intended to do—with her would-be fiancé.

But she's boxed herself in now. She turns away, head held high, gaze straight ahead. Her steps on the kitchen tile sound like gunshots.

"I'll get the broom," Braiden says.

"A mop might work better," I say.

"Mop it is, then."

And he handles the clean-up as efficiently as he does everything else.

It's only as I put the few surviving eggs into the fridge that I remember I'm still wearing bunny ears. But Braiden hasn't forgotten. He nuzzles the back of my neck, and the heat of his body kindles something deep inside me. "Come upstairs," he says.

"Aiofe," I reply, because I don't want the child watching me trail into his room.

"She'll be drawing, or reading her books." His fingers slip

beneath the elastic band of my yoga pants, and I catch my breath at how quickly he can set a rhythm that drives me mad.

"Fiona, then," I gasp.

"She'll be taking orders from her da." He turns me around, pressing my shoulders against the cold fridge door. He pins one knee between mine.

"Not here," I say. Not against the refrigerator. Not over the granite counter. Not on the hard tile floor.

He could order me to stay here and, collar or not, I'd obey. I need him, even though I'm still sore from all the other punishment I've had this week. I'm starving for him, like I starve for the air I breathe.

But he listens. He cares. He half-pulls, half-carries me into the mudroom. I don't see which coats he tosses onto the floor. I only know that he covers them with a green plaid blanket, the one Fairfax keeps on hand for picnics.

After Braiden shakes out our makeshift bed, he tugs me down, covering my lips with his, smothering my body with his, matching all his roughness to the soft, wet heat inside me.

And through it all, he tells me I'm beautiful. He tells me he needs me. He tells me I'm his.

And I drink down every word, grasping every urgent syllable, as if they can drown out Birte's evil little whisper at the back of my mind: *Punish the liar. Punish the liar. Punish the liar.*

21

BRAIDEN

Fiona's by the door to the infirmary, slouched against the paneling. Her shoulders are back, her arms crossed over her chest. The sole of one foot rests against the wall behind her.

She's been waiting a while. Samantha and I took our time downstairs.

I'm not about to justify what I've done.

Instead, I say, "No," and turn toward my bedroom, my shower, and my clean clothes.

"No, what?" She pushes off the wall and hurries around to stop me.

"No, whatever you're about to say."

"No, that wasn't a God-awful mess in the kitchen?" Her lips twist into a challenging smile.

"Accidents happen." I shrug, as if I scrub down floors and counters every day.

"No, you don't want me out of your house by midnight?" she tries, and this time, she cocks a knowing hip.

"Stop playing games, Fiona." I try to shoulder past, but she doesn't give an inch.

"No, you didn't just get the ride of your life downstairs?"

"Have a good afternoon."

I'm almost to my room when she says, "Is marrying me such a terrible thing?"

Turning back, I remember every blow her father's men gave me a week ago. I force myself to close the distance between us. I'm taller than she is by a head, and I must outweigh her two to one. But she doesn't flinch, not even when I say, "I have a wife. Two, in fact. No man needs a third."

"Birte's not your real wife."

"The church records in County Cork say different."

"Grace Poole told me what happened. You've never taken that shattered girl to bed."

Jesus Christ. I should have sent Grace home when I had the chance.

Fiona goes on: "And Madden told me about the priest who married you to Samantha."

Fucking gobshite. I'll put him on the plane with Grace. Get them both out of my life forever.

"Listen to me, Fiona. I'll only say this once. I'm not buying the annulment your father demands. I'm not leaving Samantha. There will never be a third Mrs. Kelly. Not by Easter. And not any time after that."

"Don't test my da," she says.

"Your da is a sick old man, and he won't win this time."

"I'm not sick. And I'm not old."

"You're not a man, either."

I practically hear the tumblers turn over in her brain, the crack of defiance clicking into place. "Don't test *me*," she says.

I reach out a hand to cup her cheek. Her skin is cooler than I expect it to be, as if she's been carved out of glass and left overnight in the garden. "I know you want to be a good girl," I say.

"I'm not a girl!"

She pulls away, as I knew she would. My fingers burn, because there's only one woman on earth I want to call my good girl now, and I just left her, soaked and satisfied in the kitchen downstairs.

"Good *daughter*, I should have said. You're doing what your da tells you, and there's no shame in that. But he can only play the cards *he's* been dealt. And this time he's got a losing hand."

"What about me?" she demands. "What about *my* cards?"

She doesn't know. She doesn't understand. And I know it'll break her heart when she finally learns the truth. But that doesn't keep me from saying: "Fiona, lass. You're holding no cards. You never have. No one even gave you a seat at the table."

I leave, so she doesn't have to. And as my shower pounds the scar on my forearm, I try not to think of how she looked, hearing truth for the first time in her life.

22

BRAIDEN

The air is soft outside St. Columba's as we gather after Easter Sunday Mass. Samantha and Aiofe are round the corner in the churchyard, filling an Easter basket with eggs hidden by the good ladies of the Altar Guild. Birte's at home with Grace Poole, because I don't trust either of them in public.

Fiona's holding court on the pavement, leaning against Madden's neon green McLaren and baiting my crew. The dress she's wearing is as far from an Easter frock as possible—all black leather, with belts and buckles that look like a detailed illustration of the devil's work. Her lips are bright red and shiny, and her laugh makes promises I know she'll never keep.

Madden stands on the edge of the crowd. I haven't seen him since I broke his jaw and from the set of his teeth, he's still wired shut. His necktie is pulled too tight around his throat. It looks like he's lost weight after three weeks of drinking dinner through a straw.

None of that keeps him from undressing Fiona with his eyes.

I close the distance between us, angrier than I have any right to be. When I cuff his head, I use the side of my hand so the blow is harder than it looks. "Don't mess with her."

"Or what?" The words are slurred because of the metal in his mouth, but he's clearly not backing down.

I don't have an answer for him. Same as I don't have an answer for Kieran Ingram, who's sure to nail me with today's deadline. There was never a question of my sending Birte back to Ireland, not with her as mad and broken as ever. And I won't drive Samantha away. I'll always be two marriages over the limit to meet Ingram's demand.

But I say to Madden, "Fiona Ingram's not for the likes of you." I try to emphasize my point with another swipe, but he blocks my hand with his forearm.

"Who's to say I haven't had her already?"

Sure. Like he's had his so-called contortionist and a thousand other girls.

I try not to stare at Fiona's black leather corset, even when she starts wriggling like she's just discovered a new way to drive my boys mad. It takes me a moment to realize she's digging a phone from between her tits.

The sun sparkles on the metal case as she answers a call. Turning toward me, her eyes lock on mine over the crowd. She nods. Says something. Closes the distance between us on her sky-high heels, phone extended.

Time to pay the piper.

"Happy Easter," I say into the phone, once she hands it over. I pause just long enough to make my point, and then I add, "Boss."

Kieran Ingram coughs like he's already halfway through his second pack of the day. I use the break to point a finger at Madden, then to gesture at the knot of Fishtown Boys trading lies around his eyesore of a car. My brother scowls, but he follows my silent order, herding them away to give me some semblance of privacy for the call.

When Ingram finally comes up for air, he says, "Tell me yer havin' th' priest read th' banns."

"You're living in the past, Boss. There's not a priest in America who does that anymore."

"Then ya have some other excuse fer not gettin' a ring on my daughter's hand by this morning?"

"You know my excuse. I'm already married."

"To a girl ya don't want and to a lyin' slag."

"Mind your fucking mouth," I say, before I consider the cost.

Ingram's answer is lost in yet another coughing fit. The man has to be short one lung by now. Maybe half another.

Fiona can't know exactly what her da is saying, but she has some general idea. Her teeth stand out against the scarlet lip she's caught.

I take a deep breath while Ingram fights for a shallow one. I count to five. I exhale even slower. And when the coughing finally lets up, I say, "Enough. Fiona will be home by midnight."

Her eyes narrow in defiance. Ingram's speechless for long enough that I'd think the call had dropped, if not for his raspy breathing. Finally, he says, "Yer passin' on th' best business deal o' th' century, boyo."

"I am," I say. I don't need to argue about *boyo*. I'm taking the upper hand. Finally.

"Yer leavin' behind some terrible hurt feelin's."

"That was never my intention."

"A little spondoolicks'll go a long way toward makin' things right."

Money. He's holding me up for cold, hard cash. And he's doing it using a word only an Irishman would know. We're brothers, he's saying. We're all in this together.

Has it been about money all along? He doesn't like the drop in my tithe, so he'll whore out his daughter. Make me pay up another way. It makes cold, vicious sense.

"What's your price, old man?"

From the shock on Fiona's face, she's never heard anyone

speak to her da with that tone. Or maybe she's just come to realize that Ingram's been using her for bait all along.

"Ten mill's a good start," he says. "Along with an extra five points on all ya earn fer th' next ten years."

It feels good to laugh, long and loud, like one of Ingram's coughing fits. "Not on your feckin' life," I finally say.

"Pay me now 'n' ya get off cheap. Yer goombah lawyer slag'll tie ya up in divorce court fer more—"

"See, that's where you've made a mistake," I interrupt. "An expensive one. I told you to mind your fucking mouth. But you just keep bringing the woman I love into this conversation. And that's going to cost *you*. A lot."

"Yer not th' one t' decide—"

"Fiona'll go home with a hundred thousand, and you'll both be grateful for that."

"Don't ya interrupt me, boyo!"

"Call me boyo one more time, you miserable cunt, and I'll come with Fiona, just to knock your teeth down your throat."

"I'm yer fuckin' General!"

"Then stop whoring out your daughter and act like it."

I end the call as Ingram's spluttering boils over into another coughing fit. "Your da needs you back in Boston," I say to Fiona, handing back her phone.

She shakes her head, but she takes the device. "You don't know what you're doing," she says.

"For the first time since you got here, I know *exactly* what I'm doing."

"He'll ruin you."

"I'll take my chances."

The phone in her hand starts to ring. She glances at the screen, then holds it out to me. "Tell him you're sorry. You made a mistake."

"I'm not. And I didn't."

"Tell him you need some time to think."

"I don't."

"Tell him—"

"I'm not telling him a thing, Fiona. Now answer the call and let him know you need his plane. Because I swear to God, if he doesn't send it, I'll put you on commercial."

But she doesn't answer the call. She waits until the ringing stops, and then she thumbs a button, cutting off whatever follow-up Ingram might try.

"I'm not leaving Philadelphia," she says.

"You're a grown woman. Do whatever you want. But I'm calling Fairfax right now and telling him to have your bags outside Thornfield's gate by sunset."

Fiona glares as I take my phone out of my breast pocket. "Don't bother," she says. "I'll be out of there."

I wait, not trusting her. But she turns to the men by the church steps. "Madden!" she calls, walking toward him, all hips and tits and a smile that says she eats men for breakfast. "Can I trouble you for a ride?"

My brother jumps like someone clipped live wires to his bollocks. His grin is broad as he takes his keys out of his pocket. The metal bits shine as he tosses them into the air and catches them. Fiona doesn't look back as he hands her into the McLaren.

Samantha and Aiofe come around the corner from the churchyard just as the acid-green car roars away from St. Columba's. Aiofe startles at the noise, nearly dropping the wicker basket in her hands. Samantha steadies her, bending down to say something I can't catch above the racket.

A fresh breeze catches Samantha's dress, the one I had Fairfax carry out to the pool house yesterday. It's a riot of flowers, all pinks and purples, and I spent too much of Father Regis' mass wondering what she's wearing underneath. Even now, I'm tempted to lure her back inside the church, to drag her into one of the confessionals for a few minutes of indecent privacy.

"Everything okay?" she asks as they reach me.

Without thinking, I close one hand over her hip. I lean down and brush a kiss against her lips, catching a whiff of something that smells like sunshine. Just the feel of her, the warmth of her, unlocks something in my shoulders, and I draw my first full breath since Fiona handed me her feckin' phone.

"It is now," I say.

Samantha's a lawyer. She's used to clients lying. To telling lies herself. She doesn't believe me for a second. But I direct a pointed glance toward Aiofe, and she lets it go.

"What's the craic, little one?" I ask, cementing the diversion.

Aiofe holds up her basket, which is filled with brightly colored plastic eggs, the kind that open to hold boiled sweets.

"For me?" I ask, making a show of choosing the biggest one.

She squeals a protest and pulls the basket away. But then she thinks twice and digs into her stash. She pokes around for a moment, and I'm not surprised when she comes up with a bright green egg.

"Thank you," I say, as if she's offered me the legendary Sword of Nuada. "I'll give it to Fairfax and ask him to cook it for breakfast tomorrow."

Laughing, she shakes her head. I let her take the egg from me, and she shows me how it opens, how it's filled with treats.

"Now that makes more sense," I say, which makes her laugh again.

"Time to head home?" Samantha asks.

We can't go back to Thornfield. Not until Fiona is packed and gone. "A day this lovely, I thought we'd take some air. What do you think about a trip to the zoo?"

I can tell Samantha's suspicious, but she won't push, not after I settle a warning hand on the ribbon in Aiofe's hair. So she shrugs, and Aiofe claps her hands, and I lead the way to the Bentley like I haven't a care in the world.

Like I haven't just launched a war against the General of the Grand Irish Union.

23

SAMANTHA

~

I wake before sunrise, tangled in bedclothes and fighting a nightmare. The images are hazy the way so many dreams are—I was in a courtroom, but it was also the zoo. I was pleading for my law license, but I was also explaining why I failed to feed the lions and giraffes. I was standing over three graves, but I was also locked in a concrete cage with steel bars as thick as my waist while Detective Tarrant read out loud from a Bible.

My pulse still pounds in double-time as I stagger into the bathroom and splash cold water over my face. My nose is sunburned; I spent too much time walking around the zoo yesterday with Braiden and Aiofe. My feet are sore, and I have blisters from my shoes.

By the time I've brushed my teeth and combed my hair, I'm beginning to feel more human. I didn't eat dinner last night; I couldn't face a bite of food after an afternoon of hot dogs and popcorn and cotton candy.

In fact, when we got back from the zoo, Aiofe was sound asleep, slumped against her seatbelt in the back of the Bentley. Braiden carried her into the house. With a rueful smile, I headed to the pool house, too full and too tired, too sunburned and footsore to consider heading after him for a session wearing my collar.

I'm still not hungry, but I'm bound by house rules. And honestly, I'm looking forward to the first breakfast in ages without Fiona Ingram sitting at the table.

It's Monday, and I have a full day of online meetings, so I dress in one of my favorite outfits: Double-breasted Prada blazer, matching charcoal trousers, white shell, and low black pumps, in deference to my tender feet. I head over to the main house with a smile on my face.

"Good morning," I say to Braiden.

He eyes my clothes with an approving leer before he moves to the sideboard. Pouring me a cup of coffee, he asks, "Did you sleep well?"

"Very well," I lie. "I was exhausted after all that walking."

"I can think of better ways to get tired out."

His arm brushes mine and I blush. He chuckles as he takes his place at the head of the table. I haven't seen him this relaxed...ever.

"Tired out," Birte chants from her seat across from me. "Without a doubt. Out, out, out."

Fairfax has provided his usual spread—eggs, sausage, pota-toes, and the rest. I help myself to a bowl of thick, tangy yogurt, smothering it in heaps of fresh berries to convince Braiden it's a meal.

Birte continues humming to herself, serene behind a full array of food as she sips a scalding cup of tea. Beside her, Aiofe eyes an empty plate. I push the platter of blood sausage—one of her favorites—closer so she can serve herself. Her face goes the color of skim milk.

Braiden says with a barely suppressed smile. "*Someone* woke up during the night and ate all the sweets in her Easter eggs."

I smother my own grin behind my cup of coffee. I half expect Braiden to force her to eat, just to make his point. But it's not fair to make anyone clean up the mess that will surely result.

"Try to drink some tea," I tell Aiofe. "That might settle your tummy."

She takes a courageous sip of the beige drink Braiden's given her—mostly milk, with just a splash of tea. Birte loads her own fork with potatoes as if she's trying to set a good example. "Drink some tea. Eat like me. Tea. Tea. Tea."

Braiden rests one hand on his stack of newspapers as he says to me, "I'll have Fairfax move your things back to the house this morning."

My spoon clatters into my bowl. "That won't be necessary."

"I've sent Fiona back to Boston. She's gone."

"She's gone," Birte echoes. "No more pawn. Gone. Gone. Gone."

I toss a meaningful glance toward Birte. "*Fiona* was not the issue."

"Not the issue," chants Birte. "Rip like tissue. Is-sue. Is-sue. Is-sue." She tears the word into parts, rocking with the force of her chant.

Aiofe folds her napkin by her plate before she touches Braiden's sleeve with one fragile hand. The poor thing truly does look miserable. I don't think she'll repeat her midnight-candy mistake again.

"Go on, lass," Braiden says. "I've already texted John Bell. One day's mitching won't ruin you. Try a quick kip. You'll feel better when you wake."

Birte taps the table. "Quick kip. Make trip. Kip, kip, kip!"

Aiofe hangs her head and makes for the stairs.

Birte calls after her: "When you wake. Don't you fake. Wake. Wake. Wake." Then she folds her fingers into a fist and starts pounding the table, continuing to chant, "Wake!"

I have no idea what's set her off. Maybe it's Fiona's empty seat at the table. Maybe it's Aiofe leaving early, breaking our routine. Maybe it's the broken circuits in her brain, the damage done when she watched her brother and nephew bleed out on church steps three thousand miles away.

Birte changes her chant: "Break! Break! Break!" The dishes jump on the table every time her fist lands.

"Grace!" Braiden calls, raising his voice enough to be heard in the kitchen. When the door swings open, he says, "Birte's finished with breakfast. Please help her upstairs."

Grace gives her usual scowl, but she comes to Birte's side. As they head toward the third floor, Grace coos about some new hymn Birte is learning to play.

I wait until they're out of earshot before I say, "This is getting worse."

"Don't start," he warns. "Not today."

But I ignore him. "She's chanting more, and she looks exhausted every morning. I don't think she's sleeping well. Do you think she heard anyone talking about an annulment?"

He makes an exasperated sound. "She wouldn't understand, even if she did."

"She's not a child. She understands a lot more than you think she does. She needs help, Braiden."

He bristles. "I got the priest you asked for."

"Father Regis hasn't been here in weeks."

"He was busy with Lent."

"Even if—" I cut myself off. "She needs a doctor."

"We are *not* having this conversation again."

"We never *have* conversations. You just make rules, and we all scramble to obey." I throw my napkin on the table and push back my chair.

"Samantha," he warns.

"I have work to do."

"Jaysus!" His accent's gone thick. "Can I have one feckin' meal not ruined by squabbling women?"

That doesn't deserve a reply. I turn on my heel and head upstairs to my office.

I expect to hear his chair scrape across the floor. I wait for his footsteps on the stairs behind me. I brace for his hand on my arm, for him to force me down the hall, past the nursery where Aiofe's taking her nap and into the bedroom.

But he doesn't.

I should be grateful he's not putting me in my collar and pretending there's nothing wrong in the world. If he ordered me to my knees, I might obey out of habit, and at the moment I'm not inclined to follow any of his commands.

The front door slams. I don't know if he's walking the grounds or if he's heading to the garage, but I don't care.

I storm down the hall to my office and slam my own door. Too late, I remember that Aiofe's trying to nap, but she's a child. If we wake her, she'll just roll over and go back to sleep.

I pace from my door to the windows, steps tight, fists clenched. Braiden *is* leaving the garage, pulling out in his jet-black Aston Martin. He guns the engine as he makes the turn in front of the house, sending up a spray of gravel before he speeds to the gate.

I whirl from the window to my desk. I have plenty of work to keep me busy while he sulks like a goddamn schoolboy. I have to sign off on a new brochure Trap's using to promote the freeport. And Alix has sent me a draft of her policies and procedures for in-house auctions. I need to review the new employment contracts for the catering staff Trap's brought on; some of them are members of local unions, which is a new angle for freeport staff.

And that's before I get to my own stack of papers. Sonja has sent draft replies for the ethics board, and Teddy wants to go over the testimony I gave Detective Tarrant last Friday. The second episode of Mousetrap waits on my phone.

No wonder I have nightmares.

But I never get to the freeport documents. I never pull up

the latest communication from my somewhat exasperated lawyers. I never even open my laptop.

Because a sheet of paper rests in the very center of my desk.

It's an ordinary piece of plain white printer paper. It's perfectly flat, not even a hint of a curled corner. It's filled with angry black letters, all in capitals. They seem to be scrawled with a felt-tip pen, angled so far to the right they look like they're flying off the page.

> *There once was a whore, wore a collar,*
> *Fucked anyone worth half a dollar.*
> *She spied for a wop,*
> *Gave away the whole shop,*
> *Shoot her now, before she can holler.*

The last word is covered with a scarlet lip-print, a blood-red kiss that gleams in the light from the window.

Fiona's going-away present. A limerick like the one I couldn't deliver at the party in the ballroom.

She has no right.

No fucking right.

And just like that, I know I need to get out of this madhouse.

I grab the paper from my desk, shove it into my briefcase, and fly down the stairs. Braiden isn't the only person with a fast little sports car. Four months ago, when I fled my condo in Dover, he had one of his men drive my Mercedes up here. It's sat in the garage ever since. I only know it's been tended to because I've seen it on the driveway once a week, washed and waxed and polished till it gleams.

The keys hang on a hook inside the garage door. I grab them and open the driver-side door as Liam appears from the office at the back. "Need a ride, Sam?" He's already heading toward the Bentley.

"I'm going for a drive."

He looks unsure. "I don't think that's a good idea."

"I'm one hundred percent certain it is."

He looks at me across the roof of my car. "Fine," he says evenly. "I'll ride shotgun."

There once was a whore, wore a collar...

I don't want anyone riding shotgun. I don't want anyone managing me. Controlling me. For five fucking minutes, I want to do whatever I want to do, whenever and wherever I want to do it.

I slide behind the wheel of the Mercedes and punch the ignition button. The engine purrs to life, perfectly maintained, because everything is flawlessly managed in Braiden Kelly's domain. That's what he's purchased with his billions.

Fucked anyone worth half a dollar...

Stabbing at the screen for the radio, I crank a classic rock station so loud my ears bleed. Liam's standing by the passenger door, saying something I can't hear. He reaches for the handle, but I peel out of the garage before he has a chance to open the door.

Approaching the gate, I blare the horn. Liam hasn't thought to call down to the guards yet. I've always been such a good little prisoner. Always done exactly what I've been ordered to do.

She spied for a wop...

The gate grinds open. The instant I can clear the iron bars, I gun the car through.

The paparazzi are taken by surprise; they barely jump out of the way in time to avoid being hit. The protesters scramble too. A few shake their signs, but most of them are still fighting to display their hateful words as I roar past.

I take turns faster than I should, getting to the main road. For one quick moment, I consider driving down to Dover. It's a work day. The freeport needs me.

The hell with work days. The hell with Dover. The hell with anyone and anything telling me what I'm supposed to do.

I skid onto the on-ramp for the freeway, heading north

because that traffic light is green, and I don't want to stop. Maneuvering into the fast lane, I rely on my mirrors to know the coast is clear.

My tires thunder over dividers in the road, falling into a rhythm that matches the doggerel in my head.

Gave away the whole shop...

Gave away the whole shop...

Gave away the whole shop...

As I near Trenton, a bright green sign announces that New York City is 61 miles away. Blue signs point me toward rest areas. The traffic is moving fast—ten miles over the speed limit, fifteen, twenty.

Shoot her now, before she can holler.

I press down on the gas pedal, trying to outpace the limerick in my head. I never make a conscious decision. I never tell myself the truth. But in my heart of hearts, I know I'm driving all the way to Boston.

24

BRAIDEN

~

I n the past, when I needed a break from Thornfield, I drove downtown to the Hare and Harp. I drowned my sorrows in a glass of the black stuff. I called my Council to meet in my private office at the back of the pub.

But that isn't an option today. It hasn't been for over two months—since Russo burned my bar to the ground.

Time for that to change.

I place three calls as I drive downtown. The first is to Seamus, my Quartermaster. He manages the clan's finances— dozens of bank accounts spread out across the city, along with the off-shore dealings we need to keep things craic. I tell him to meet me at the corner of Frankford and Master.

My second call is to Patrick, my Warlord, back from Ireland nearly two weeks since he collected the Book of Skreen. Technically, he's my chief enforcer, in charge of all the muscle the clan can wield. But at forty-eight, he's my oldest advisor, the one I trust most to tell me when my arse is showing. Plus, he's lived in

Philadelphia for thirty years, and he knows every block of down-town like a priest knows the Bible.

My third call is to Madden. He's still my Clan Chief, my second-in-command. His driving off with Fiona yesterday didn't change that, any more than my breaking his jaw did, weeks back.

I'm his Captain. And his brother. We need to talk. Clear the air. Get back to doing what we do best—making money for the Fishtown Boys.

When he doesn't answer his phone, I leave him a message: "Call me when you get this. I'm settling on a new place for the Hare this morning, and I'd like your input."

See? I can be perfectly reasonable, when people around me aren't doing their level best to drive me mad.

Before I can put my phone back in my pocket, it sings out "Sunday, Bloody Sunday." So much for not driving me mad.

"What?" I snap when I answer the call.

"Ya hurt my Fiona's feelin's, boyo."

"She shouldn't have been surprised. Not if her eyes were open. Not if she paid an ounce of attention, the entire time she was here."

"Ya have one chance t' make this right."

"Don't bother giving me a deadline, old man. I won't play your game. I've struck out on two wives, and I won't try a third."

"Ya seem t' think I'm askin'."

"*You* seem to think I'm one of your Boston boys, pissing my pants every time you start to roar."

"They call it a union fer a reason, boyo!"

"Because that's how they do things over in Dublin. Because that gives you a chance to lord it over the rest of us. Because that's how you make your fucking money, tapping your Captains to pay up their tithes, like scared little boys topping off the collection plate. I'm not scared, Ingram. I'm not little. And by Jesus, Mary, and Joseph, I'm not a boy."

He starts coughing when I'm only halfway through, and he

hasn't caught his breath by the time I get to the end. I could wait for his threats, for his telling me to watch my back, for his twin demands of obedience and tribute.

But nothing he can say will make me take back my words. I'm tired of bending a knee to an old man whose days are numbered. So I tap the call done before he splutters another word, and head off to my meeting in Fishtown.

I get there first. There's a coffee shop on the corner, and they're doing good business, which would ordinarily please me, because what's good for the neighborhood is good for the Boys.

But every time someone opens the shop door, the smell of coffee wafts to where I'm waiting. Of course, that makes me think of Samantha, and that makes me think of the feckin' disaster I left at breakfast and that makes me wonder what the hell I'm actually going to do about Birte.

Because Samantha is right: Birte's getting worse. Maybe she's overwhelmed by spending time outside of the attic. Maybe Easter was too much for her religious sensibilities. Maybe…

I don't have a feckin' clue.

Then call a doctor and get one.

I need Samantha out of my feckin' head.

My phone rings, and I know the boys would laugh if they saw how fast I take it from my pocket. It's not Samantha, though.

It's Liam. And he starts off apologizing, which can't be good. "I'm sorry, Boss."

I sigh. "What's she done now?"

He hesitates a moment, but not too long because he's one of my best men. "Took her Mercedes," he says. "I tried to go with her—"

I interrupt him with a curse. Truth be told, I forgot Samantha's car was in my feckin' garage. "Just pull up the tracker. Keep an eye—"

"There isn't a tracker, Boss."

I pinch my lower lip. Of course there isn't a tracker. When I had the car brought to Thornfield, Samantha and I had already had ructions about my selling off her condo. It wasn't worth another fifteen rounds over the Mercedes. I figured I'd sell it soon enough, after she had a chance to settle in. No need to add the tracker I put in all my cars.

"Did she say where she was going?"

"No, Boss."

Did she take a suitcase with her? I can't make myself ask it. Part of me doesn't want to know.

I force more confidence into my voice than I feel. "Let me know when she's back."

"I will, Boss. I'm sorry. I didn't think she'd go like that. I should have forced her to stop. I should have dived in front of the car. I should have—"

"We'll talk after she's home."

I end the call while he's still groveling.

Liam's sole job was keeping an eye on the woman I call my wife. I want to hang him from the ceiling by his bollocks.

But I want her home more. And if there's a chance she'll call him from the road… Better to keep Liam on my side. For now.

Samantha's been driving herself around for well over a decade. She's a responsible, capable woman. She keeps her head in challenging situations; she's a capable enough fighter that she bloodied Madden's nose.

But she's never been out in Philadelphia with so many enemies on the streets.

We still don't know who sent the man—Terrence King—to attack her at the freeport. I've done my digging, and Prince has too. Even Best has gotten in on the game. But whoever hired that piece of shite could be planning another attack, this very moment.

Russo's been quiet since he made out like a king at our Rittenhouse summit, but I don't trust that peace to last much longer. Once he wakes, he'll be loud, and if he decides to settle all of this, once and for all…

There's Ingram, too. I declared open war with him yesterday. This morning's skirmish only proves I'm not backing down. I assumed getting rid of Fiona would cost me money, maybe even some territory. But if Ingram's angry enough to hand the Fishtown Boys over to a man of his own choosing, he'll start by hitting me in my soft bits. And there's nothing softer than Samantha…

Christ. Even Fiona could work her own scheme. She acted calm yesterday, but my rejection had to sting. She's a viper in her own right—seven men she's taken down. If she decides getting at Samantha's the way to even things up with me…

And there's Madden. He's bullin' at me, but he's not eejit enough to touch Samantha. Unless Fiona puts him up to it. Unless he's ready to make a break with the Fishtown Boys… Unless…

He can't. He won't. Despite all the shite over the last four months, we're brothers.

But the Mafia, the GIU, a woman scorned, and an enemy I can't begin to name? Those are more than enough reasons to get Patrick back on the phone.

"I'm five minutes out, Boss," he says. "Just parking now."

"Change of plans. I need four men with me, here in Fishtown. Now."

"Did someone—"

"And once I'm home, I want them backing up the guards on the gate. With machine guns. Walking patrols at the fence. Visible."

He doesn't waste time arguing. "My best men are on their way. You're safe until I get there?"

I want to believe I'm over-reacting. I'm putting on a show here in Fishtown and protecting the piece of property I call home because I can't get a man to Samantha.

But glancing around, I realize that a late-model Ford has

been idling in the loading zone across the street since before Liam called. And a man hurrying down the sidewalk—shoulders hunched, hands in his pockets—is heading on a straight line to me. And that woman going into the coffee shop could be reaching for anything in her ragged, stained backpack.

My scarred forearm burns, and I'm back in the closet, eyes squeezed shut, waiting for a storm of bullets to tear me apart. I'm supposed to be strong. I'm supposed to be brave. But I'm six years old and I'm pissing my pants as Sister Mary Margaret dies.

The car pulls away. The man veers into a drug store. The woman comes up with a wallet, even more worn than her pack.

Patrick's still on the line, professional enough to have kept his silence while he waited. "Yeah," I say. "I'm fine." But I add, "Hurry."

Patrick arrives in under two minutes. He's got one hand tucked into his jacket; fingers on the Glock he keeps in a shoulder holster. "Boss," he says, his eyes sweeping the street with steady concentration.

Seamus saunters over five minutes later. It only takes him a moment to pick up on Patrick's tension. He studies the rooflines above us like he's thinking about funding an award for urban architecture.

"Forget about walking Fishtown today," I tell them. "But I want a list of possible properties for a new Hare and Harp on my desk by Friday."

I give them my specifics—square footage, ideal location, a basement I can outfit the way I need. Chances are, the place will already be occupied, but Seamus is an expert at manufacturing financial incentives. And Patrick can pick up the slack if anyone makes the mistake of being unreasonable.

Patrick's men show up as I finish outlining my expectations. All four enforcers are big enough to offer intimidation just on sight. Two have shoulder holsters. Another has a pistol in the small of his back. The fourth looks like he's got a gun strapped to his ankle—not my choice, but it's a free world.

If they're Patrick's best, they've also got weapons I can't clock, which is fine with me. They'll pick up machine guns from the stash at the house.

One of the men climbs in the Aston Martin with me. The others go with Patrick and Seamus. Opening the throttle once I'm back on the freeway, I call Fairfax, and he says the house is quiet.

Thornfield is safe.

Birte and Aiofe are safe.

But Samantha... I call her, and I'm not surprised when I drop into her voicemail. I try her work phone, too. Voicemail, again. I try her landline in Dover, which is ridiculous, because she hasn't had time to get there, even if that's her destination. When Mary answers, I ask her to have Samantha call. I say it's urgent.

After that, I have to wait.

I pick up my speed—not because I think that will get Samantha home faster, but because that requires a faster reaction time. My brain has to focus on something other than all the possible threats to my wife's safety.

It works.

By the time I weave through the reporters and sign-carrying eejits at Thornfield's front gate, my mind is calm. I've left behind that feeling of helpless urgency. I'm back to being a Captain, to making the hard decisions no one else can make.

It's not until I sit behind my office desk that I realize Madden never returned my call.

25

SAMANTHA

~

This morning, I told Braiden that Fiona wasn't the problem.

I was wrong.

Fiona arrived the first day Birte was out of the attic. That made it difficult to calculate how much household chaos could fairly be attributed to Braiden's first wife and what belonged on Fiona's own doorstep.

But those leather outfits... That constant smirk... The never-ending sexual energy she brought to everything from breakfast to business meetings... From the first moment Fiona crossed Thornfield's gate, she did her utmost to undermine me.

There once was a whore, wore a collar...

This isn't a mob thing. It's a *woman* thing. Fiona wants my man, and she'll stop at nothing—even immature, threatening limericks—to get him.

I refuse to let her win.

When I'm an hour outside of Boston, I pull into a rest stop.

With the car engine running, I take out my phone and call up Lexis-Nexis, a legal research app I use every day at the office.

Lexis can tell me a lot about individuals. I can find out if someone owns a car, boat, or plane. I can track down their driver's license number and their passport number. I can locate outstanding judgments and liens, along with any bankruptcies they might have filed. And I can find a home address.

All I need to do is lie.

The system asks if I have a legitimate need to know the information I seek. There's a long list of justifications, but none applies to my current situation. I don't hesitate before I tap the button that says I'm a law enforcement officer.

I'm accepting a wide range of penalties if I'm caught, but five minutes later, I have a home address for Fiona and Kieran Ingram.

Plugging the information into a map, I discover it's a massive three-story home taking up half a city block in South Boston. That makes sense. Southie has been an Irish-Catholic neighborhood for ages. Just the type of place an Irish Mob boss would frequent.

I tap the screen on my phone and follow turn-by-turn directions to the Ingram family home.

Growing up in Philadelphia, I lived in the shadow of Antonio Russo's sprawling downtown compound. I've spent the past four months at Braiden's suburban mansion. I understand mobsters' strongholds. But the Ingram family home is something completely different.

The street looks like any other road in Southie—narrow, well-worn, with clapboard houses sagging on their foundations as if they're too exhausted to stand straight any longer. On most blocks, cars are parked nose to tail, so close together they look like they've been lifted into place with a crane.

But one block is different. There are no cars on the street. A couple of kids slouch on the corner, shoulders slumped, hands in their pockets. They look young enough for junior high. I wonder if school has already let out for the day, or if they're playing hooky.

Two grown men stand on either side of the Ingrams' front door. Massachusetts must be an open-carry state—these guys make no attempt to hide their shoulder holsters or the textured grips of their handguns. They're wired, too, with visible plastic earpieces hinting at easily summoned reinforcements.

The thugs stare at me as I drive past the dark gray house. I keep my eyes on the road, but I get a vague impression of slicked-back hair a couple of decades out of date and determined jaws just begging someone, anyone, to say the wrong thing.

Two more dropouts hunch against the lamppost at the far corner. One of them whistles—at me or at the Mercedes, I can't be sure. His buddy cuffs him hard across the back of his head.

It takes me two blocks to find legal parking, and then I'm grateful for the Mercedes' smooth power steering. I nail the space with less than an inch to spare. It feels wrong to leave the car here, unattended, but I don't have a choice.

My fingers have just closed on the grip of my briefcase when my phone rings. Glancing at the screen, I'm not surprised to see Braiden's name. He's already called two dozen times, precisely on each quarter hour, the entire time I drove north.

Clearly, he's over his tantrum from breakfast, and he's back to his trademark control. I've glanced at all the transcribed voicemails he's left. They're identical: *Samantha, this is urgent. Phone me immediately.*

If Braiden wants to apologize, he can do that by message too. And if he doesn't, I'm not ready to talk to him.

I clutch my briefcase and get out of my car.

The juvenile delinquents on the street corner stand straight as I approach. The one who wolf-whistled reaches into his jeans pocket and produces a phone. Barely glancing down, he taps the screen. I feel as if I've rung a doorbell.

The kids have no right to stop me from using a public sidewalk, but the weight of their combined stares feels like a javelin between my shoulder blades. Trying not to twitch, I make my way to the serious enforcers at the main door.

"I'm here to see Fiona Ingram," I say.

"There's no one here by that name," Tweedledum says, almost before I get out the last syllable.

I shift my briefcase, not afraid to make this look like an official visit. "We both know that's not true."

"*If* a Fiona Ingram lived here, she'd accept service through her attorney." Tweedledee chimes in. His Boston accent is thick; her name sounds like Fioner.

"I'm not serving process."

"We have to ask you to move along now." Tweedledum takes a step forward, intentionally crowding into my comfort zone.

I square my shoulders. "No, you don't. You have to let me in to see Fiona."

Sunlight glints off the butt of Tweedledee's pistol. "If you know enough to ask about the Ingrams here, then you know enough to understand why it's a very bad idea to outstay your welcome."

The man has a point. One I intend to ignore, but a point, all the same.

Pretending my heart isn't pounding, I cross to the far side of the street. I plant my feet in front of the run-down house there and cup my hands around my mouth. "Fiona!" I shout. "Fiona Ingram!"

Tweedledum lunges across the street to pin my biceps in a grip so tight I know I'll be bruised for a week. A curtain twitches at a window on the Ingrams' third floor, but falls back before I glimpse a face. A door opens behind me, but it slams closed so quickly I wonder if it was caught by a localized hurricane. At the far end of the street, a man and woman approach, only to be held back by the kids at the corner.

"Let that be the last stupid mistake you make today, Samantha Mott," Tweedledum growls.

Someone has fed him information through his earpiece. They must have noted my Mercedes, out of place in this neighborhood. They ran my license plate through a database like LexisNexis.

Tweedledum clearly thinks his using my name will terrify me. But from Day One, Kieran Ingram has taken the position that my marriage to Braiden doesn't exist. I'm not a proper wife because Father Brennan wasn't a proper priest.

That makes me a civilian. And the Mob can't hurt an outsider. They can't harm one woman bringing a private complaint to another woman's doorstep. Not if Kieran Ingram intends to live by his own code.

Tweedledee presses his fingertips to his ear, clearly receiving instructions from someone inside the Ingram castle. Ignoring him, I shout to the third-floor window: "Fiona! Call off your dogs!"

Tweedledum snarls and tightens his grip on my arm. Involuntary tears spark in the corners of my eyes, but I raise my chin and call out again. "Fiona! How's this for a limerick? There once was a woman from Southie!"

I don't have a second line in mind, but I'm spared the need to scramble for one because the Ingrams' door opens. A kid, even younger than the boys on the corner, steps onto the stoop.

Tweedledee glances over his shoulder and barks, "What?"

The kid pipes, "Let her in."

Tweedledum drags me across the street. He keeps his grip tight as Tweedledee frisks me. The scowling goon makes sure I'm not hiding anything in my bra. He spends a lot more time than necessary checking for a weapon in the waistband of my pants, and he uses the excuse of potential ankle holsters to shove his face into my crotch.

I refuse to let him see a reaction. And when he finally decides I'm not an armed threat, I stand straight, stepping into the clapboard house like I have every right to be here.

I don't know what I expected—maybe an armory guard

room with a dozen soldiers, or a secret passage to a basement lair, or a blinding white reception area like some exclusive doctor's office.

But what I find is a parlor that looks like it was decorated in the middle of the last century. There's a plastic-covered couch with a huge floral print. It faces a pair of matching armchairs with sagging seats. A coffee table is covered with water stains from years of drinking glasses placed without coasters. The entire room reeks of stale cigarette smoke.

No. Not the room. It's the man standing in front of me who reeks.

He's shorter than I am by half a foot. His face is an unhealthy yellow-gray, and his eyes are set deep in fans of wrinkles. His chin is cobbled, as if something broke up the underlying bone a century or two ago. His wool suit hangs loosely from his shoulders, making me think he's recently lost a lot of weight.

"Yer makin' a mistake, lass." His accent is thicker than anything I've ever heard from Braiden's lips.

"Kieran Ingram." I don't pretend it's a question.

"Tell yer man t' fight his own battles."

"Braiden didn't send me. He doesn't know I'm here."

"Then yer a lot more foolish than th' stories I hear."

I don't ask what stories. I don't want to know. "I want to see Fiona."

"If she wanted t' see ya, she'd be here instead o' me."

"With all due respect, I don't care what Fiona wants."

I'm not surprised my reply makes him angry. But I *am* surprised when his sharp intake of breath sets off a coughing fit. He digs his fist into his thigh, fighting for breath. His sallow face flushes, then turns red, then purple.

When he finally regains control, he drags a handkerchief from his pocket. I catch a glimpse of bright red after he spits, but he hides it quickly.

Before he can say a word, I pull the limerick out of my briefcase. There's no way Ingram can read the words from across the room, but his eyes narrow when he sees the smear of lipstick at the end.

"Tell Fiona this is the last time she threatens me."

He asks, "Do I look like a feckin' message boy?"

"Tell her," I say. "And if anything happens to me, if I so much as stumble and stub my toe, my lawyer has orders to send the original straight to the FBI." I'm lying about the last bit, but I'll call Teddy the moment I'm back at Thornfield. Sonja too, for good measure.

"Yer man's too smart t' run t' the feds."

"I already told you. Braiden didn't send me. This isn't Fishtown business. Not the Union's, either. This is just between Fiona and me. Tell her."

I drop the goddamn poem back into my briefcase and turn on my heel, leaving the room while Ingram's still spluttering threats. Out on the sidewalk, Tweedledum and Tweedledee startle to attention, but I ignore them. I pass the corner boys without looking left or right.

I'm so grateful to reach the Mercedes unmolested that I have to swallow the urge to sob. But I maneuver out of my parking space with a minimum of turning the wheel. I head back to the freeway. To Thornfield. To home.

I've done what I came here to do. I've told Fiona I won't tolerate her threats.

So *now* it's time to deal with Braiden Kelly.

26

BRAIDEN

"Samantha, this is urgent. Phone me immediately." I refuse to change my intonation. I already expressed my anger this morning, and that's why we're in this mess.

But if she thinks I'll give up first, she clearly hasn't been paying attention the past four months.

Plus, she hasn't blocked me.

A call comes in before I can return my phone to my pocket. "Sunday, Bloody Sunday." Possibly the last sound in the world I want to hear right now.

"Boss," I answer, because Ingram might get off the phone faster if I don't purposely antagonize him.

"If ya don't curb yer bitch, boyo, she'll get a bullet in her head."

My stomach tightens. He ordered me to make Fiona my bitch, and I refused. Birte and Aiofe and Grace are all secure at Thornfield; none of them can be the bitch who's feeding Ingram's rage.

184 | ALIX KEY

"If you set one finger on Samantha, I'll see you buried in a shallow grave, old man."

How the fuck did she get all the way to Boston in the time she's been gone? She must have averaged seventy on the Interstate, and still been lucky with traffic. I don't bother wondering how she found Ingram; she's smart and she's strong, and apparently she's highly motivated.

"Yer bitch came into *my* home, talkin' about goin' t' th' FBI."

"Call her that again, and I'll be the one in your home."

"Yer not listenin', boyo. *F. B. I.* She said it like she was writin' up her grocery list."

Oh, Samantha… What have you done now?

I can take a hard line, telling Ingram he's brought this on himself, sending Fiona down here in the first place, upping the ante with his Easter deadline. I can remind him Samantha's a lawyer, that she doesn't make idle threats, and if she mentioned the feds, she must have had good reason. I can tell him he's old and sick and he must have misunderstood.

But the truth is, Ingram's taken out men for less than Samantha's done. Everyone knows the old man had Finn Monahan executed—rat in mouth, the whole nine yards—just for wearing a gag t-shirt he bought on a street corner in Washington, DC. *FBI*, it said in big block letters. And smaller, around a fake badge: Female Body Inspector.

Kieran Ingram won't tolerate any mention of the feds in his territory. And I can't imagine what possessed Samantha to drive three hundred miles to taunt him.

At least I know why she hasn't responded to my voicemail messages.

"What're ya gonna do about her, boyo?"

"She's not going to any feds."

"I hear yer voice. 'N' I understand yer words. But ya don't have any way o' knowin' what yer one's about to do."

Yer one. That's better than *bitch*. He's not ready to pull the trigger yet. Not ready to force my hand.

"She's on her way home now," I say. I don't know if I'm lying. I have no idea where Samantha is. And I'd be incriminating myself, to even imply she's been out of touch.

His voice ratchets higher. "Ya take her in hand, boyo."

"I will." That grim promise is easy to make.

His tone rises a few more notes. "Ya make her understand what she can and cannot say."

"She'll understand."

"If I—" He's worked himself into a proper fit. He breaks into one of his coughing jags.

This time is worse than the others. His cough is deeper. Wetter. It goes on for long enough that I wonder if I should end the call and reach out to 911. Or, at least to Fiona, so she can get him the medical care he clearly needs.

"Jaysus, Mary, and Joseph," he finally groans. And then he's right back in the thick of our argument. "Yer one," he says, and something's shifted. He's angrier. More determined. "She's not just talkin' t' th' feds. She's sellin' ya out t' th' dagos."

I roll my eyes. Fiona must have passed on Madden's paranoid fantasies.

"She isn't," I tell Ingram. "Antonio Russo killed her parents. Her cousin, too. She'd die before she'd tell Russo the first thing about how I run the Fishtown Boys."

"She'd die," Ingram repeats. "Then ya understand what has t' happen."

A chill knifes through my gut, but I argue with the old man. "You're not listening. Samantha hates Russo."

"But she told him about yer shipment at th' docks."

"She didn't—"

"And she let him into yer pub."

Jesus. Fiona's trotted out all the old lies. "Samantha had nothing to do with Russo burning down the Hare and Harp."

"She told that wop where t' find yer man. Donovan O'Keefe."

Just the name is enough to make me picture the live video feed on my phone. Donny lashed to a chair, broken and beaten. Donny soaked with petrol, an Irish flag jammed down his throat. Donny writhing in flames, screaming for longer than I thought any man could.

Cold sweat coats my palms. When I remember how to swallow, all I taste is battery acid.

"Samantha didn't hand over Donny."

"Stop listenin' t' yer prick, boyo. Start seein' th' facts."

I close my eyes, searching for the magic words that will make Ingram understand. I start: "I don't know who's been telling you stories."

But it has to be Fiona. She had to tell him something about why I sent her packing. She had to justify my choosing Samantha over her.

"This isn't about stories, boyo. This is about trust. And if I can't trust one o' my own captains—"

"You can trust me," I say through gritted teeth.

"I *thought* I could trust ya wi' Fiona," he shouts. "We had a plan!"

I wonder if one of his men is in the room with him. Maybe he's embarrassed by that coughing fit, by what it took out of him. He has to prove he's still strong enough to be general. That's why he's being so stubborn.

I purposely pitch my voice low, still hoping to calm him. Hoping he'll let me end this feckin' call so I can leave Samantha another voicemail and get her home where she belongs. "There wasn't a plan," I remind him. "I never said I'd marry Fiona. *You* said that."

"Well, I'm sayin' this, too, boyo. Ya take care o' yer one, once and fer all. Ya make sure she never talks t' th' feds. Can I trust ya with *that*? Or is it time fer someone else t' run Philly?"

It's a fucking loyalty test. I kill Samantha, and I'm allowed to keep the clan. I refuse, and someone else takes over the Fishtown Boys.

And Ingram takes out Samantha and me, both. That's the bit he hasn't said out loud.

"You don't want to do that," I say with false calm. "Not with all the attention on her now, the press about her car crash."

"About th' weans she killed? She's poison, boyo. Get rid of her."

"If something happens to her now, important people will ask a lot of questions. Questions that will attract too much attention."

Attention from the FBI.

I think about saying that last bit out loud. But that might overplay my hand. I can't sign my own death warrant while I'm fighting against Samantha's.

Ingram says, "Don't think I'm fergettin' my Fiona. With yer side bit gone, ya can do what ya should've done th' first time yer general gave ya orders."

"Samantha's not my si—"

He cuts me off. "Do. It."

He ends the call before I can.

Fingers shaking, I place yet another call to Samantha. I don't care that it's not the quarter hour. I don't care about keeping my voice perfectly even. I don't care about making her more angry, or frightened, or sad.

"Samantha," I say when she doesn't pick up. "Game's over, *piscín*. This just turned life or death. Get your arse home now."

27

SAMANTHA

I t's after ten by the time I get back to Thornfield. The second Mousetrap podcast has spawned more protesters and signs that weren't there this morning: *No One Should Die Like a Dog in a Ditch. Drugs Kill. No More Victims. John 3:16.*

The knot of paparazzi sends out tentacles the moment my Mercedes comes into sight. Cameras flash, and the two most persistent reporters stake out positions directly in front of the gate.

This is the first time I've needed to negotiate the bloodsuckers on my own. Braiden and Liam have always made it seem simple, keeping a slow, steady pace to the property line, as if they're easing past rabid dogs in the middle of the road.

It's harder than it looks. Too fast, and I chance clipping one of the crazies with my front bumper. Too slow, and they can swarm my windows, blinding me with their cameras.

I finally make it to the gatehouse without causing a disaster. An extra man stands inside the shelter, his hands locked on a machine gun. Looking toward the house, I realize three more guards wait just inside the fence, similarly armed. Thornfield looks like it's under military siege.

Swallowing hard, I place my sweating palm on the electronic reader. I stare directly into the laser that scans my retinas. I focus hard so I don't blink.

A century goes by before the gate starts to roll back. The extra guards scowl at the paparazzi and the protesters. They don't shift their weapons as I drive past, not even a millimeter.

Somehow, I expect Liam to be waiting at the garage, but he's nowhere in sight as I back the Mercedes into its bay. I start to return my keys to their hook on the wall, but then I hesitate. This morning, I taught Braiden how easy it was for me to take my car. Given my refusal to respond to his voicemails and texts, I'm certain I'll have a much harder time leaving in the future.

I pocket the keys and slip out of the garage.

The guards at the gate must have let Braiden know I'm home. I imagine him waiting for me in the dining room or—worse—in the bedroom we once shared.

I can't confront him tonight. I'm stiff from sitting in the car for so many hours. My arms are tired from gripping the wheel. The roof of my mouth hums a little, now that I'm finally free of the moving car's vibrations.

Tomorrow is soon enough to face Braiden Kelly.

Making my way around the corner of the house, I take the path to the back, to the pool, to my own private apartment. I miss the lock on my first try. I'm even more tired than I thought. It turns easily, though, on my second attempt.

I kick off my shoes the instant I step over the threshold. Crossing to the sink, I fill a glass of water from the tap and drink it down without stopping. I haven't eaten a real meal all day—just a few spoonfuls of yogurt before breakfast became a battle—but the thought of food leaves me nauseated. I hang my head and dig my fingertips into the nape of my neck, trying to massage away my miserable day.

"House. Rules."

I catch a scream at the back of my throat, already recognizing Braiden's voice before I turn toward the bed. He's sitting on the edge of the high mattress, dressed all in black—jacket, shirt, trousers, even his necktie.

"Jesus," I say. "You scared the crap out of me."

"That was my intention." His voice is flat, as if he's reading lines from a cue card. He repeats his first two words: "House. Rules."

I stifle a groan. I've broken every one of his fucking house rules today. I didn't eat all my breakfast. I worked long past six —if confronting the woman who threatened my life can be called work. I'm still dressed in my charcoal suit, no hint of the flowery skirt I'm required to wear at the end of every day. And I am absolutely, positively wearing panties.

"Not tonight, Braiden," I say. "I'm exhausted."

"Do I look like I give a fuck how tired you are?"

"Fine," I snap. "Tie me up. Smack me around. Want to beat me with your belt? Go ahead. Just get it over with. I don't need my collar."

There once was a whore, wore a collar...

He rises from the bed like a cobra striking. One hand clamps my left wrist. The other pinches the nape of my neck. Before I know what's happened, he has me bent over the edge of the bed.

I know how to defend myself; I've taken classes and worked one-on-one with trainers. I understand how to turn toward a captor, how to shift my body so I can use his weight against him. I'm well versed in going for eyes, for the soft flesh beneath a nose. I can jam the heel of my hand into a man's Adam's apple or drop him with a sharp blow to the crotch.

But Braiden's too big for any of that. He's too big and he's too heavy and he's too furious for me to shift him even one inch. He's crushing me, all his weight on the small of my back. With my cheek pressed into the mattress, I can barely draw a breath, much less fight for freedom.

"Open your eyes, Samantha."

I didn't realize I'd closed them.

He squeezes his fingers around the base of my skull. "Open your goddamn eyes."

I do. And for a moment, I can't figure out what I'm staring at. The room is too dark. My heart is racing too fast. I'm fighting too hard to draw a full breath against the weight of the man on top of me.

But I blink. And I look again. And I realize I'm staring down the barrel of a pistol.

It's on top of the comforter, nestled amid tulips and honeysuckle. Braiden can reach it easily from his position on my spine. He could plant the muzzle at the base of my skull and pull the trigger. The bedclothes would catch most of the mess.

I want to close my eyes again, but I won't give him the satisfaction.

I was raised in the lap of the Mafia, side by side with my cousin Eliza. Antonio Russo raped her with his gun, then tore her apart with a single bullet just because he could. Braiden saved me from that madman's grasp; bringing me to Thornfield and telling the world I was his bride.

But in the end, violent men use violent means. I pushed Braiden over the edge at breakfast this morning, and now he's proving who he really is.

I'll never let him see my fear. "So this is my punishment for driving around in my car? At least Eliza got to fuck her boyfriend before Russo shot her."

His fingers tighten around my neck. He's leaving bruises my collar would cover, if I ever agreed to wear his fucking emerald again. "This is what you get for breaking the rules."

"You never said I couldn't take my car."

"I gave you a goddamn driver."

"To go to the freeport. I didn't drive to Dover."

"No. You drove to Boston. To Kieran Ingram. To my fucking general."

"You *tracked* me?" My voice cracks with indignation.

"I wish I had. Then I could have sent a man to intercept you."

"News flash, Braiden. It's a free world. I'm allowed to drive my own car. I can go where I want. Talk to who I want. Heading up the Fishtown Boys doesn't give you the right to change that."

"Heading up the Fishtown Boys——" His voice drips with venom as he repeats my words. "Gives me the need to kill you."

Need. Not *right.*

He's already made up his mind. I've been tried, convicted, and sentenced, without a chance to say a single word in my own defense. That's why he's brought a gun to our game.

Braiden has done things to my body before, things I never believed I'd let a man do. Things I never imagined wanting. He's left me bruised, left me battered, left me broken and spent.

But always, *always*, that's been with my consent. *Say* red *and I'll stop.* That's been our rule.

"Let me go," I whisper.

"I can't do that."

"Braiden, you're scaring me."

"If only you'd been scared before… Just a little. Just enough to follow my rules."

"I followed your goddamn rules!" But getting angry won't help here. No amount of shouting will make me big enough, strong enough to escape. So I try the opposite. I make myself very, very small. "I don't understand," I whisper.

"You went to Boston, right?"

"Yes." My answer is barely audible.

"You spoke to Ingram, right?"

"Yes." My answer is so soft, I wonder if he can hear it.

"You threatened him with the fucking FBI, right?"

I threatened *Fiona.* Not Ingram. His daughter. But I know I have to say *yes*. My mouth shapes the word, but I can't say it out loud.

"He's the general of the Grand Irish Union, Samantha. In charge of us all. He got there by facing down every threat that's ever stood in his way, every challenge to his authority. What did you think would happen? What did you think Kieran Ingram would do when you said you'd call the feds on him?"

"That's not what I said."

"So Kieran Ingram's a liar?" Braiden's voice shreds like silk over sandpaper.

"I was talking about Fiona. Not about her father."

But Braiden doesn't hear me. He's still talking. "Ingram's heard all the stories. He knows all the lies, about all you've done for Russo. All the Fishtown secrets you've given away. And today you gave him the one excuse he needed. You made a threat he can't ignore."

I want to protest. I want to explain. But Braiden doesn't give me a chance.

"He could have sent one of his own men to do it. He could have called someone over from Dublin. But it's not enough for him to see you dead. He wants *me* to do the killing. He wants me to prove I'm loyal."

"*Shoot her now,*" I whisper. "*Before she can holler.*"

"What the fuck?"

"Fiona wrote it. She left a note on my desk before she cleared out of here yesterday."

When Braiden finally speaks, his words feel like an ancient earthquake. "What note?"

I barely have the range of motion to nod toward my briefcase, where I dropped it by the door. "I found it this morning."

Finally, he releases my neck, shifting his hand to grip his gun. He holds the weapon far out of my reach as he eases his body off mine, and then he slips the pistol into his belt, at the small of his back.

"Let me see," he commands.

I grimace as I stand. I don't know if I'm unsteady because of his weight, or because of my adrenaline, or because I haven't eaten all day. Nevertheless, I manage to cross the room, and I retrieve the lipstick-marked note.

He scans the lines, all five of them, his eyes flicking from the end of one phrase to the beginning of the next. His attention lingers on the scarlet stain for so long I want to scream.

When he finally speaks, his voice is washed clean of every atom of emotion. "You didn't bring this to me?"

"You weren't here." *Asshole.* I think it, but that's another thing I don't say out loud.

A muscle twitches in his jaw. "So you found this in your office. And instead of waiting for me, instead of mentioning it to *Liam,* instead of telling Fairfax for God's sake, you hopped in your car and drove all the way up to Boston. To Kieran Fucking Ingram."

"You. Weren't. Here," I repeat, packing each word with frustration.

"Did you think I'd driven off forever?"

"I didn't know where you went! For all I knew, you changed your mind about Fiona. You could have been off to Boston yourself, making her the third Mrs. Kelly. Wait. She wouldn't have been third. Because *I* wasn't second."

"Don't start on that—"

"Start on what? The fact that you lied at the altar? That you made me a laughingstock in front of your brother? In front of every one of your men? You set me up for Fiona."

"I *protected* you! Father Brennan—"

A wordless cry of frustration rips my throat. "No! Father Brennan wasn't for me. Father Brennan was for *you.* So you could keep Birte and me both. So you could have a virgin in your attic and a whore in your bed."

"I never treated you like a whore."

"You bought me clothes. Gave me an office. Set your goddamn *house rules* so you could fuck me anytime you chose."

"I never laid a finger on you that you didn't beg for."

"Tell yourself whatever lies you need so you can sleep at night."

"You could have stopped me with a single word."

Red. I want to scream it now. I want to make him stop. I want to make him leave. I want him out of my life forever.

But I don't need my safeword. I have another weapon. One he gave me a month ago, when I moved back to Thornfield after the last time we fought.

I have words that will silence him forever.

And then we can both get on with our lives. We can forget the worst mistake we ever made together—thinking we could love each other like normal human beings. Him—a mob boss whose daily life is so drenched in violence that he brought a gun to my bed. Me—a woman who killed three innocent people and lied for over a decade.

Enough. It's time to end this farce.

I feel like I'm chambering a bullet as I ask, "Want to know the truth? Want the real reason I didn't wait to give you the note?"

He glares.

I know my next words. It's like they're the truth, like they're truly what I thought when I saw Fiona's note this morning. I know exactly how deep they'll cut. I cock the hammer, making sure to enunciate every word. "I knew you couldn't help me. You can't keep me safe."

"I killed—"

"Right." I fake a yawn. "You killed a man for me. At the freeport. You've said that once or twice."

I can still stop. I can still keep from shattering everything we have.

But if I back off now, we'll fight again tomorrow, or the next day, or the day after that. We'll be trapped on this same precipice forever—doomed mobster and lawyer, broken man and woman, ruined Dom and sub.

I need this pain to end. I don't want to ever hurt like this again. So I curl my finger around the trigger of my words and I say, "That was a month ago. And we still don't know who sent that man, because you shoved a gun in his mouth."

"Are you honestly saying you'd prefer—"

"I'd *prefer* being with a man who has some shred of impulse control. Someone who doesn't shoot first and ask questions later. Someone who doesn't storm away from breakfast like a petulant child."

This is it. This is where I destroy him. Destroy us. This is where I say the words I can never take back.

I take a deep breath, and I fire.

"You think you're a grown man, but you're still the same six-year-old coward who hid first and counted bodies later. So, yes. Yes, I went to Boston. Yes, I tried to reach Fiona. Yes, I tried to protect myself. Because I couldn't count on you to do a goddamn thing."

28

BRAIDEN

The scar on my forearm flares with rage and remembered pain. I want to keep my fingers from clutching it, but my body isn't taking orders from my brain. I feel the rough surface, the permanent reminder of the worst day of my life.

It's not the words that hurt. They're nothing worse than what I've told myself for years.

But it's the fact that Samantha says them. She chose to use my past against me.

I'm responsible for sharpening her claws. I've let her say things before, challenge me in ways I'd never allow from any other lover. I've let her push me to the edge and beyond, all because I didn't trust her to stay in my bed if I called her on topping from below.

But she's wrong. I'm not a hopeless, helpless boy. Not anymore.

I'm a man. A man who was stupid enough to trust her with my story. A man who can't afford to trust her ever again.

"You're a lousy fuck," I say.

Her laugh is a single incredulous bark.

And she's right. I wasn't precise. I didn't say exactly what I meant. So I correct myself. "No. You're a lousy *sub*."

"You managed to put me in that collar often enough."

"And you fought me every fucking step of the way. But you can't top your way out this time. We're done, you and I. Finished. Whatever you thought we had, it's over."

She softens her voice like she's mocking a child. "Did I hurt your little feelings?"

"This isn't a game, Samantha."

She flares at that. "I promise I don't think—"

"Stop." I lash out with my Captain's voice. The single syllable is strong enough to clamp her mouth shut. It's my turn to laugh—a short, sharp sneer at the shock on her face. I speak very slowly so she won't miss a word. "I let you interrupt before because you were scared."

"I wasn't—"

"One more word now, and I'll put you in a gag."

Her mouth opens. Her throat works. She's about to speak, but I see the instant she decides not to test me.

It's the first smart thing she's done since walking through the pool house door. Since leaving Thornfield and driving up to Boston. Since finding that fucking note and deciding not to wait for me.

She broke something this morning—an essential trust between us. And now, after what she's said tonight, there's no way we can ever glue it back together.

"You think this is all a game. I'm pretending to be a gangster. You're acting like my sub. But this isn't smoke and mirrors. This isn't a play." I pull my pistol from the waistband of my trousers. "This gun is real."

She snorts in disdain, as if she knows I never loaded it with bullets. As if she's certain I would never hurt her.

That was this afternoon, when Ingram called. This is now, when she's cut me to the quick.

"Not one fucking word," I warn.

I dig harder into my forearm. My scar itches like I'm six years old again, like I'm days past failing Sister, not decades. The burn keeps my fingers from wrapping around Samantha's long, black hair. I'm too angry to touch her.

"At first it was just Madden, blowing off steam. Then it was Fiona, writing a dirty poem. But Ingram believes every fucking word. So you can be sure he'll have every other captain in the Union on board soon. Every single one of them will know about you and Russo."

She talks back. Of course she does. She can't help herself. "That's a goddamn lie."

I won't hurt her physically. I've got enough control left to keep from that. But I strike with the sharpest weapon I possess.

"How many times does a man have to hear about a bitch taking it up the arse before he knows it's true?"

Her voice trembles. "You *know* what Russo did to Eliza."

There. She's opened the door. She's shown me how to win.

I want to be a better man than I am. But my arm burns and my head aches and I just want this to end.

So I let my accent off its leash and say the worst words I can. "I know what yer man did t' yer feckin' cousin. And I know what ya let me do t' ya. Ya like it rough, lass. Ya love it. Do you think o' him when yer in my bed? Do ya close yer eyes 'n' picture yer guinea boss?"

One moment, she's standing tall and straight, chin raised high like the woman I used to love. The next, she folds around herself, caving in, sinking deep, as if I've landed a physical blow to her gut. When she rights herself, she's trembling.

"You're a fucking asshole," she says.

She's foolish enough to turn her back on me. She slips her feet into the shoes she left at the door. She picks up her briefcase, as if she has some important meeting to get to, even though it's well past midnight.

I let her get halfway out the door before I land my killer blow. I manage my accent this time, because I want to make sure she doesn't miss a word. "Go on, Samantha. Run away and don't look back. It's just like leaving three dead bodies on a twisting mountain road. You're good at that."

The glass door shatters when she slams it.

29

SAMANTHA

I take the guards at the gate by surprise; they're not expecting anyone to come in or out this late at night. Of course, one of them reaches out to Braiden to find out if he should let me go. Braiden is king of this rotten land. His word is law.

I half expect him to deny me the right to leave. After all, that's the sort of control he craves. But the guard nods as he pockets his phone, and he snaps a command to the other men. The machine guns look like parade flags as I pass through to the street.

Unfortunately, both paparazzi and protesters were warned by my headlights. Their ranks have thinned; most seem to have homes to return to, warm beds to sleep in. But the ones that remains are even more aggressive than usual, spurred on by the prize of my late-night exit.

I want to roll down my window and scream at them, make them understand how they're ruining my life. But I know that won't work, any more than flashing both middle fingers will make them back off.

I grip the wheel and stare straight ahead until I've cleared the pack. That same semblance of control gets me down the street, around the corner, and all the way to the interstate.

I've driven hundreds of miles today, from Philadelphia to Boston and back again. The last thing I want is to spend more time in the car.

But the decision's been taken out of my hands.

Braiden is under orders to kill me.

He won't do it. I know that. If he meant to execute me, he would have fired the instant I stepped through the pool house door. One shot through the head or the heart, and he'd be done. Clean up would be easy enough—just order one of the enforcers at the gate to take care of my body. I'd end up in a shallow grave somewhere in the woods of western Pennsylvania, or at the bottom of the Schuylkill, or miles off-shore in the Atlantic Ocean.

Braiden's already decided to disobey Ingram's order. But that doesn't mean I'm safe. All it would take is one hothead hoping to impress his boss—one of Braiden's soldiers trying to ease his captain's burden, one of Ingram's runners trying to move up...

Better for me to get out of Philadelphia. To get somewhere safe.

By reflex, I'm on the road to Dover.

I can't beg a cottage at the freeport, not this time. Sure, Trap Prince is a friend. Alix, even more. But they're my employers. My career is on shaky enough footing, with my law license near suspension. I can't run back to them for shelter even though— especially because—they gave it to me last time.

Last time.

How have I let my life get to this point? Where I'm running for the second time from the man I thought I loved?

Braiden has changed me. He's turned me into a woman I no longer recognize.

I don't recognize the woman who just screamed like a fishwife, digging for the sharpest words, going for the deepest cut.

I don't recognize the woman who drove all the way to Boston on a whim, who confronted a mob boss—a mob boss!—because she had a dispute with his daughter.

I don't recognize the woman who craves submission, the woman who chooses to wear a collar, the woman who interrupted her husband's *business meeting* so she could give him the crudest sort of lap dance.

I let Braiden sell my condo. I let Birte sit at our table. I let Fiona live in our house. I did it all, but I can no longer explain how or why or what hold Braiden has over me.

That's why I need to drive to Dover. That's why I need to return to the freeport, to my career, to the very core of who and what I am—in hopes that I'm not too late. That I'm not lost forever.

At two in the morning, I arrive at one of the executive hotels just a few miles from my office. I startle a sleepy desk clerk, who taps on her computer keyboard long enough to book me into a room. I pay for two nights up front, putting the charge on my credit card.

I'm too wired to sleep.

I force myself to lie on the bed for a couple of hours, staring at the ceiling. I order myself not to replay the vicious things Braiden and I said to each other. When the sky starts to turn gray outside my room, I realize I never even pulled the curtains.

I take a shower in the neutral-tone bathroom, standing under a scalding spray until my skin aches. I dry myself with rough white towels. I apply makeup from the touch-up bag in my briefcase—eyeliner, mascara, stark burgundy lips. I gulp two cups of horrible coffee from the single-serve machine on the dresser, and then I'm back in my car.

My first stop is the gun shop on Dupont Highway. Just north

of the Air Force base, it boasts a wide range of weapons. I'm the easiest sale of the day; I know I want a Glock nine millimeter, just like the one I used to own. Before Braiden.

The yawning man behind the counter runs a background check. I half expect him to react when I hand over my ID, spelling out the name that's been splashed across the front pages of newspapers for weeks. But apparently the owner of Dover Armory isn't up on current events. And I haven't yet been convicted of a felony.

It's only a matter of minutes before I leave with a pistol, an extra magazine, and two boxes of ammunition. I feel a lot safer with them in my briefcase as I head into the office.

Freeport security is a lot like the system at Thornfield, but I try not to think about that. My office setup with its executive chair and dual monitors resembles my workspace at Thornfield, but I ignore that too.

My office has a closet, intended to hold a couple of coats, maybe an umbrella or two. It's crowded with the clothes I bought the last time I fled Braiden. Everything was moved here from Goldenrod Cottage when I foolishly went back to Thornfield.

I change out of yesterday's suit, making a mental note to take it to the dry cleaner. With fresh clothes, I'm ready to tackle all the work I ignored yesterday.

I start with email. There's a message from Sonja Heller, uncharacteristically subdued. The ethics board has set a hearing date—June 4. We have five weeks to pull together all our evidence, every possible argument that I should be allowed to continue my career.

I make a note on my calendar with mechanical precision, and then I dig into the rest of the emails. Teddy Newland sent a bill, without a cover letter or comment. Connor Boyle wants to schedule a meeting about charitable donations. Cole Wolf asks for a formal legal opinion about the tax implications of loaning a Monet to a university in Lithuania.

Phone messages are next. There are dozens from Braiden. I delete them unheard.

I turn to texts from various colleagues at the freeport. I answer questions about statutes, about regulations, about government initiatives and international organizations.

I work through breakfast. I work through lunch. Trap comes in mid-afternoon, with an emergency inquiry about Swiss banking law. Alix stops by, but I tell her I don't have time to chat. I work through dinner. Mary stays late, without my asking her to change her plans.

Once, I stand too quickly to cross the office for a file, and I sway on my feet, absurdly light-headed. But I touch my fingers to my desk and take a few deep breaths, and then I'm back to normal.

Normal. I've missed it.

This is what I'm supposed to be doing. This is who I am. A few more days, a few more nights, and I won't even think about the unrecognizable woman I left behind in Philadelphia.

30

BRAIDEN

I wait until Fairfax sets his platter of roasted tomatoes on the table before I say, "The door to the pool house needs to be replaced."

"Again?" he asks, his voice perfectly toneless.

The glare I give him is meant to make him question his choice of profession and the likelihood that he'll live long enough to spend his next paycheck. The effect is somewhat marred by Birte crooning, "Replace the door. What a chore. Someone's sore."

"Have it done by noon," I tell Fairfax. I suspect that's an impossible deadline, even for him. But I want to have something to holler about later.

"Of course," Fairfax says, nodding and returning to the kitchen, as if my request is no more difficult than his providing an extra fork.

Birte is still chanting—sore, sore, sore. "Eat your breakfast,"

I tell her, pointing to her plate. She picks up her fork and starts to eat her beans, stabbing them one by one.

Aiofe watches for a moment, curiosity tilting her head. She picks up her own fork, clearly intending to imitate her aunt, but she casts a quick glance toward me first.

"No," I say.

She pouts, but she shoves her beans onto toast like a normal person.

I push back from the table and head to the sideboard, meaning to pour myself some tea. Reflexes take over, and I fill a mug with coffee first. I realize my mistake before half the cup is full, but the damage is done. The entire room smells like coffee. Like Samantha.

"Fairfax!" I holler.

He pushes through the swinging door, his face a carefully blank mask.

"Take this." I hand him the mug. "And I want that samovar out of here by lunch."

"Of course," he says again.

My phone rings before he clears the room: "Sunday, Bloody Sunday." I answer, because I have no choice, not if I'm to keep my position as Captain of the Fishtown Boys. Trying to scrub a lifetime of rage from my voice, I say, "Boss."

"Tell me yer diggin' a grave this mornin'."

Jesus Christ. But I say, "It's been less than twenty-four hours."

My answer irritates him as much as his demand grates on me. But whatever he starts to shout turns into the longest coughing fit I've heard yet from the old sod. His voice sounds like a broken reed when he finally croaks, "How long does it take fer a man t' fire a pistol?

"I need some time."

"Fer what, boyo? One last poke, t' remember th' good times?"

Now I'm the one who can't talk. I can't push words past the scarlet fire in my brain.

Ingram says, "Don't wait too long, boyo. Or I'll start t' think yer wantin' t' leave th' Fishtown Boys behind."

"The Boys are mine, Ingram."

The deep breath he draws sounds like oil sloshing in a barrel. "Will they stay yers, boyo? When they find ya've lost yer bollocks?"

"I haven't—"

"Today, boyo. Get rid o' that skirt today."

I nearly break my finger stabbing the call away. Aiofe and Birte are staring, eyes as big as Fairfax's serving bowls. I snatch up *The Philadelphia Enquirer* so I don't have to speak.

I'm halfway through the front page before I realize I forgot to get tea. I'm willing to skip it, myself, but there's no reason for Birte and Aiofe to go without.

I make the child's first, pouring milk into a cup and adding just a splash of tea. The beige liquid slops into the saucer as I set it on the table. Aiofe frowns and pushes it away.

"Don't start," I warn her. She turns her attention to a sausage, as if she's practicing brain surgery.

Back at the sideboard, I pour for Birte. I stir in her four spoons of sugar, grimacing at the thought of that much sweetness. "Careful," I say, as I place it beside her plate. "It's hot."

"Hot, hot, hot," she chants. "Fought, fought, fought. Rot, rot, rot."

I gulp my own tea, black and bracing. It sears my lips like lava, scoring a gulley through my chest. The fire matches the burn of my scarred forearm, which hasn't let up since Samantha set it throbbing hours ago. "Goddammit!" I shout.

Aiofe bolts upright. The look on her face is pure terror, which drives a stake through my heart because I've never raised a hand to the wean.

Birte reaches for the rosary that hangs from her belt and starts muttering over her beads. "I believe in God…"

I snatch my papers up from the table because I've lost all hope of reading in peace, and I'm not hungry, and I don't want more tea, and breakfast isn't right anyway without Samantha. That's rubbish, though, because Aiofe and I ate together every feckin' morning for seven years, and nothing should be any different now.

I shove my chair into the table, hard enough to make a peony fall from the bowl of flowers in the center. Samantha wore a skirt with peonies on it—the petals scattered across black silk, along with tulips and chrysanthemums. The last thing I want to see this morning is a peony. I snatch the flower from the tablecloth and crush it in my fist.

"Our Father—" Birte chants, her voice rising to match my rage.

"Shut it," I tell her.

"—who art in heaven," she continues, even louder.

I swipe at her beads, trying to snag them from her fingers.

"Hallowed be thy name," she shouts.

"Dammit, woman!" I holler, raising my voice to cover hers.

Birte bellows, "Thy kingdom come…"

Aiofe squeezes her eyes shut and covers her ears, rocking back and forth in her chair.

"Fairfax!" I shout, but he's already barreling through the swinging door.

"What's all this foolishness?" he asks Aiofe, closing gentle fingers around her wrists. The instant he touches her, she freezes. "There you go," he says calmly, easing her hands from her ears. "Be a good girl. Go on up to your room. Draw me a picture of Coinín before John Bell gets here. Can you do that for me, love?"

She stares at him like he's an anchor and she's a tiny rowboat tossed on stormy seas. When she nods, I realize I've been holding my breath.

"Go on then," Fairfax says. "Take a piece of toast with you. That one in the holder, already spread with butter."

Aiofe grabs the toast without taking her eyes from Fairfax.

"Go on then," Fairfax repeats. "Start your drawing. I'll be upstairs in just a mo."

Aiofe finally leaves.

Birte's been shouting the entire time. She's finished her Our Father and two Hail Marys; she's halfway through the third.

Fairfax closes his hands over hers, so they're both clasping the onyx rosary beads. He keeps his own voice low and steady as he joins her: "Pray for us sinners…"

And like a feckin' miracle, Birte lowers her volume to match his. "Glory be to the father," she starts.

Fairfax calls over his shoulder, into the kitchen. "Grace? Can you help us out a bit?"

Grace Poole slouches into the dining room. Her eyes are bloodshot, and I don't know when her hair last saw a comb. But she takes Birte's hands between her own and starts crooning in Irish. I don't catch the words, but the tone is a mother settling a child after a bout of bad dreams.

Fairfax says to Grace, "Why don't you take her upstairs? A kip and a bath and she'll be right as rain."

Grace nods over Birte's head before helping her from her chair. As they disappear upstairs a silence falls over the entire house.

"This isn't working," I finally say.

Fairfax's face is bare of any emotion. It occurs to me that this is how he manages *me*, much as he's managed Aiofe and Birte into calm. The thought pricks along the back of my neck. I'm better than this. I have been. I can be.

"Birte's not strong enough to join us down here," I say. "See to it that she's kept comfortable on the third floor."

"Sir," Fairfax says.

That means he disagrees with me. And I know Samantha would disagree too. She'd say the answer isn't locking Birte up. The answer is a doctor, same as she's been insisting for weeks.

But Samantha left. She doesn't get a vote in how I run my house.

"Do you have something you want to say?" I challenge Fairfax.

"No, sir," he says. His formality tells me he's thinking volumes.

"Then get back in the kitchen." Because I don't want to hear it, not one word.

"Sir," he says. His back is stiff as he leaves.

I almost call him back. But if I apologize to Fairfax, that'll just open doors to all the other words I owe. And I'm not saying them to anyone, not when I'm right, not when I meant every feckin' syllable.

By reflex, though, I take my phone from my pocket. My finger hovers over Samantha's name.

No. I'm not calling her. Not when she'll eat my head off about Birte. When she's the one who lit Ingram's fuse. When she broke the feckin' pool house door, despite Fairfax's snide conclusions.

I slam my finger down on the icon, blocking Samantha Kelly on my phone forever.

For the second day in a row, I storm out of my own dining room. And this time, when I head to the garage, it takes all my concentration not to see the gaping hole where the Mercedes used to sit.

I order Seamus and Patrick to meet me in Fishtown. We look at three properties, and I choose the one I like best. Seamus makes the necessary calls, finding the owner, making a bid, doubling it to drown out any conflict.

I call my chief foreman at Kelly Construction and order him to meet us on the site within the hour. When he arrives, I tell him I want the ugly mid-century building leveled. I long to see something broken. Ruined. Destroyed.

I give him four months to build a new Hare and Harp. When he protests that he needs more time, I tell him to get the job done, or I'll find someone who can. Seamus and Patrick stay behind when I stalk back to my Jaguar.

I don't care if every man who works for me sneers behind my back. I just want the Hare back. I want a place I can work, away from Thornfield, away from Aiofe and Birte and yes, away from memories of Samantha.

I want to turn back time. And failing that, I want to forget the past four months and go back to when being Captain of the Fishtown Boys was all I ever needed to be happy.

31

SAMANTHA

❧

I can't do anything to clear the bloodsucking paparazzi and their Mousetrap minions from the freeport gates. I can't speed up the ethics board process about my keeping my law license. I can't force Detective Tarrant to decide if he has enough facts to complete his investigation or if he needs to dig deeper into my personal life. I can't change what happened on a mountaintop eleven years ago, and I can't take back the angry words I threw at Braiden two nights back.

Wait. I don't want to take back those words. Maybe I fought dirty, hitting him with the one thing I knew would shatter him. But he hit back even harder.

There is no force on Earth that would make me run to Antonio Russo. The fact that Braiden could even frame the thought—much less say it out loud—confirms that we'll never reconcile.

Even if he killed a man for me.

He killed Terrence King. That's why we still don't know who hired the waiter. Was it Russo, breaking his truce with Braiden? Was killing me supposed to be the first shot in a new war?

Or do I have yet another enemy? Someone I can't name, can't see, can't predict?

I need answers. Now.

I pull up a list of contacts, official contractors the freeport is approved to hire. There's a private investigator there, someone Trap has relied on in the past—Harry Asher.

I call from the landline on my desk. The phone rings three times, and I'm preparing to leave a bland voicemail when a gravelly voice answers.

"Asher."

I introduce myself, but neither my name nor my title seems to make an impression. "I have an important matter for you to investigate, Mr. Asher. I'd like to discuss it in person."

"When?"

"Can you come to the freeport now?"

"Tonight?"

His surprise makes me glance at the clock in the upper right corner of my computer screen. It's almost eight o'clock. I've worked through dinner again.

"Yes, please," I say. "I'd like this matter resolved as soon as possible."

He sighs and he grumbles, and he clarifies that he charges for travel time, but he agrees to be here within the hour.

He makes it in forty-five minutes. I use the time to review the internal file the freeport keeps on him.

Harry Asher put in twenty years at the Dover Police Department before he hung out his shingle as a private investigator. He still has contacts on the force, along with connections to a wide range of forensic laboratories. He's a one-man shop, but he'll work plenty of overtime if the pay is right.

One thing the file doesn't say: Asher reeks of stale cigar

smoke. The instant I meet him at the security desk, I change my initial plan. I don't want his rumpled brown trousers or his stained short-sleeve dress shirt anywhere near my office. A few minutes of his sitting on my upholstered chairs, and I'll never get out the stench.

I escort him into one of the conference rooms and close the door for privacy. He's not much on small talk; I can tell that by the way he takes a small notepad out of his breast pocket. He punches a ball-point pen and waits for me to talk.

Perfect. I need a man who's all business.

"I'm trying to confirm who sent a man to kill me."

Asher keeps a perfect poker face. "When did the attack occur?"

I give him all the details. An envelope arrived at the freeport gate with an FBI return address, an "Eyes Only" stamp, and Trap Prince's name. I interrupted a Diamond Ring meeting to bring the thing to Trap. A waiter went after me with a gun. Braiden stopped him. Braiden fought him. Braiden killed him with his own weapon.

"I don't remember reading about that in the paper," Asher says. His tone is even. He's watching me closely, though, and I'm pretty sure he was a damn good cop.

"Diamond Freeport values clients' privacy." I wait to see if he'll challenge me, because dead men should be a bit more important than corporate-speak on a business brochure. When Asher keeps his mouth shut, I say, "The waiter's name was Terrence King."

Something shifts on Asher's face.

"You know him?" I ask.

"White guy. Five ten, five eleven. Two-twenty maybe, all of it muscle. Prison tats on his face, arms, knuckles."

The description opens a hollow inside me. I thought I was all right with that night, that I'd accepted how close I came to dying. Apparently, I was wrong.

Asher says, "I caught him on his third B&E. He pleaded it down to trespass. With his priors, he still went away for two years."

"When was that?"

"Thirteen years ago, come June."

"And you remember him that clearly? After so much time?"

"Sometimes I don't like a guy."

I nod. "I didn't like him either. But I think I know who hired him. That's what I want you to prove."

"Who's that?" he asks.

"Antonio Russo." I wait to see if he'll flinch.

He doesn't. But he sounds skeptical as he asks, "The Philly capo?"

"Russo and I have some history."

"That's some dangerous history," Asher says.

"I'm well aware of Russo's reputation."

"It's not just a reputation."

"I'm aware of that too."

Asher studies me for a long time. I wouldn't want to face him in a poker game. I can't imagine what he's thinking.

Finally, he says, "It's dangerous, poking around the Mafia. I get time and a half for hazard pay."

"That's fine. I need an answer by close of business on Friday."

"Forty-eight hours?" He shakes his head. "COB Monday. That's the best I can do."

Five days sounds like forever, but I've already pushed him past his comfort zone, making him go after Russo. "Monday," I agree. I give him my private email address. I don't want his work mixing with freeport business.

He puts his little notebook back in his pocket and pushes back his chair. When he stands, he exhales decades-old cigar smoke into the room. He shakes my hand, firm, but not like he's trying to crush my fingers.

"Monday," he says.

"You can reach me here at the office."

He looks around the room, and if he wants to criticize my hours he thinks better before the words cross his lips. As we head back to the security desk, I leave the conference room door open, hoping the cigar smell will be gone by morning.

32

BRAIDEN

~

Ingram yanks my chain at breakfast, same as he has every day this week. The rain is lashing down outside, making it hard for me to hear his creaky voice. "It's Friday, boyo. Clock is tickin'."

"I wear my own watch, Boss."

"So ya know yer late gettin' the job done."

I debate how much information to share. I want him off my feckin' back, at least for a few more days. I settle on: "She's out of town. I can't get to her till she's back."

That sets him off, exactly the way I thought it would. He coughs for a while, and it takes him three tries to hawk up enough phlegm to speak. He finally bleats, "That's a load of shite, and ya know it."

"If I do it outside of Thornfield, I'll have to answer questions. And I can't guarantee your name would stay out of it."

That earns me another coughing fit. He barely manages to whisper, "When'll yer bitch be back?"

She's not mine. And she's not a bitch, no matter what she said to me in rage. But I give him a vague answer to buy more time. "Next week."

"Have her home by Monday, boyo. Or I'll send a man who can."

Aiofe's sitting at the table, so I don't tell him what I'm thinking. Instead, I end the call and scowl at my newspapers until I can manage a civil word.

I've just managed to send Aiofe up to the nursery to wait for John Bell when my phone rings again. I glare, wondering if Ingram's using a new number to torment me. He isn't, but this call is nearly as bad. Seamus is calling with the weekly report I've ordered him to make.

He starts off with: "It's bad."

I stare out the window at the vicious rain while he gives me the grim financial rundown. I've heisted all the funds from Kelly Construction that I can manage without landing unwelcome questions from tax officials, labor unions, and more.

But we're really feeling that shipment of cocaine Russo boosted last month. Ingram's insisting on his ten percent, even though I never saw a penny from the docks. Every one of my gambling fronts is in the red—shite timing, and there's no way of knowing when the tide will turn. The land for the new Hare and Harp was more dear than we planned, and we're paying a king's ransom to make the fire inspectors look the other way over the wetwork room in the old place. And then there's "that matter" in Dublin, the one Seamus is careful not to name, as if he fears I'll take his head off just for mentioning it. He thinks we've closed the books on that one, all that's left is paperwork, but he can't be sure for a few more days.

"Sorry, Boss," Seamus says.

"Can't be helped," I tell him. But when I end the call, I send a text to Patrick, letting him know I'll do the milk run today. I need to see who I can lean on for a little extra cash.

I start at Mimi's.

The madam looks up from her Bailey's in surprise. "Wasn't expecting to see you," she says, barely hiding a yawn behind her red-painted nails. "Want me to wake one of the girls?"

The thought of taking a ride turns my belly like milk left on the counter for a week.

I shake my head and say, "Just your envelope."

Mimi laughs and flutters a hand over her chest, where her heart would be if she had one. "Well, your sense of humor's fine as ever."

I stand a little straighter. "Come on, Mimi. Hand it over."

A quick glance at the counter between us tells me where she keeps her gun, or maybe it's just a baseball bat. "Good one," she says, looking straight in my eyes. "I'll see you next week."

She's smarter than that. I plant both hands on the counter and lean forward, hoping all she needs is a little encouragement to turn back into the solid, reliable account she's always been. "I need my money, Mimi."

"Then talk to your brother."

"To— Madden was here?"

"Him and the girl you brought in. The one that looks like someone forgot to cage a tiger."

Fiona.

Fiona Ingram is supposed to be in Boston. But that's not actually true, I realize in a rush. When I sent her packing at Easter, she hitched a ride with Madden. I assumed my brother drove her to Thornfield, collected her things, and took her to the private airfield north of Philly. I thought he put her on her father's plane and sent her home—good riddance.

But Samantha never saw Fiona in Boston.

And Fiona herself said she was staying in Philly.

Fiona toyed with Madden the whole time she lived at Thornfield. He took her for a walk in the garden. He played her feckin' limerick game at the party. He drove off with her in his acid-green McLaren, like he found the golden egg on his very own Easter egg hunt.

Christ.

"Madden and Fiona made collections?" I can't afford to make any more mistakes.

"This morning," she says.

"What time?"

"Seven o'clock, maybe? Eight? Early enough that I was still asleep when they came pounding on the door."

I mutter under my breath in Irish.

Mimi whines: "Madden said you had him on the milk run today. And since you came around with that girl before... How was I supposed to know?"

Their plan is genius. First, they steal my money. Then, they steal my time, because I'll have to finish the whole run now, tell every eejit who owes me an envelope that he puts it in my hand from this day forward. I don't trust anyone else.

Maybe Madden did it to impress Fiona. Maybe she put him up to it, pushing him to fight for her honor. In the end, I can't worry about why and wherefore. I just need to get things back on track.

I start with Mimi. "From here on out, envelopes only go to me."

She nods. And when she realizes I'm not going to make her pay for Madden's lying, cheating soul, she offers me a tilt of the head and a sly suggestion. "Sure you don't want one of the girls? On the house. Take the edge off. Make it worth your while, coming down here in the first place."

I don't want a roll with one of Mimi's whores. I never have. My own right hand is faster and doesn't come with complications from a girl who dreams about life with the Fishtown Boys.

But even if I did lean toward taking a taste, I don't have time today. I have to check out the rest of the milk run.

Within an hour, it's obvious that Madden's cleared me out. The bars, the after-hours clubs, the day-to-day protection... He and Fiona stopped by every one.

I take out my phone after I leave Mikey's gambling joint.

Madden doesn't answer, but I'm not surprised. I figured the feckin' coward wouldn't have the bollocks. "I assume you and Ingram's girl are doing me a favor, *dearthái*," I tell him. "Making the milk run so I can concentrate on what's important for the Boys. If those envelopes aren't on my desk by midnight, there'll be hell to pay."

I almost hope he'll miss my deadline, so I can give him all that's due.

33

BRAIDEN

~

S itting in my home office, I sip my third Jameson of the night and stare at the document I never should have needed. Just dropped off by courier, it has a fancy border, heavy black letters, and three separate signatures. A heavy red stamp covers it all.

Annulled.

My marriage to Birte is over.

When the envelope arrived, my first thought was to show it to Samantha. I wanted her to know I've finally done something right. I've settled the old debt. Too little, perhaps. Too late. But Birte is finally free.

Of course, Samantha isn't here. She'll never be here again.

I could call Ingram. Wake the old bastard. Thank him for getting me to do one good thing. But then I'll have to duck his kill order, yet again.

I pinch my lip. At least Seamus should be happy. The books

are, indeed, closed on "that matter." I won't spend another penny buying off half the Catholic church in Ireland.

This paper has cost me millions. It's worth it. But I'm desperate for a change in cash flow.

I drink my whiskey. Midnight comes. Midnight goes. There's not a word from Madden.

I've tried to give my brother the benefit of the doubt. He's sulking because I broke his jaw. He's cunt-drunk on Fiona Ingram. He wants to impress Kieran Ingram, wants to make a name for himself with the General.

But now I can't deny the truth: Madden stole the milk run. After years of chafing under my authority, my brother has finally lashed out in a way I can't ignore.

Part of me wants to strike back, hard and fast. Call Patrick and tell him to bring Madden in—walking, if the gobshite has any sense of self-preservation. Carried in, if the eejit puts up a fight. I don't care what it takes—a bullet to his kneecap, a base-ball bat to the head. Knock him out, tie him up, take a finger or two. Just let the fucker know I won't put up with his shite.

I sit back in my chair and pour another whiskey. The annulment stares at me—a stark reminder that *some* mistakes can be undone. But not this. Not with Madden. There's no going back if I send Patrick to fetch him.

I'm Captain of the Fishtown Boys. I make hard decisions every day.

But in my heart of hearts, I know I acted too fast with Samantha. I said things no man should ever say. No *Dom* should ever admit.

I can afford to slow things down with Madden. He's my *brother*. I can wait through the weekend. Till Monday even.

And if he hasn't come to his senses by then, I'll do what has to be done.

34

SAMANTHA

Thursday. I check out of my hotel room before dawn. It might be safe to spend another night there. Maybe no one's looking for me. But it feels smarter to move to another chain hotel, to book another room. It's easy enough to flee when I can pile all my possessions on the passenger seat of my car.

Friday. The third Mousetrap podcast drops. They've interviewed people who attended the graduation party, witnesses who say I was drunk, I was high, that they tried to stop me from leaving. I don't remember any of the names; I don't know if they're telling the truth or trying to bask in the glory of podcast celebrity. The episode ends with the sound of tires squealing on a road, followed by an ominous thud.

By noon, someone has tracked down my freeport email address. Truth be told, I'm surprised it's taken this long. Within fifteen minutes, my inbox is flooded with the worst kind of trash: *U should B dead 2. Die, bitch, die. Choke on this*—that last one with a dick pic attached. I delete the first dozen emails before I realize I need to save them as evidence in case someone takes so-called justice into their own hands.

Traffic only picks up in the afternoon. IT says the servers can't handle the load. I sign off on an emergency spend for cloud storage. Trap authorizes more money for a team to filter the foul stream, to make sure client matters actually reach my desk. I work until midnight, just to catch up. And to avoid my sterile hotel room.

Saturday, finally. I change hotels and, after an icy shower to drive away the worst of my fatigue, I'm back in the office by seven. I feel like a soldier marching miles from dawn to dusk. A dull headache pounds between my eyes, radiating through the scars along my hairline. I catch myself rubbing my wrists, as if they're raw from handcuffs.

Sunday. New hotel. Sunrise at the freeport. A dozen messages on my office telephone, another ten on the cell I turned off for the few hours I tried to sleep. My email inbox continues to overflow.

The Philadelphia Enquirer has turned my life into a full Sunday feature. Someone's talked from my old neighborhood. There's a photo from my first communion, and another of Eliza and me in our school uniforms. The newspaper raided my senior yearbook to get black-and-white smiles: Me, Eliza, Giorgia, and Gianni. There's a four-column-wide view of the twisting mountain road, of the ditch yawning like the mouth of hell. And there's a snap from Monday night, when I fled Thornfield—overexposed, my face pale, my eyes wild as I gripped the wheel of the Mercedes.

I don't have to worry about Mousetrap anymore. The *Enquirer* has scooped them. It's there, all of it: My "family association" with Mafia capo Antonio Russo. My flight to New York and my adoption of a new name. My marriage to Irish mob boss Braiden Kelly; my fleeing the marital home after midnight.

I look desperate. I look like a criminal. I look deranged.

Sonja leaves a message. "This is a fucking nightmare," she

says. "I strongly recommend that you retain counsel and consider suing them for defamation."

But truth is a defense to a claim for libel. There's nothing the *Enquirer* has written that isn't true. Sure, they've built up the drama. They've made my life look like every gangster movie ever filmed. But they've researched their facts, and they've sprinkled in the word "allegedly" when absolutely necessary.

There's nothing I can do.

I'm preparing my letter of resignation for Trap when he sends a text:

TRAP

Don't even think about it.

I try to follow his orders. I try not to think. The only thing that can begin to make me forget the hell of my current life is work. I stay at the freeport till two in the morning, trying to make up for everything I've ever done wrong in my entire life.

Monday. Change hotels. Cold shower. Strong coffee. Work.

The office feels like a funeral home. Everyone speaks in soft tones, and no one—not even Mary—meets my eyes. I keep my office door closed, trying to make it easier for everyone.

Asher calls at 4:59.

"Tell me you've got proof it's Russo," I say.

He sighs, and my memory supplies the cigar stench wafting across my office. "You aren't going to like this."

No shit. We're talking about the man who tried to kill me.

But I keep my weary response to myself. Asher goes on: "There's no record of Russo or any of his soldiers being in contact with King. No one from the East Falls Crew traveled to Dover. There's no indication that King ever went to Philadelphia. I checked phone records, bank records, traffic cameras. Nothing."

Asher is wrong. Russo has to be involved. It's the only thing that makes sense.

I feel scooped out, like I'm a dented tin can kicked to the side of the road. It's hard for me to draw a full breath; something's crushing my sternum. My fingers tingle, and I wonder how I've kept from dropping my phone.

But Asher's still talking. "...ninety-two miles per hour. Under Delaware law, that's an automatic reckless."

"I'm sorry," I say. "*Who* was driving reckless?"

"Madden Kelly. Your brother-in-law, right?"

I dig my fingernails into my palms, trying to make myself concentrate. "Madden was here? In Delaware?"

Asher harrumphs. He doesn't like repeating himself. "The ticket was issued at 5:17 p.m. on March 24. Madden Kelly. Driving a green McLaren, Pennsylvania license plate..."

I don't listen to the numbers and letters. March 24 was the night of the Diamond Ring event. The night Terrence King tried to kill me.

"I didn't make the connection," Asher says. "Until I read that article in yesterday's paper."

I'm still confused. "You're saying Madden Kelly was here, in Delaware, the night King tried to kill me."

"And that's not all." He's a professional, but he can't keep from gloating.

"Go on." I do my best to sound professional too.

"I've still got contacts with the Philly PD so I called in some debts. They keep plenty of surveillance on your friend Russo."

"He's not my friend," I say automatically, when I *want* to tell Asher to cut the crap and get to the real news.

"I'm sending you pictures now," Asher says, and my computer chimes a few seconds later. My fingers move out of habit, double-clicking on an attached file.

"What am I looking at?" I ask, even though some part of my brain already knows.

"That's Madden Kelly's McLaren at the gate of Antonio Russo's East Falls compound in Philadelphia. The time-stamp on this one says March 24. I've got a dozen more from the past four months, going in and out. Seven in the last week. And the most recent one is from this afternoon. Madden Kelly and Antonio Russo are working together."

35

BRAIDEN

Ingram calls at five sharp, as if he's got me working on a factory line. I let the call go to voicemail.

He calls at 5:01.

5:02.

5:03.

I know exactly how this technique works. And I know it failed spectacularly when I tried to get Samantha home from Boston. Next up—

Sure enough, he texts.

INGRAM

Pick up or I send my own man to do the job

Then:

He'll do two for one

So I'm in the crosshairs too.

I calculate how long it'll take me to get to Boston. My plane can be in the air in less than an hour. Ninety minutes to Hanscom, northwest of the city. I can hire someone to meet me at the airfield with a car, and I can be in Southie an hour after that.

Ingram can be dead by ten tonight.

And I'll be at war with every captain in the continental United States. Plenty of men in Dublin, too. And half my own crew, who've looked up to the Grand Irish Union since they were in nappies.

My phone rings again. I answer half-way through the first "Sunday".

"No."

"Don't get smart with me, boyo."

I say it again: "No."

Ingram won't listen to any argument I make. He's made me his bumboy. Today, it's kill Samantha. Tomorrow, it'll be hand over half my take. The next day: Put Fiona in charge of Philly. I do what he says or he kills me.

Fuck it. I'm skipping to the end.

He splutters. "The bitch isn't home yet?"

"No." This is easier than I ever dreamed it would be.

"Ya haven't killed her."

"No."

"Ya had a deadline, boyo!"

"No."

"Stop sayin' that 'n' give me a real answer!"

"No."

"Ya fuckin' eejit—"

I'm sure he's got more to say, but he starts coughing. And I can tell from the start this is a different type of fit. Even over a phone line, it sounds like wet cloth tearing, a blood-soaked curtain being dragged across a stage.

I hear noise behind him. Someone says he should take a seat. Someone else gives him a glass of water.

There's a clatter and a rumble, and the pounding of feet. A man shouts for a doctor. Another says he's calling 911.

I can still hear Ingram, but his coughing sounds like boking now. From the cries of his men, he's bringing up blood, a lot of it. He pisses himself. He starts to seize.

The shouting grows more frantic. The men seem far more lost. One man starts a frantic Hail Mary. Another blubbers like a child.

And then: Silence.

At first I think the call's been cut off, but the numbers still tick up on my screen, second after second after second. I want to ask what's happened, but I already know. I think about crossing myself, but the old bastard isn't worth the effort.

Finally there's a scraping sound, and my ear fills with broken breathing. Someone sniffs hard, like he's just downed a kilo of cocaine. When he speaks, his voice is clogged, thick with equal measures of sorrow and hate.

"He's gone, Kelly. Now you're a dead man too."

36

SAMANTHA

❧

M adden Kelly is working with Russo.

Asher's still telling me the details—where the surveillance crews were located, when the other photos were taken, how often Madden arrived in the McLaren and when he drove other cars.

None of it matters. Not now.

A week ago, Braiden broke my heart. He said horrible things to me, things I'm not sure I can ever forgive. But those words shouldn't be a death sentence. Braiden has to know his brother is a traitor. If Madden is working with Russo—*the most recent one is from this afternoon*—no one in Thornfield is safe.

"Thank you," I say, cutting Asher off. "Get me your invoice, and I'll pay it immediately."

That's the magic formula to get him off the line. I scramble for my cell and tap Braiden's number.

It goes straight to voicemail. He's blocked me.

Swearing, I call Liam, my former driver. His phone rings

four times, but it goes to voicemail too. I tell him to call me, tell him it's urgent, but I have no idea how long it will take for him to call back. For all I know, he could be half a dozen time zones away. Braiden could have sent him to Ireland. Could have fired him altogether.

I don't have a number for Fairfax. I don't even know if Grace Poole owns a phone. Birte doesn't have one, nor does Aiofe. There are guards at the gate, but I don't know their names, much less their phone numbers.

I'm sitting in front of one of the most powerful computers sold on the open market. It only takes me a moment to dive into LexisNexis, the same research software I used to track down Ingram's location in Boston. I make the same promises, tell the same lies to get past the nanny filters designed to keep personal data private.

The database gives me Braiden's address. Registrations for all of his cars. His plane. A boat I didn't know he owns. Fairfax's name is listed as a person who might be living at the same location. Grace Poole, too.

But there's no phone number.

Groaning in frustration, I pull up the freeport's official records. We have client contracts, government forms, tax documents—hundreds of files under Braiden's ten-digit client number.

I race through the first three documents. The only one that requires a phone contact lists the freeport's number.

This is hopeless.

I remember the muzzle of Madden's pistol, jammed against my throat. I hear his crude threats in the Thornfield ballroom, his promise to rape me. I think about all the things Russo has done, killing my parents, killing my cousin, threatening to murder me.

Seven in the last week. Madden and Russo are stepping up their partnership.

I grab my keys and head to the freeport parking lot.

The Mercedes' engine whispers to life at the touch of a button. I reach across the console to open the glove box. My new Glock waits with a full magazine, ready at an instant's notice.

Now, I set the weapon on the seat beside me. My head feels light, as if it's filled with helium, floating high above the paved road outside the freeport. I realize the last thing I ate was a granola bar Mary forced on me at lunch. I washed it down with an over-size coffee, my third of the day. No, fourth.

Merging onto the interstate helps me to concentrate. The dashed white lines hurl me forward. I camp out in the left lane, beating the speed limit by a good twenty miles an hour.

The trip should take two hours. I make it in an hour and a half.

Approaching the gate, I find a fresh flock of paparazzi, congregating with podcast protesters around the last street lamp before the fence that surrounds the mansion. The *Enquirer* article must have dumped fresh blood into the water; they're all restless for prey.

I come in fast, like a missile locked on target. The sharks are smarter than they look. They get out of the way before I have to slam on my brakes.

The guards don't expect me. I see surprise on their faces, and one of them starts talking into his phone. But my credentials still work—hand scan and eye scan both. The gate glides open and I gun the Mercedes toward the house.

37

BRAIDEN

P atrick and Seamus have arrived in record time. Soldiers are still trickling in—four of them standing watchfully in the corner of my office, another eight on their way.

Ingram's men will come looking for vengeance, ready to hit me hard. The most logical place to start is Fishtown, the heart of my life in this city. Every place on the milk run is vulnerable.

My lieutenants study an old-fashioned paper map spread on my desk. Patrick's second-in-command, Rory O'Hare, double-checks boundaries on his phone. They're breaking down streets into manageable plots, assigning sections of my territory to the waiting enforcers.

"That won't work," Rory points out, stabbing the map with a crooked index finger. "There's six blocks exposed, with Mimi in the middle. The girls will be one of their first targets."

Patrick swears and tugs the paper closer to the edge of my desk.

I'm about to weigh in when my phone rings. One glance at

the screen, and my heart tumbles into triple-time. I'm being haunted by a ghost.

But I didn't read quickly enough. The phone doesn't say *Ingram, Kieran*, and the ringtone isn't "Sunday, Bloody Sunday".

It's *Ingram, Fiona*.

Not a hell of a lot better.

But the girl's just lost her da, and my ignoring her will only make things worse. And maybe, just maybe, she's calling to make peace before I'm forced to go to war with the Boston clan.

Yeah. And leprechauns hand out gold at the end of the rainbow.

I cross to the curtained window and tap the screen. "Fiona." I do my level best to scrub emotion from my voice.

"Your brother's a fucking bastard."

Christ. It's taken something as disastrous as Ingram's death to make me put Madden's treachery on the back burner. Glancing over my shoulder at the map, I say, "Tell me something I don't know."

"He took it all," she says. I realize her words sound thick. Slurred. Like she's talking through swollen lips and a broken nose.

"Took what?"

"The milk run."

"The money you two stole from me?"

"He beat me up," she says, like that's a reasonable apology.

My brother's always been a shite to women. He started in ninth grade, bragging about Katie Monahan sucking him off beneath the bleachers. Her four brothers beat Madden to a pulp for ruining her reputation and then they turned on me, just for good measure. I've refused to get between Madden and his girls ever since—not my circus, not my feckin' monkeys.

"I'm not your knight in shining armor," I say.

Her snort sounds painful. "If you don't kick his ass, my father will. And you'll end up caught in the middle. Is your piece-of-shit brother worth burning every bridge to the Union?"

Jesus Christ. She doesn't know her da is dead.

"Braiden..." Fiona says, and I hear something in her voice I've never heard before: Desperation.

My phone vibrates in my hand. I pull it away from my face just long enough to see that a text's come in. It's from Fiona.

I tap the screen, and it fills with a photo.

Her lip is split. Her nose is broken. There's blood on her teeth, her lips, her chin. Her left eye is swelling closed, and a dark bruise blooms on her cheekbone.

"Christ, Fiona," I finally say.

"Make him pay."

I will. Because only an animal would do that to a woman.

And also because when Madden was beating the shite out of Fiona, he thought Kieran Ingram was still alive. He had to know the old man would hold me responsible for my brother's violence. Ingram would make me feel every blow Fiona took.

I'm trying to decide if my brother will ever walk again, when Fiona starts to sob. "Please... Come get me, Braiden."

I can't have Fiona Ingram at Thornfield while I'm building a defense against her father's men. Once she's back on her feet, she'll hate herself for making this call, for admitting human weakness. She'll be a thousand times more dangerous than she's ever been before.

But for now, her da's dead. My brother beat her. I'm the one she called.

I swear under my breath, long enough that Patrick, Seamus, and Rory all look up from the map. I shake my head; they can't fix this problem.

But Patrick can help. He's been my Warlord for years, managing all my enforcers. His hard work has created the machine we're about to deploy tonight, the defensive barrier we're building.

But over the last four months Patrick's acted more like my Clan Chief than Madden ever did. Patrick is my true second-in-command. I can send him in my stead.

Fiona's still on the phone, waiting.

"I can't leave Thornfield," I say. "But I'll send my Warlord, Patrick Moran."

A question peaks Patrick's eyebrows when he hears his name. His gray eyes look black as he stares across the room. The overhead light glints off the silver in his hair.

It's a shite job, telling a girl her da has died. But Patrick is calm and level-headed. Even better, he moved to Philadelphia from Boston thirty years ago. He might even have a kind word to say about Ingram, something he can dig up from his past. Or he'll lie. Whatever's necessary.

"Please..." Fiona says. "Come get me yourself." It's the second time she's begged, and it's not a good tone for her.

"Text me your address," I say. "Patrick's on his way."

That's the only solution I have on offer. And Fiona must hear the resolution in my voice, because she says. "Tell him to hurry."

I forward the text to Patrick with the flick of a finger. He's not happy to go. "You need me here, Boss."

"I need Fiona squared away. And in a manner that won't egg on her father's men."

He wants to argue, but he's too well-trained to put any more objections into words.

I tell him: "If Madden's eejit enough to be anywhere near Fiona, you can take care of business. I don't trust anyone else to handle a Kelly man."

Patrick nods his understanding. He's followed his Captains' orders for decades. Now, he says to his second, "Rory. Keep an eye on the waterfront. Those warehouses will be hell to take back if Ingram's men get in."

Rory pulls the map closer. My Warlord claps a hand on his shoulder as he hurries out the door.

I shoulder in beside Rory. Another four soldiers have arrived. They're standing in the corner, trying to look casual, but the room is growing thick with a toxic mix of testosterone and adrenaline.

Seamus argues for my pilot to be put on call, ready to ferry me up to Boston to launch settlement talks with Ingram's Warlord *before* bodies start dropping. Rory takes out his phone and places a call, staring at the map with narrowed eyes. He starts to give out to the person who answers, telling him he should have been here fifteen minutes ago.

I'm studying the warehouse district. Patrick's right. If Ingram's men get in there, it'll be door-to-door combat getting them out. In the past, I've seen good men wounded in raids down there. I have to protect my Boys.

All of a sudden, the room falls silent. I figure Patrick must have come back. He forgot something. Or someone's blocked in his car. I look up, annoyed, because I need Fiona neutralized without delay.

But Patrick isn't standing in the doorway.

Samantha is.

38

SAMANTHA

~

Braiden looks up from the map spread across his desk, annoyance scribbled across his face. The fingers of his left hand dig into his right forearm, prying at the scar I know is hidden beneath his shirt.

His hair is ruffled, and I can tell he's been clawing through it, frustrated by whatever has prompted this evening war session. His cheekbones are sharp, and I wonder if Fairfax has been feeding him properly. His muscles are strung as tightly as laundry on a line. He's ready to bark, to snarl.

But when he sees me, everything changes.

Shock. That's his first emotion. It's there on his face, in the widening of his eyes, the twist of his lips.

Worry comes next. His eyebrows pinch together. His jaw tightens.

Then comes relief. His eyes close for a heartbeat that might include a prayer. His lungs fill. His mouth relaxes into something that might grow into a smile.

"Samantha," he breathes. I don't think he realizes he's taken two steps toward me. I don't think he knows his hands are out, reaching for me, welcoming me home.

I want to run to him. I want to bury my face in the crease of his neck. I want to breathe the cedar and spice scent of him, fill my lungs, fill my soul.

But there are too many words we have to say, too many mistakes we have to make right. His men are watching, and something important is at stake. The Fishtown Boys look like they're plotting a campaign.

And I have to tell them they have a new enemy.

I should take Braiden aside. I should spare him hearing the news in front of everyone. I should give him a chance to absorb the blow before he has to act.

But there isn't time to be kind. There isn't space for softness. Not when Madden and Russo have met seven times in the past week. Not when Madden was in East Falls last night.

So I meet Braiden's gaze. I swallow all the things I *want* to say—that I'm sorry, that I didn't fight fair, that I'm back. I shove aside all the emotion, all the longing, all the sleeplessness and sorrow of the past week.

And I say, "Madden."

Braiden doesn't blink. "What about him?"

"He's working with Russo."

"He—"

"I have proof. Pictures. Time stamps."

"How—"

The world explodes before he can finish his sentence.

39

BRAIDEN

∽

The sound is a fighter jet skimming low over a factory floor. It's a forest of transformers blowing all at once. It's a hurricane locked inside a shipping container, and only the bulletproof glass behind me prevents the windows from shattering into a million jagged knives.

My ears feel like they're packed with cotton as I yank back the curtains. It takes me a moment to parse the scene outside.

The garage is filled with orange-yellow fire. The framework for each bay stands out, black against the blaze, like Hell has opened up with six toothless mouths.

Part of my mind floods with rage. Samantha's announcement makes everything fall into place. Madden took the milk run for his guinea boss. Madden turned on Fiona because she'd never accept his betraying Irishmen for the Mafia.

Madden's working for Russo. And now he's attacked Thornfield. He's bombed my garage. I know it in my bones.

My brother got a taste for explosions when we were kids

—cherry bombs at first, then M80s, then honest-to-God pipe bombs, set off in the fields behind the house, wreaking havoc on the lawn. He added to his knowledge each trip he took to Dublin, talking to the old-timers who fought through the Troubles. He set bombs when we went after Russo, in the tit-for-tat after I married Samantha. He even proposed explosives as a growth business for the Fishtown Boys.

And now he's bombed my home.

Another part of my mind, stays coldly mechanical. That's the part that registers my Aston Martin is wreathed in fire. The Jaguar too. The Jeep won't be safe for much longer, but the Bentley might make it, at the far end of the garage. If—

The petrol tank on the Aston Martin blows.

As I watch, Fairfax runs from the front door of the house, coming up short beside Samantha's Mercedes on the drive. Silhouetted by the flames, he reaches into his pocket and produces a phone. I assume he's calling emergency, getting fire-fighters on their way.

Turning back to the war room, I find a dozen gaping men. They're staring out the window like they're watching a film, like they're deciding if *these* special effects are worth a little gold statue.

But it's not the men who have my attention.

"Samantha," I say, my voice low, like we're the only ones in the room.

One hand is spread across her chest, as if her heart is beating so hard it hurts. The other fingers the web of tight white scars at her temple.

Russo firebombed her parents' car when she was only ten years old, and the shattered glass marked her forever. But my windows are made out of bulletproof glass. They didn't break. And I won't ever let her be hurt like that again.

"Samantha." I repeat her name, more urgent now, because she doesn't believe I'll keep her safe. But her gaze is lost in the past. Her lips move, and I don't know if she's shaping a prayer or sharing some nightmare from long ago.

"Samantha!" I say one last time, dropping into the power of my Captain's voice.

She blinks and finds my face. She seems surprised that she's a grown woman. That she's at Thornfield. That she's mine.

"Get Aiofe from the nursery," I tell her. "Go to the safe room." And when she starts to protest, I say, "Now!"

She leaves like a sprinter from the blocks.

That's enough to startle my men from their trances. I'm gratified that half of them already have weapons in hand. "Madden," I snap. He's a feckin' firebug. He's watching his handiwork from somewhere close by. "He's here at Thornfield," I tell my men. "I want him in this office within the hour. Alive."

Patrick's gone, but he's trained his troops well. Not one of them stops to question Samantha's half-delivered message. Instead, they accept their assignments from Rory—one each to the gatehouse, the greenhouse, the pool house. A pair get the grounds, and all the smaller outbuildings. Another two are sent to the cottages. Rory follows them out, saying he wants reports texted to his phone, every five minute.

Once they've left, I say to Seamus, "Let's check the house."

We start with the door to the third floor. I open the lock with the key in my pocket. Seamus takes his post by the right of the jamb. I count down with silent fingers—three, two, one. I use the door as a shield after I yank it open. Seamus springs into place, his arms locked in a tactical firing stance.

"Jaysus, Mary and Joseph!" Grace Poole shrieks as I peer around the door. She's gripping her own key, as if there's any situation in the world where she'd be better off unlocking the door and facing whoever's been rattling the knob.

There's a flurry of question-and-answer, half in English, half in Irish, as Grace screeches and clutches her heart and calls on half the saints in Christendom. Madden isn't upstairs, though. She and Birte haven't seen him.

"Stay here," I tell her. "Don't answer the door for anyone."

Seamus and I make short work of the rest of the second floor—Samantha's office, the guest rooms and their jacks, my bedroom suite. The ground floor is empty as well, both wings. Each cleared room sharpens my concentration, honing my thoughts like a razor strapped against leather.

Madden stole the milk run. Madden beat Fiona. Madden blew up my garage.

Madden's making his bid to run the Fishtown Boys. I have one chance to stop him before he takes Thornfield, Philadelphia, and all of Clan Kelly.

40

SAMANTHA

⁓

B raiden's command jangles in my head: *Get Aiofe from the nursery. Go to the safe room.*

My legs move before my brain catches up. By the time I slip open the nursery door, I've shoved down the worst of my horror. I'm not a child in my parents' home any longer. The glass at Thornfield didn't shatter. Braiden is managing the explosion.

My fingers brush against the Glock I nestled at the base of my spine. The feel of the textured grip is enough to steady me. There's no need to terrify Aiofe by drawing it now.

She's tangled in her sheets, her bright red hair spilling over her pillow. Curled up on her side, she has her stuffed rabbit— Coinín—tucked beneath her arm. I'm astonished the sound of the bomb didn't wake her. I can't remember ever sleeping that soundly.

"Aiofe," I call softly, hurrying across the room. I don't want to startle her, but I can't waste too much time being gentle. I smooth her hair from her face.

A frown creases her forehead as she stirs. "Come on, Aiofe," I say, pushing back her covers. She's all arms and legs, too big for me to carry down the stairs. "We need to go."

I get her on her feet and halfway to the door. She's left Coinín on her pillow, though, and turns back to get him. "Hurry," I urge. "Braiden wants us downstairs."

Her uncle's name must unlock something in her drowsy mind, because she stops resisting. The corridor on the ground floor is cool. Windows march down one side, looking out over the driveway, toward the garage. Orange light flickers weirdly.

Every time I think about the *boom* of the explosion, my knees threaten to buckle. That sound tore apart my life when I was Aiofe's age. That sound killed my parents.

I hear men outside, shouting over the crackle of fire. Someone hollers that the front gate is open. The fire department is on its way.

I don't have to worry about any of that. I don't have to think about the cars. I don't have to remember the glass that shattered when I was a child. I only have to do what Braiden taught me to do, my first full day at Thornfield.

I haven't worked the safe room door since Braiden showed me how to access it, months ago. But he drilled me then, testing me three times, making sure I could work the latch alone, blindfolded, with a madman on my heels.

Now, the door glides open silently, heavier than the entrance to a bank vault. As Aiofe and I cross the threshold, sensors bring up the lights inside. Just as Braiden taught me, I take care to lock us in, testing the door twice to make sure no one can follow us into the refuge.

The room looks like a den in someone's well-furnished basement. A pair of heavy couches face each other, upholstered in forest-green leather. A huge television screen sits between them, filling most of the wall.

"We're safe now," I tell Aiofe. "No one can get in."

A thick rug swallows the sound of my footsteps as I cross the room to a small refrigerator. Finding a bottle of water, I crack the seal before I pass it to her.

"We're safe," I say again. I don't know if I'm trying to convince her or myself. I take the Glock from my waistband, and the pistol's weight is comforting, even though no one can reach us here. I know how to use the weapon. I know how to protect myself, and Aiofe too.

She's still standing in the middle of the room. In her long white nightgown, she looks like an angel, or maybe a girl in a choir. Her lips form a tight little circle of displeasure.

"Drink up," I say. And then I try to make things better. "I wish we had a plate of Fairfax's cookies to go with that. We'll ask him to make lemon snaps once we're out of here. Maybe ginger cakes too."

Aiofe only stares. Her eerie silence makes me long for a fall-back, for more firepower than my Glock provides.

A gun safe is built into the far wall. Braiden taught me how to open it, the same day he gave me access to the room. I'll feel better with a second gun in easy reach.

Turning my back on the frozen Aiofe, I cross to the safe. Desperate for the child to feel more secure, I keep up a constant patter.

"My father taught me how to fire a pistol on my eighth birthday. He took me to a firing range, an outdoor one, with targets that looked like they were miles away. He showed me his pistol and taught me the names for all the parts."

I set my Glock on the credenza beneath the safe. Hands free, I lower my thumb to the biometric pad. "They had all different types of targets." I continue speaking to Aiofe, pushing a smile into my voice because she can't see my face. "My father said it was just like Pin the Tail on the Donkey."

The lighted dial on the safe turns green. I go on: "None of the targets looked like donkeys, though. And I knew better than to go all the way down the range to pin anything on—"

"*Samantha! Look—*"

I snatch up the Glock and whirl to face the impossible.

Aiofe doesn't speak. Aiofe hasn't said a word in the four months I've lived in this house—not when she's happy, not when she's sad, not when she's protesting one of Braiden's edicts.

But my ears ring with the sound of her voice now—higher than I expected, louder than I ever dreamed. The vowels pull like taffy through an Irish brogue that matches Birte's and Grace's and Braiden's.

And no wonder Aiofe screamed.

Madden Kelly is clutching her close to his chest. His forearm arches across her throat. He's forcing her head back. Her eyes are so wide, I can see white around her pupils. Coinín's collapsed in a heap by her feet.

An evil black pistol presses against her temple.

"She's just a child," I tell Madden. I try to pitch my voice like I'm talking to a jury, like I'm sharing simple facts that can't possibly be in dispute. "Let her go."

Aiofe sobs. "He was going to shoot you!"

His grip tightens on her throat. "Shut the fuck up."

Aiofe ignores him. "He came out of the jacks," she says. "While you weren't looking. He pointed his gun. He wanted to kill you. Samantha! He wanted—"

She cries out—in surprise or pain or fury—as he pushes his gun into her flesh. I've felt Madden's rage before. I know it leaves a mark.

"Hush, Aiofe." I keep my weapon aimed at Madden's head. "You're okay," I tell her. "We both are. Take a deep breath. Everything's fine."

I take my own deep breath, trying to get her to imitate me. My throat is immediately coated with the scent of citrus and wood. It's the smell of my childhood, of my father when he pulled me onto his lap and called me his *principessa*. It's Acqua di Parma, the cologne worn by Antonio Russo.

And by every man under his command.

The cologne means more than Asher's photos, more than the bomb exploding in the garage, more than the gun pushing against poor Aiofe's temple right now… Russo has branded Madden Kelly as clearly as if the Mafia boss pissed down the leg of his dark jeans.

In my mind, I hear the limerick Fiona left on my desk: *She spied for a wop. Gave away the whole shop.* "Fiona got it wrong," I say.

"Fiona?" Madden sounds confused.

"*You* were the spy. You always were. But the limerick Fiona…" *Left on my desk.* I'm about to say it, when I realize the truth. "She didn't write the limerick," I say flatly. "*You* did."

He laughs like I just shared the punchline to a filthy joke. "Took you long enough." He smacks his lips as if he never learned the difference between kissing and devouring. "All I did was borrow Fiona's lipstick."

I fight the urge to slip my finger past the trigger guard. Aiofe squirms, trying to turn her face away.

Madden grunts as he tightens his grip around her throat. "Ingram said you made quite an impression in Southie. Demanding to see Fiona. Threatening to bring the FBI. But Fiona was with me in Philly, the whole fucking time."

My entire trip to Boston… The nightmare fight with Braiden that followed… Moving from hotel to hotel to hotel in Dover… Trying to duck my death sentence…

All because of Madden.

The urge to shoot him is a hot wire threaded into the base of my skull. But if I fire, his hand might spasm. He might get off a shot. He might hurt Aiofe.

So for now, I need to make Madden feel smart. Feel safe. Feel like the type of man who would never dream of harming the terrified child he's holding hostage.

I look into his flat brown eyes and try to sound like we're two ordinary people having an everyday conversation, like neither one of us holds a gun. "You must have been planning this a long time. Blowing up the garage tonight... How did you know Aiofe and I would come to the safe room?"

He cackles like a child torching an anthill with a magnifying glass. "Fuck the two of you. I knew my pussy brother would come. He'd hide like a little girl."

But he didn't. Before I can point out Madden's mistake, Aiofe starts to struggle. I don't know if it's the "little girl" that sets her off or the thought that Braiden's a coward. But she spits something in Irish and tries to land an elbow in Madden's ribs.

He yanks her neck back like he's jointing a chicken.

"Aiofe!" I say, more terrified than I let myself sound. I stiffen my arms, resigned to taking a shot, because I see no other way to save her.

Madden counters by digging his weapon into the bone beside her eye. She stops fighting, but her entire body vibrates, her hair swirling like she's charged with static electricity.

No.

Her curls don't move in an electric current. They sway in an *air* current.

I glance over her shoulder. Down the hallway. Toward the door I closed and locked. Into the shadows—where Braiden crouches, body taut as wire, a pistol glinting in his hand.

41

BRAIDEN

Samantha is beautiful and she's terrible, like Ireland's ancient goddess of war, the Morrigan. She's shrouded in black and white, the unforgiving uniform of a lethal lawyer. She was only gone a week, but her cheekbones are sharper here in the safe room. Her chin is more pointed. Her whiskey eyes boil with fierce certainty, and the scars along her hairline stand out like a silver aura.

She holds her pistol like it's an extension of her arm. This is the life she was born to. This is the life she's embraced.

Standing on the drive as my garage burned to its foundation, I wasn't afraid to face Madden. But watching Fairfax talk to the firefighters, I wasn't a fool either. My brother had to know he'd be fighting for his life. He had to be desperate. And desperate men are the most dangerous.

I came to the safe room because I couldn't risk dying without kissing Samantha one last time.

I'm not a total lovesick fool. I left Seamus standing guard at the doorway.

Now, Samantha feels me before she sees me. She *knows*. We're bound by the rings she still wears, the one with the Celtic knot of my Fishtown Boys and the engraved one I gave her at our wedding.

Is liomsa tú.

You are mine.

I'll die before I see her harmed. Even if—*especially* if—that means killing my brother in the very heart of Thornfield.

42

SAMANTHA

❧

In one hand, Braiden holds a pistol. With his other, he raises a single finger to his lips, warning me to silence.

But it's not silence Braiden needs. It's noise. I have to provide a distraction as Braiden maneuvers for a clear shot.

So I lower my Glock just a fraction, and I offer Madden the chance to brag some more. "How did you get in here? Without anyone knowing?"

His one-shoulder shrug is dismissive. "This was my da's house before it was Braiden's. I've been sneaking in and out of Thornfield since I was ten."

If Braiden's surprised, he doesn't give a sign. I try another line to distract Madden. "That bomb in the garage. Did you learn that from Russo?"

He snorts hard enough that his own weapon slips toward Aiofe's ear. She whimpers as he boasts, "I've known that shite since I was this one's age."

Braiden can't get off a shot yet, not without putting Aiofe at risk. But I edge a little to my right, trying to get Madden to shift to a more vulnerable position. "But you've been working with Russo all along, haven't you?"

He sneers. "So the penny finally drops."

"You hid things well." And he did. Or maybe I didn't want to see. "At the Rittenhouse, at the summit. You accused *me* of spying for Russo to take attention from you."

"Couldn't let Baby Brother know *I* was responsible for East Falls taking that cocaine."

A quarter of a billion dollars. I wonder how much Russo paid for the tipoff.

My gun is still lowered, an outward show of my good intentions. I shift my weight, taking another half step toward the closest green couch. Madden obliges by squaring his body to face me—not enough of a shift to bring him into range for Braiden, but something.

"You were responsible. And Fiona too?"

"Fiona didn't know shite. She was Daddy's Little Princess, running that meeting. Gave me good cover." He laughs. "Gave me good head too."

Aiofe flinches. I don't think she understands his words, but she can't miss the cruelty in his tone. Madden digs his gun deeper into her skull. Braiden tenses, ready to pounce, but the child's still not safe.

I slump a little more to my right, trying not to sound frantic as I clutch at straws to keep him talking. "You and Fiona met at the summit?"

This time his laugh is a single harsh bark, contrasting with Aiofe's moan. "I was nailing Fiona months before she came here. Met her on my trip to Dublin—not that my jackeen brother paid enough attention to figure *that* out. Who the fuck bones a contortionist? He'd believe anything."

I don't know what he's talking about, but from the thunder on Braiden's face, it's some sort of dirty joke. Horny men boasting about conquests. Naughty boys trying out new lies.

Braiden gestures with his chin toward my Glock. He wants me to raise it. He wants us to go after Madden together. But I still can't be sure a death spasm won't kill Aiofe.

Instead, I try to distract Madden one more time. Maybe Braiden can get close enough to grab Aiofe, to pull her away. "You and Fiona met in *Dublin*? Before she ever came to the Rittenhouse?"

He nods, one tight toss of his head. "As *if* she'd settle down with a trip to the old country. Her da's a feckin' eejit. She's a schemer, that one. Her and me both."

Braiden's face is dark with barely harnessed rage. I'm almost out of time to make Madden drop his guard. But I have one last point to leverage, the one Asher gave me. Was that only this evening?

I keep my tone even, intent on distracting Madden with a known lie. "But Fiona acted alone, didn't she? Hiring the waiter to kill me at Diamond Freeport?"

"Fiona? Fuck, no." Madden's voice is slimy with scorn. His smile is obscene. "I wanted to prove Russo could trust me. Give him a little present—you. Your body, anyway. *I'm* the one who hired that gobshite."

Braiden bellows.

Aiofe screams.

And I do the only thing I can do, to keep Madden from executing his hostage.

43

BRAIDEN

～

"Aiofe!" Samantha's shout echoes in the safe room, loud and clear. "Bring me Coinín!"

The child drops to her knees as if Madden's already pulled his trigger. Clutching her stuffed rabbit like it's some sort of heavenly angel or maybe a bulletproof vest, she scramble-crawls toward Samantha.

I do my best to cover her escape. Hollering like one of the banshees that haunted my granny's dreams, I leap from the shadows into the main room. My arms come up fast. My knees lock. I'm ready to kill Madden with a single shot.

But he fires first.

The bullet goes wide, because my brother never bothered with the hard work of building up skills. He's never invested a minute on a firing range. He's weak and he's wild, and he staggers back until his shoulders are braced against the wall.

Pinned by his own retreat, he shifts his focus like he's driving a road filled with potholes. His pistol twitches toward the nearest sofa. Samantha's taken shelter behind the green leather; I can hear her comforting a weeping Aiofe. Madden flips his gun toward me, aiming at my head, my heart, then back again to my head. His wrists snap, and he's focused behind me, which makes me realize Seamus has my back.

I barely shift my chin toward the man I can trust. "Stand down," I order. Seamus hesitates, but only for a moment. I hear him take a step back and I imagine he's lowered his weapon.

Madden's focus is back on me.

I couldn't shoot him while Samantha played him like a star witness. Most men shot in the head drop like butchered hogs, dead before they hit the ground. But some—all it takes is one— convulse as they die. I couldn't chance Madden sending a bullet into Aiofe's brain.

He deserves to die for sending that fecker after Samantha. Hell, he was destined for one of my bullets the instant he put a gun to Aiofe's head. After the photo Fiona sent, I'd even do it for her.

But Madden's done more than threaten the women under my protection. He went to Russo. He sold me out in the Philadelphia port. He schemed to break the Fishtown Boys.

Madden shouldn't *die* for that.

He should suffer.

I would take him to the basement of the Hare and Harp and string him up over the grate in the cold tile floor, but his guinea friend burned the Hare to the ground.

I would lock him in the trunk of Russo's blood-red Huracán and set fire to the car, but I ruined the Lambo with a baseball bat after Madden failed to steal it from his goombah boss's garage.

I would tie my brother up in the safe room here and let the Boys go at him one by one, but Donovan O'Keefe was one of my Boys, and he burned to death before my very eyes. Donny'll never get revenge for Madden selling out to Russo, so it's up to me to settle the account.

Madden's one shot filled the room with the sharp tang of a match that's just been lit. I long to add to that, squeezing off shot after shot, pulverizing his wrists and shattering his kneecaps, standing over his writhing body and blowing away his bollocks.

So I lie. "Set down your gun, and we can talk like men."

Madden is a traitor. He's lazy and he's cruel. But he was raised beside me, both of us at Da's right hand. My brother knows I'll never let him off that easy. "You'll kill me," he says.

"I won't." I lie again.

"Let's set them down together," he bargains.

"You're in my house, *deartháir*. You follow my rules here. Drop your fucking gun."

I'm braced for him to fire at me. I half expect him to point his weapon toward the green couch that's shielding Samantha and Aiofe. But I'm surprised when he takes the coward's way out, pressing his gun to his own head, leveling the muzzle just above his ear.

"No!" I roar, because I want to be the one to take the shot. I don't want him stealing this last prize from me.

He flinches and pulls the trigger.

44

SAMANTHA

❧

A shot fires, and Braiden bellows again, and a body falls to the floor. Aiofe's trembling beneath me like a rabbit cowering in its burrow. I know I should stay hidden, but I can't, not after I hear the clatter of a gun kicked across the room.

Braiden's standing over his brother. Madden is twitching, flailing, making a horrible noise that's part scream, part gurgle, part moan. His cheek is a mass of bloody splinters, his nose reduced to a bleeding hole.

Braiden presses the barrel of his gun against his brother's shoulder. "You couldn't even do that right, shitehawk," he says. "Count to three, *dearthàir*, and then we'll start to dance."

"Stop!"

The shout comes from beside me. Aiofe's gripping the back of the couch. Her fingers stand out like jagged icicles against the dark green leather. Her face is covered in snot and tears.

"Uncle Braiden!" she shouts. "Stop!"

Aiofe's voice hits him like a two-by-four. Shock stiffens every muscle in his body. But I know the code he lives by. Madden betrayed him, betrayed every one of the Fishtown Boys. Madden sold out his clan to Russo, and that can never be forgiven.

Still, Aiofe is the child Braiden has protected for the last seven years. He was there when bright red blood stole her voice. If he fires that gun, he'll do more than torture Madden. He'll ruin Aiofe forever.

He settles for snarling over his shoulder to Seamus. "Let's get him upstairs."

Seamus reaches for his phone. "Want me to call Kelleher?"

"No." Braiden puts force into the word. It's a direct command.

Seamus nods as if he expected the order. Now he knows what will happen in the infirmary room on the second floor. All four of us adults know. "I'll tell the others we have him."

"No," Braiden says again, and this time Seamus is surprised. "I need to be certain Russo's kept in the dark."

That admission costs Braiden something. Madden fooled him for weeks, for months even, working secretly with Russo. There may be other traitors in the ranks. Braiden will have to scour the Fishtown Boys, test their loyalty from top to bottom.

And Madden will pay for that too, once he's upstairs.

As Seamus bends over the writhing Madden, Braiden turns to me. There are a thousand things I want to say—every thought I've had in the past week, every discovery I made when I saw him standing in the hallway. But we'll have time for all of that later, when the house is quiet, when we're alone.

"Get her out of here," he says, jutting his chin toward Aiofe. And he's right. She's already seen far too much.

Aiofe's hand is limp in mine. I ease her through the doorway and down he hall lined with bookcases. Red lights flash outside the windows. A quick glance shows three fire engines and at least a dozen firefighters in full turn-out gear. The flames are already out.

The men start to swear behind us. From the range of curses, they're forcing Madden to his feet. Aiofe tries to turn back, but I keep my body between her and the bloodshed. After a moment's resistance, she lets me guide her toward the kitchen.

Fairfax frets beside the stove, shifting a kettle over an open flame as if that will make the water boil faster. A stack of foam cups waits on the counter, waiting to restore the firefighters. I suspect there isn't a crisis in Fairfax's life that wasn't made better with tea.

His face is marked with soot, and I spy a burn on his wrist, as if he was caught by an ember. But he smiles weakly as I lead Aiofe into the room. "Such a fuss all those men are making outside. Did they wake you, little one?"

Instead of answering, Aiofe says, "You're hurt!"

He startles and looks at me, as if I'm the one pulling puppet strings, making the once-mute child speak. Of course, being Fairfax, he recovers so quickly I wonder if I imagined his surprise. "I'll be right as rain by tomorrow," he promises Aiofe.

He glances past me, at sudden chaos in the foyer. Braiden and Seamus are getting Madden upstairs, being none too gentle about it. Aiofe's paying too much attention again, so I ask her, "Why don't we help Fairfax with his tea?"

"Chamomile?" Aiofe asks. "That always makes me feel better."

"Chamomile it is," I say. "Lets find the strainer."

Fairfax shakes his head slowly. "I didn't think I'd live to see the day." I don't know which amazes him more—Madden's injury or Aiofe's speaking or my voluntarily taking on the task of drowning foul leaves in water.

But then he keeps Aiofe busy, asking her to choose a favorite teacup and saucer. He directs her toward a step stool so she can retrieve a decorated tin filled with fresh toffee cookies. It's not until she's lining up the foam cups for all the men outside that Fairfax says to me, "Go on, then. Aiofe's the only assistant I need."

"I—" I start to tell him I'm happy to stay. But the truth is, I'm desperate to know what's happening upstairs. "Thank you," I say.

Before I can leave, Aiofe gives me a fierce hug. "And thank *you*," I whisper into her hair. "Thank you for keeping an eye on Fairfax." But I mean more than that. I mean, *thank you for warning me about Madden.* I mean, *thank you for choosing to speak.*

"All right, Aiofe," Fairfax says. "After we take care of the men outside, you can help me back to my cottage. In fact, why don't we have a sleepover out there? You can stay the night, and I'll make us both waffles in the morning?"

I suspect Fairfax will be needed back at the house, once he gets Aiofe into bed. But I slip free while the child is still distracted by the promise of breakfast.

The door is closed to the infirmary on the second floor, but I don't let that stop me. Braiden has rolled up his shirtsleeves. The scar on his forearm looks purple in the bright light, raised like a mountain range and twisted like a snake.

He looks past me. "Aiofe?" he asks.

"She's with Fairfax. He's taking her back to his cottage."

He nods once before he says, "You don't need to see this."

"I do."

He won't argue. He never does. He'll just issue a single command—*no*—in that tone I can't resist.

But he doesn't do it. Instead, he says, "Close the door. If you need to boke, there's a trashcan in the corner."

Madden lies naked on the paper-covered table. Medical scissors and clumps of blood-stained cloth tell the story of someone cutting him free from his ruined clothes. Vinyl cuffs are buckled around his wrists and ankles, holding him fast.

The restraints didn't come easy. Seamus is shaking his right hand; his knuckles are split. A spray of blood paints the floor. There's a smear of handprints on Madden's heaving chest. The mess that used to be his face pulses with every breath he gasps.

Drawers stand open, and cabinets gape. One counter is

covered with bandages and sutures, syringes and vials of drugs. Another is lined with the sterile blue of a freshly opened surgery pack. Stainless steel tools gleam in the cold bright light—forceps and clamps, retractors and scalpels, heavy-duty tweezers and a bone saw.

Madden's moaning is a constant low rumble. His lips are the color of liver.

Braiden selects the forceps and runs his thumb along its ridged jaw. "Let's go all the way back, *deartháir*. When did you first meet with Russo behind my back?"

Madden barely sounds human as he spits, "Go to hell. *Deartháir.*"

Braiden strikes like he's delivering a boxing jab, stepping between me and the table. I can't see what he does with the forceps, but Madden's keening is loud enough that I want to cover my ears. The cry goes on, longer and louder than I ever thought possible. The smell of piss is sharp in the air.

Braiden drops something bloody onto the floor. Madden pants, "Thank God we live in Philly. City of Brotherly Love."

Braiden shifts his grip on the forceps, holding them just above Madden's ruined face. "How much did he pay you to save his fucking cars?"

"Why, *deartháir*? Need a loan?" Madden asks, the words pulled and twisted through blood.

Another strike from Braiden, but this time he holds on longer, and his shoulders shake with the effort. Madden's screams turn my stomach to fire-washed stone. The reek of shit floods the room. Both men are gasping like beached sharks when Braiden finally steps back.

I can't watch. I can't leave. I look at Seamus to see how he can bear this, but he's leaning against the wall, shoulders back, studying his thumbnail like his cuticles have done something to offend him.

Braiden drops the forceps on the floor. As he moves to select a scalpel from the counter, I can finally see Madden's newly ravaged face. I swallow hard, telling myself I don't need the trashcan in the corner. I'm stronger than that. I have to be.

Madden opens his eyes as Braiden moves back into position. I can't see where Braiden presses the scalpel—on his brother's chest or his belly—but I watch Madden's lips stretch tight.

Braiden demands, "How much did you get for Donovan O'Keefe, motherfucker?"

"Didn't...fuck...my...mam." Madden fights for each word. "Fucked...yours."

I expect Braiden to make one quick cut but he doesn't. Instead, his shoulders tense and his arm moves slowly—inching, inching, inching his way down Madden's body like he's sculpting a masterpiece.

Madden's shriek would shatter glass, if there was any in this torture chamber. Tears stream from his eyes into the mangled hole where his nose used to be. Every muscle in his body convulses; he strains so hard I'm certain he'll break his bonds. I wait for the table to collapse.

But the buckles hold. The straps too. The table stands.

Madden pants through his teeth, foul air whistling out of him. He tosses his head, and I wonder if he can still see, if he's still able to hear. I can't imagine how much more of this he can take.

But before Braiden can ask another question, Madden's thrashing stops. His eyes open. He turns toward me and grasps with his near hand, as if he wants to feel the fabric of my suit.

When he speaks, he seems to have found some new well of strength. His words are slurred because his face is shattered, but he manages complete sentences, gasping just a little, every few words.

"Thanks for leaving...my cock, *dearthálr*. I need it...to fuck your guinea whore...up the arse." He purses his lips in parody of a kiss. "Russo's waiting, Giovanna."

Braiden doesn't shout. He doesn't strike. He doesn't falter.

He simply swipes beneath Madden's body, filling his hand

with an unholy mess of piss and shit and blood. He shoves his palm against his brother's bleeding mouth. He swipes his fingers through the ruins of Madden's nose and cheek.

Only when Madden is gagging, when his chest is heaving, when his belly is rising and falling like he's about to give birth, does Braiden jam the scalpel deep into his groin. He twists. He carves. And he jams the resulting link of flesh past Madden's filthy lips, choking him on his own cock.

It takes Madden a century to die.

When it's finally over, Braiden hangs his head, breathing like a bull. I'm pretty sure he didn't intend to kill Madden—not so soon, not without getting at least one honest answer to his questions. Madden goaded him on purpose, ending his torture by pushing Braiden past reason.

Braiden drops the scalpel between his brother's mutilated legs. He strips off his shirt and uses it to wipe his hands, sponging up as much of the muck as he can with the white cotton fabric. He drops the ruined shirt on Madden's body and crosses to the surgical sink. Lathering up like he's scrubbing in for surgery, he washes all the way up to his elbows, taking care to soap between each finger, under his nails, around the sinews of his wrists. After he finally rinses, Seamus pushes off from the wall and hands him a towel.

"Thanks," Braiden says, as if he's just been passed a cocktail napkin.

"Where should I take him?" Seamus asks.

Braiden says, "Leave it for now."

It. Madden is gone forever.

Braiden goes on. "We'll send pieces to Russo—put them in that fucking McLaren and leave them at his gate. But we all need sleep first. There'll be pushback once this gets out."

Seamus shakes his head, keeping his voice mild. "Russo doesn't give a shit about that guy."

"He'll bite. I took his toy away." Seamus still wants to argue, but Braiden interrupts. "Not a word to anyone. Not until I say."

"Not a word," Seamus agrees after a few heartbeats.

"Go on, then," Braiden tells him.

Seamus barely glances at me before he opens the infirmary door. His head is high as he takes the stairs. He doesn't look back.

So there's no one to see what happens, when Braiden finally turns to me.

45

BRAIDEN

~'

I can't take my eyes off Samantha. She's my bridge to the future. She's the way I leave behind the butchered animal on the table and come back to the world of men.

But she has to know the truth. She has to understand, or anything else between us will be built on lies.

I show her my hands—still flushed from my scrubbing. My fingers spread wide, not a hint of tremor. "I won't apologize for this," I say. "You've seen who I am. What I'll do. You have to know that."

"I see." Her chin trembles a little as she says it but her eyes meet mine. "I know." And then she takes a deep breath. "Braiden—" But she cuts herself off. "Please. Can we talk somewhere else?"

I've made my point, so there's no reason to stay in this stinking hellhole. I gesture for her to leave first, but I take time to lock the door behind us. The last thing I need tonight is Aiofe stumbling on her uncle's mangled body.

Samantha begins to relax the instant the door is closed. Her shoulders come down from around her ears. The lines on her forehead ease, the ones that look like she's fighting a migraine.

I want her in my bed.

But I take her to my office.

From the windows, I can see two firetrucks left on a driveway pocked with puddles. A few men in turnout gear explore what's left of the garage—blackened timbers and stone tumbled around the carcasses of cars. More stand around, drinking from foam cups. Fairfax is talking to someone who seems to be in charge.

Of course Fairfax has the situation under control. He always does. Nevertheless, I should get out there.

But Samantha starts again, matching her tone precisely to the one she used in the surgery. "I had to come here, Braiden. I hired an investigator, and he made his report tonight. That's how I knew Madden was working with Russo. I had to let you know, even though... Even with... Even after we..."

Jesus Christ. She thinks I'm going to throw her out. She thinks I don't want her here.

"Stop," I say.

She's still explaining. "You blocked my number—"

"Stop!"

"I looked online, using databases. I went through freeport records—"

"*Stop.*"

I use my Captain's voice. The look of relief that dawns on her face is something a thousand painters could try to capture for a thousand years and never come close.

She needs that sort of command. She needs that type of control. But more than anything, she needs to know exactly what I thought when I looked up from the map that's still sprawled across my desk—that moment when I saw her standing in the doorway.

"You came home," I say. "I never should have let you go, not like that, not in anger. And after you left, I should have chased after you. Should have followed you to Delaware, to the freeport, whatever it took."

"I wouldn't have let you past the door," she says.

"You wouldn't have had a choice, *piscín*."

She catches her breath at that. Her mouth softens at the pet name, but she won't give up control. Not yet. "You scared me," she said. "Bringing that gun to the pool house."

"You *terrified* me," I admit. "The fact that you went to Ingram. That I couldn't ignore what he ordered."

"The things I said... They weren't fair. I knew you could protect me. You already had, at the freeport. Against the man Madden sent."

I hold her gaze. "You knew exactly where to put your knife." I know she'll flinch. I know she'll look over her shoulder and down the hallway. I know she'll think of Madden dying under a knife.

But I say it because she can never forget who I am. She has to remember what I can do, what I *will* do to anyone who crosses me. And she has to know I'd never harm her like that, never hurt her in any way she doesn't beg for first.

I speak because she isn't ready to. "The only reason we could fight like that is because we know each other so well. We know the words to say. The wounds to open. You know my secrets and you know my shame, the same as I know yours."

She nods, because she recognizes truth. I can barely hear her when she whispers. "Promise. Promise you'll never do that again."

I take my time, because she has to know I mean it. I look directly in her eyes. I swallow before I open my lips. And then I say, "I promise."

"I won't either," she says. And now her voice is stronger. "I swear."

I need to touch her then, need to feel her body against my still-bare chest. My arms fold around her, and I spread one hand across the back of her head. I measure the moment she accepts that she's home again. That she's mine.

She's thinner than she should be. It's only been one week, but the hard wings of her shoulder blades tell me she's skipped meals. She's pale, too, her face washed out by the white silk of her top, by the harsh black of her suit.

If I kiss her, I'll never get out of this office. And my men still need me. It takes all my strength to step away. "I can't," I say. "Not yet."

She nods, because she understands. Samantha always understands.

"I have to take care of things downstairs. Fairfax shouldn't have to deal with the firefighters on his own. And I need to call off O'Hara's search for Madden."

She winces a little at my dead brother's name. This time, I pretend I don't see her discomfort. Instead, I say, "And *you* need to eat something."

"I don't—"

She stops when I raise both eyebrows.

But then she tries again. She glances toward the door, toward the hall, toward the locked infirmary. "I can't—"

"You will."

God help me, I want to feed her myself. I want to sit her on my lap and bring ripe strawberries to her lips. I want to watch her chew. I want to see her swallow.

A heavy engine revs outside, one of the firetrucks moving. Men shout to each other, the steady call of experts, wrapping up a job. I need to go.

"*Piscín*," I say, letting one hand tangle in her hair.

She turns her face and rests her cheek against my palm. "I'll eat," she says. And then she straightens. Her spine grows stiff. She's the one who finds the strength to step away. Eyeing me steadily, she says, "I'll be here when you get back. Go."

So I do.

46

SAMANTHA

~

I'm a little surprised he listens to me.

But Braiden stalks to the bedroom. I keep my distance as he ransacks his dresser, coming up with a clean black T-shirt. I watch him tug it over his head, and then I follow him downstairs as he heads out to manage his empire.

I told him I'd eat. So I go to the kitchen and make myself a plate—cold roast chicken and thick slices of cheddar cheese and a pair of tiny clementines. Rinsing the dish when I'm done, I discover it's grown quiet outside. Both trucks are gone, along with all the firefighters.

I wonder what Braiden is telling his men. Whether he's directing them to search for Madden elsewhere in Philadelphia. How long he'll draw out the charade.

Glancing at my watch, I see that it's well past midnight. I should be exhausted, especially after my frantic drive from Dover. But I'm not tired at all. Instead, I feel like I've drunk a vat of dark roast coffee. Like a million fireflies flutter inside my veins. Like I'm waiting for a starting pistol before a hundred-meter sprint.

I wipe my palms against my wool-covered thighs. I'm still dressed for the office, even though my work day ended hours ago. I should be wearing a skirt. I should be dressed in flowers.

My belly twists in a long, slow somersault.

I don't want to change. I don't want to follow the rules. But I'm willing to wait in the bedroom.

It's another hour before Braiden returns. I hear him long before I see him. He locks the front door. He climbs the stairs. He makes his way down the endless hallway.

And he freezes in the doorway, when he finds me sitting on the edge of the bed. His hair stands on end; he's been running his fingers through it again. Tight lines bracket his lips, frowning remnants of all the lies he's told about Madden.

I don't realize I've stood until his arms close around me. He grips me like a drowning man. I feel his heartbeat through his tight black T-shirt.

"Samantha," he breathes against my hair, melting something deep inside me.

This is what I needed, the past week in Dover. The steadiness of his body holding mine. The strength of his certainty.

His fingers tangle in my hair. He brushes his lips against the net of scars at my temple. His soft caress sends a shiver down my spine, and he tightens his arms around me. I barely hear him when he whispers, "You've broken the rules, *piscín*."

This is what I wanted. This is why I came upstairs. So I sink to my knees before him. I bow my head, like I'm waiting for a crown. When I look up at him through my lashes, I hear his breath catch in his throat.

"Please, sir," I say, and the words sound *right*. They're what I long for. They're who I am. "Put me in my collar. Teach me the lesson I deserve."

The platinum is cold when Braiden takes it from its velvet case. I shudder as he settles it around my neck, a delicious wave rolling from the crown of my head to my toes. He kisses my nape after he fastens the lock, and he makes a show of nestling the key deep in the pocket of his pants. To steady myself, I press the emerald into the hollow of my throat.

He pulls me to my feet and orders, "Out of those feckin' clothes, *piscín.*"

He watches me undress, really studies me. I'm suddenly shy as I slip out of my jacket. I'm awkward as I work the button on my pants, as I slide down the zipper. A smirk curls his lips as I shimmy out of the trousers and step free, right foot first, then left. He's focused on the plain white cotton of my panties, at the suddenly damp V between my thighs. Embarrassed, I turn away to unbutton my top.

"Not on your fucking life," he says.

I catch my lower lip between my teeth and work the buttons, one by one. The heat of his gaze unleashes a flock of humming-birds in my belly. I loosen my bra and drop it to the floor. I step out of my panties. And when I'm standing in front of him, wearing only my shoes, I remember the words he told me the first time we met in the safe room, the morning after our wedding.

You'll be terrified I'll hurt you and petrified I won't, and every time you come again you'll thank God for the day you became my wife.

He's never lied. He's never hidden who he is. He's never pretended he isn't capable of doing horrific things.

So when he says, "Forearms on the bed," I know exactly what he's offering. I know what I'm accepting. My knees threaten to collapse.

I do what he says. I support myself on my arms, gripping the hunter green comforter with both fists.

The position is absurd. Because I wear heels, my ass is high in the air. My breasts hang above the mattress, weighed down by nipples that have gone rock-hard.

After an approving growl, Braiden moves to the dresser. I

know the things he keeps there, the paddles and floggers. There's a cat o' nine tails and a riding crop.

And a cane.

I've tried to get him to use the cane on me before. Once, I moved it to the front of the drawer, tempting him, inviting him. It's a wicked toy. It calls to me and it scares me and I want to know that I'm strong enough to take it, even though I fear I'll break at the very first blow.

As I look over my shoulder, my knees grow weak when I see him take the cane from the drawer. He flexes it between his palms. It bends, but it doesn't break. That's what makes it dangerous. That's what gives it strength.

For Braiden, I've flexed every rule I've ever had for myself. Don't let a man control you. Don't give in. Don't let yourself be hurt. I've bent nearly double. But I haven't broken. Not yet.

He hasn't touched me yet, but I'm already wrapped as tight as an iron spring. He traces the backs of my thighs with the end of the cane, writing some secret message that sends me up on tip-toe. He rests the cane across the small of my back, letting it balance on my trembling flesh.

"Say red," he says. "And I'll stop."

I know the rules. I know he gives me a safeword to protect me. And I know I'll never use it.

But I nod, all the same.

"I need to hear you, *piscín*. Tell me you understand."

"I understand. Red, and you'll stop. Sir."

I expect him to hesitate for a moment longer, to give me a chance to change my mind. But Braiden Kelly doesn't pause for anyone.

The sound of the cane slicing the air is like Fairfax's teakettle shrieking in the kitchen. I barely have time to brace my legs before the blow falls across the widest part of my ass.

I can't keep myself from yelping. The cane is ice, melted immediately by fire. It bites into my skin, a white-hot laser. For a heartbeat, I think I've shattered like glass in the pool house door, but then Braiden's palm smooths over the line, soothing me, calming me, bringing me back from the edge.

"You're brave, *piscín*," he says.

My knees sag toward the bed. My nipples brush the dark green comforter. My fingers clutch the fabric, grabbing so hard I hear my knuckles squeak.

He strikes again.

The second blow is lower on my body, closer to my thighs. I feel it all the way to the chambers of my heart—hot-white-ice-fire. But this time I know what to expect. This time I don't cry out.

But I whimper a little as Braiden caresses me and says, "You're so strong."

I don't feel strong. My ankles are shaking above my high heels. My breasts are crushed against the bed. I fight the urge to bury my face in the mattress, to scream and scream and scream, but I can't do that, I won't do that, because I need to prove to both of us that I can take it.

The third blow falls at an angle, crossing the other two.

Constellations spin behind my eyes. Sparks fly from the intersections of the marks, from the raw places where the cane has doubled its bite.

I scream. I have to. I've never felt a pain like this. Never felt such a ferocious fire banked inside me.

I'm suspended over a chasm, falling, spinning. I want him to go on. I need to say *red*.

My mouth is open. My throat is stretched. Want. Need. Want. Need.

"You're beautiful," Braiden whispers as he slips one hand between my quivering thighs. One fingertip settles against my clit, and I'm instantly shredded. I transform into a messy, sobbing animal, a desperate creature who pushes back against that finger, who takes it inside, who rides its hooking pressure over an even higher cliff, spinning and warping and falling into wordless, mindless nothingness.

I'll make you come so hard you'll think you've gone blind. That's another thing he told me in the safe room. That's another thing he promised, and now I know he didn't lie.

I moan when his hand slips free from the vise of my thighs. He bends over me. He brushes his lips against the burning stripes he's left on my ass.

My arse, Braiden would say, with his Irish lilt.

Braiden would say that, and Madden too. I shouldn't let the memory of Madden's dying taunt into this room: He needed his cock to fuck my arse.

I've never done anal before. I've never given any man the option.

But lying here, marked and bruised and already eager again, I know what I want. What I need.

"Fuck me," I say to Braiden. "Take my ass."

He runs his hand over the welts from the cane. He sounds amused when he says, "Already back to topping from below, *piscín?*"

I'm not topping. I'm not playing games. I need to know this is something no one can ever steal from me, a threat no man can make again. I have to be certain the first man there is the one I choose, the man I've given myself to, heart and body and soul.

I push back from the mattress, just enough to drop to my knees beside the bed. At this level, I can see the bulge in Braiden's pants, measure how much my orgasm turned him on.

But I don't reach for his buckle.

He's my Dom and I'm his sub, no matter how much he lets me break the rules. He taught me a lesson my second day in this house: How to beg.

"Please," I say. "I'll never ask for anything again."

A smile breaks his stern lips. "I don't believe that for a moment."

But he gave me my response that first day in the safe room. "I'm girl enough to beg for what I really want," I tell him. "And you're man enough to give me what I really need."

I don't know if he remembers the filthy words he burned into my brain that first morning. But he knows I'd never call myself a *girl* for any man but him.

Still, he's holding back. He's weighing whether to deny me for speaking out of turn. I have to convince him. I have to force a ghost into the room, make him see the reason why, same as I do. "Madden said he'd do it. Russo too. Madden can't anymore. And you'll never let Russo. You'll protect me. You'll keep me safe. That's why I want you to be the one. I need you... Only you... You have to... Please..."

Sweet God, help me out here. I've lost my words just when I need them the most.

"You want me to be the first to fuck your sweet little arse."

And those are words he said in the safe room too. He does remember. Those are words he promised.

"Yes, please," I beg. "Sir. Master."

He strips then, more brutally efficient than I was when he ordered me naked. His cock stands at full mast, for all our talk about topping and power, about who makes the rules and who gets to break them. I watch him stride to his nightstand and yank the drawer open, fishing around for something toward the back.

When he produces a bottle of lube, I see that it's Fuck Water. That's the brand I know, the one I chose, the one he learned about the first night he saved me from Russo.

It's not just lube he's found in the drawer. He's holding a pair of handcuffs too.

He rips the comforter from the bed and throws it onto the floor.

"On your back," he orders. "In the middle."

He's the one in charge now. His hands are firm as he closes my right wrist in one metal cuff. He loops the chain around one of the posts in the headboard, then secures my left hand.

"Red," he growls again, like he hasn't already reminded me of my power.

I don't know why he tells me again. I *know* the rules. He's made them clear from the very beginning. But I nod, never taking my eyes from his. "Red," I say. "And you'll stop."

My knees are already bent, easing the pressure on my lower back. Kneeling between them, he uses one shoulder to angle them wide, baring me to his feral gaze. He's already opened the bottle of lube, already covered one of his palms. He strokes himself twice, thoroughly bathing his cock.

My belly tightens at the sight of him, even larger than I remember, and harder too. He's back to calling me *piscín*, telling me I'm beautiful, reminding me I'm strong.

Swiping between my legs, he makes me twitch when the back of his wrist finds my swollen clit. But his attention is focused on the rosebud beneath my fluttering pussy lips. Leaning forward, he slips in one drenched thumb.

I buck in surprise, gasping out something that isn't a word. He grins wickedly and kisses the inside of my knee, pressing down with that unexpected thumb until my mouth stretches into a raw, needy O.

He strikes like lightning then, rocking back on his heels. His hands grip my ankles, bringing them to rest on his shoulders. I barely have time to curl my fingers around the posts of the bed, and then he's easing into me, guiding his cock where his thumb just played.

He takes his time, giving me a chance to relax around him. He was generous with the lube and clever with his hand, but he's so much larger than anything I ever imagined going there. I catch my breath, fighting the pressure, bearing down against the pain.

"Easy, *piscín*," he murmurs, turning his head to kiss my ankle. "Breathe, sweet girl. You can do this. Breathe…"

I still feel the stripes from the cane, and maybe that's a good thing, because they distract me from the pressure of what he's doing now. I breathe like he tells me to, shallow at first, but deeper when I realize that a long, slow exhale lets him fill me more.

"You're so tight, *piscín*. So beautiful. So strong." His fingers close around one ankle, feeding me determination.

One breath. Another. One breath more. And then I feel the heat of his body pressed against mine.

"*Mo chailín maith*," he breathes. *My good girl.* I *am* his good girl. I've taken every inch of him. I'm stretched more than I ever imagined I could be. I'm more full than I ever dreamed.

"Eyes on me, *piscín*," he says, and I didn't know I'd closed them. But I find his burning ocean gaze, and neither of us blinks as he starts to move.

I've never felt anything like this before. He's strung a harp to play every nerve in my body. He's gliding between my legs, but I feel him in my chest, in my throat, in my skull.

My arms arc over my head, secured by the cuffs. My belly grows taut, so close, so close, almost there. My toes point. My thighs turn to steel.

I want him to move faster and I want him to slow down and I want this endless spiral of sensation to last through the cold death of the universe.

But it can't. Nothing stays forever. His own jaw is tight. The cords in his neck stretch like lines on a sailboat. He drops one hand from my ankle, slips a knuckle against my clit, tapping once, twice, three times.

I shatter.

Every nerve he's kindled bursts into holy flame. The lines from the cane ignite, incinerating every last shred of my reserve. I call on God. I call on Braiden, screaming his name until my throat is raw, and then I whisper it, over and over and over again.

And as the waves of sensation roll inside me, echoing at the backs of my eyes and down my spine again, Braiden loses his own control. He spills inside of me, pulse after pulse, somehow driving deeper when every cell in our bodies is already perfectly matched.

I lose every one of my thoughts. I forget every word I've ever known. I'm pure pleasure… I'm pure… I'm…

~

Legs. I have legs.

Arms. I have arms.

Lungs. I have lungs, and they're pumping and breathing, bringing me back to life after I don't know how long.

I hear Braiden, whispering to me in Irish, calling me *mo chailín maith*, his *piscín*, other sweet half-swallowed words I've never heard before.

I smell sex on the sheets and sweat on my skin and the cedar-and-spice that is Braiden.

I taste ambrosia melting across my tongue, a food of the gods, and it takes me a lifetime to remember that this joy is called chocolate.

I feel Braiden's fingers on my face, coaxing me to sip from a smooth, cool glass. And then I feel a warm cloth between my legs, gentle, gentle, cleaning me. There's the soft glow of arnica melting into my stripes, smoothing away the cane's remembered fire before I'm gathered into the velvet-steel circle of Braiden's arms.

I open my eyes. Moonlight seeps in around the curtains at the window.

Braiden's back is against the headboard. He's cradling me inside the V of his legs, arms around me, my head nestled against his chest.

"Braiden," I whisper, surprised that I can't manage anything more.

"Shh," he says, pulling me a little closer. And then, so low I barely hear him, "Stay here?" he asks. "Don't go sleep in the pool house?"

The pool house. I can remember how important it was not to spend the night in Braiden's bed. How I needed to maintain my own territory.

But that was a lifetime ago. I can't imagine wanting to sleep anywhere but here.

"I'm staying," I whisper. "*Is liomsa tú,*" Those are the words inside my wedding band, the ones he used to claim me. I'm staking the same claim. I'm demanding the same rights. Braiden is mine, and I'll never leave him again.

"*Is liomsa tú,*" he agrees. *You are mine.*

"I love you," I tell him. The words are simple and clear. Easy to say because they're a perfect truth.

"I love *you.*" Then, "Close your eyes. Rest a while."

I do what he says. I close my eyes. And because he's Braiden, because I trust him, because I'm still wearing his collar, I sleep.

47

SAMANTHA

~

I don't dream. I don't toss and turn, seeking a more comfortable position. I don't fight my pillow.

I just sleep.

And when I wake, I can't tell how long I've been out. Only a few hours, I guess, because it's still dark outside. But I'm so well-rested—despite our marathon reunion—that I feel like I'll never sleep again.

Braiden and I are spooning, his chest to my back. His arm falls loosely across my hip. He's kept his claim, even in sleep.

When I slide to the edge of the bed, he murmurs, reaching out for the warmth he's lost. I turn back to kiss his cheek, and he mutters, but he's out again before he fully awakes.

It's chilly in the bedroom. Our clothes are strewn around the bed. I can't imagine putting on my suit again. I settle for Braiden's black T-shirt and his rumpled boxer shorts.

There's something else on the floor. It's by the door, as if someone dropped off a hotel bill while we were sleeping.

A paper. Printed on heavy bond. There's an ornate border and heavy black letters, like a diploma. The words are partially obscured by a large dark stamp. I can make out three signatures at the bottom, but it's too dark to read any details.

I take it over to the window and tilt it toward the moonlight.

Annulled, says the one word printed across all the others.

My eyes fill. I fight to pick out the names written on the fancy document. Braiden Fergal Kelly. Birte Antóinín Mason.

At least, that's what it used to say. Someone has scribbled through Birte's name, using a blood-red crayon. The lines are sloppy. Frantic. I squint at the rest of the wording, but even by the window, I can't make out the small print.

Looking up from the paper, I realize it's not emotion clouding my senses. Wisps of smoke are stealing in around the door.

"Braiden!" I shout.

Even as his name leaves my lips, a piercing siren slices through the room—the smoke detector on the ceiling, just inside the door. The electronic box shoots a beam of light onto the floor, and a mechanical voice announces, "A fire has been detected. Leave the building at once. A fire has been detected. Leave the building at once. A—"

"Samantha!" Braiden roars. He's tugging on the pants he discarded last night. He shoves his feet into his abandoned shoes, not bothering with socks.

Dazed, I say, "I'm fine."

He's cursing in Irish, laying his palm against the door. He tries to listen too, but no one could hear over the smoke detector.

This doesn't make sense. This isn't possible. Madden bombed the garage. The garage was on fire. Madden's dead on the infirmary table. There's no way he started another fire in the house.

"Stand back," Braiden says, but I'm already back. I'm

hovering by the bed, looking at the windows, trying to remember how far a drop it is to the ground from the second floor.

I watch as Braiden cracks open the door. I don't need to be standing beside him to hear the roar of the flames outside. His face flashes orange before he slams the door closed again.

"Birte!" I say. "And Grace."

This time he doesn't bother swearing. He grabs his phone on the nightstand and unlocks the screen. Tossing it to me, he orders, "Call 911." I don't need his Captain's voice to make me tap the numbers.

He's in the bathroom, running water.

An operator answers: "911. What's your emergency?"

I tell her, trying to crush the panic where my heart should be. I give her the address. I tell her there are four of us in the house, because I pray to God Fairfax didn't change plans, didn't bring Aiofe back to the nursery. I tell the woman on the phone I don't know where the fire started, how it started, how much of the house is in flames.

I wait for her to say the fire station already responded to a call at this address tonight. I'm ready to bargain. I'm ready to cry. But she merely confirms the destination and says help is on the way.

Braiden's out of the bathroom. He's carrying towels, the huge bath sheets he keeps by the shower. They're so soaked with water they're dripping onto the floor. He drapes one over my shoulders and drags me to the door.

"When I open it," he says. "Run for the stairs."

"I can't—"

"Don't look back," he says. "Don't stop."

"You're coming with me," I say, and I realize I'm pleading. I'd drop to my knees and beg, but I know it won't do any good.

"There are eleven steps to the landing. Ten to the ground floor."

"You need to—"

"I need to get Birte and Grace."

"You can't—"

"I need you to go."

He won't listen. He won't stop. If I waste any more time arguing, I'm only putting him in greater danger.

He crowds me close to the door. He crushes his lips against mine, unbearably hard, unbearably fast. "Ready?" he asks. "On three."

I nod because I can't speak.

"One," he says. "Two."

On *three* he opens the door and shoves me into the hallway. The walls are catching fire. They seem to waver, and paint bubbles up like water in a pot. Flames are eating their way into the ceiling.

With one hand, I clutch the towel over my head and race for the stairs. Past the guest room. Past Aiofe's room.

Eleven steps to the landing.

Ten to the ground floor.

I shoot the deadbolt on the front door and yank it open. Staggering outside, I stumble halfway to the ruined garage on pure momentum.

Glass explodes in one of the upstairs windows. I can't tell if it's our bedroom or Aiofe's, or even one of the offices in the other wing. I scream for Braiden, as if ripping my throat raw can carry him out of that hellhole.

I'm closer than I should be.

I'm farther than I ever wanted to go.

And I stare into the black pit of the doorway, waiting, hoping, praying to see the man I love.

Thank you for reading *Irish Vice*! I hope you enjoyed reading

Samantha and Braiden's love story as much as I've enjoyed sharing it with you.

Their story concludes in *Irish Reign*.

Buy *Irish Reign* Now!
https://alixkey.com/PB6US

BONUS SCENE

~

Things got pretty rough when Braiden and Samantha were separated. Want to learn more about how miserable Braiden's life became?

Get your bonus scene by typing:

https://alixkey.com/Bonus5

into your phone or computer browser.

MORE DIAMOND RING

~

Or maybe you'd like to learn more about foul-mouthed Trap Prince, and how he came to create the Diamond Ring? (And, um, you're curious about my super-spicy, very dark, Cinderella-retelling romance with Trap, now available in a completed series!) Start the Kidnapped Series by typing:

https://alixkey.com/dring0

into your phone or computer browser.

~

One last thing: If you want an absolutely free full-length, totally stand-alone Diamond Ring novel, featuring a gender-switch Jack and the Beanstalk retelling and starring Irish mobster Connor Boyle, I've got you covered! Just type:

https://alixkey.com/sins

into your phone or computer browser.

THANK YOU

I can't thank you enough for choosing *Irish Vice* from among all the dark Mafia romances out there! Without readers like you, I would never have my writing career.

You may not realize it, but *you* can be my hero. Study after study shows that the number one reason a person reads a book is because that book was recommended by a friend.

So will you tell one friend about *Irish Vice*?

Of course, if you're dead-set on reviewing my book on Amazon and Goodreads, I won't complain! Honest reviews are hugely helpful because many advertisers require me to have a certain number of reviews before I can buy ads.

Leave a review on Amazon
Leave a review on Goodreads

Whatever you do, don't be a stranger! I look forward to hearing from you soon!

www.alixkey.com
alix@alixkey.com

ABOUT THE AUTHOR

Alix Key was born in Potomac, Maryland, where she grew up making her twin brother and all her dolls act out her favorite fairytales. When an all-grown-up Alix discovered that very real dangers lurk in the woods, she figured out how to rescue herself. She now lives outside Dover, Delaware with her own Prince Charming. When not writing dark romance, Alix serves as the Chief Operations Officer of Diamond Freeport.

You can learn more about Alix at her website, www.alixkey.com.